PRAISE F

"The teen drama is center-court Compton, with enough plots and sub-plots to fill a few episodes of any reality show."
—*Ebony* magazine on *Drama High: Courtin' Jayd*

"Abundant, juicy drama."
—*Kirkus Reviews* on *Drama High: Holidaze*

"You'll definitely feel for Jayd Jackson, the bold sixteen-year-old Compton, California, junior at the center of keep-it-real Drama High stories."
—*Essence* magazine on *Drama High: Jayd's Legacy*

"Edged with comedy and a provoking street-savvy plot line, Compton native and Drama High author L. Divine writes a fascinating story capturing the voice of young black America."
—the *Cincinnati Herald* on the *Drama High* series

"Filled with all the elements that make for a good book—young love, non-stop drama and a taste of the supernatural—it is sure to please."
—THE RAWSISTAZ REVIEWERS on *Drama High: The Fight*

"If you grew up on a steady diet of saccharine-*Sweet Valley* novels and think there aren't enough books specifically for African American teens, you're in luck."
—*Prince George's Sentinel* on *Drama High: The Fight*

"Through a healthy mix of book smarts, life experiences, and down-to-earth flavor, L. Divine has crafted a well-nuanced coming-of-age tale for African-American youth."
—*The Atlanta Voice* on *Drama High: The Fight*

Also by L. Divine

THE FIGHT

SECOND CHANCE

JAYD'S LEGACY

FRENEMIES

LADY J

COURTIN' JAYD

HUSTLIN'

KEEP IT MOVIN'

HOLIDAZE

CULTURE CLASH

COLD AS ICE

PUSHIN'

Published by Kensington Publishing Corporation

Drama High, Vol. 13
Super Edition

THE MELTDOWN

L. Divine

Dafina KTeen Books
KENSINGTON PUBLISHING CORP.
http://www.kensingtonbooks.com

DAFINA KTEEN BOOKS are published by

Kensington Publishing Corp.
119 West 40th Street
New York, NY 10018

All Kensington titles, imprints, and distributed lines are available at special quantity discounts for bulk purchases for sales promotion, premiums, fund-raising, educational, or institutional use.

Special book excerpts or customized printings can also be created to fit specific needs. For details, write or phone the office of the Kensington Special Sales Manager: Kensington Publishing Corp., 119 West 40th Street, New York, NY 10018. Attn. Special Sales Department. Phone: 1-800-221-2647.

KTeen Reg. U.S. Pat. & TM Off.
Sunburst logo Reg. U.S. Pat. & TM Off.

ISBN-13: 978-0-7582-3117-8
ISBN-10: 0-7582-3117-2

First Printing: February 2011

10 9 8 7 6 5

Printed in the United States of America

This volume is dedicated to my readers. Every time I visit a new city or have a signing at home I am amazed by how much Jayd's drama reaches you all. Thank you for sharing the journey with my characters and me.

I would also like to say a special thank you to my dear friend and fellow writer Tina McElroy Ansa, who has on countless occasions reassured me that I'm on the right path. Thank you, sis, for reminding me to respect my process and follow my spirit.

And, as always, thank you to my publisher, Dafina / Kensington, for allowing my pen to flow freely.

Odu Ogbe Ogunda 31:1

An uncontrolled temper does not create
anything for anyone.
Patience is the father of good character.
A person who is patient will become the
master of all things.
She will reach a ripe old age.
He will live a healthy life.
And she will enjoy life thoroughly
Like a person tasting honey.

—As interpreted by Maulana Karenga

Acknowledgments

When I read about several of the Haitian earthquake survivors building shelters on top of their dilapidated homes and bartering whatever resources they had to survive, I was struck by the urge to live and to keep moving forward no matter the conditions. They are a spiritual inspiration, indeed.

I would also like to acknowledge all of the hardworking folks out there who never give up and who always choose the positive side of life no matter what your current circumstances may be. One of my favorite quotes from the HBO show *The No. 1 Ladies' Detective Agency* is, "Don't worry about me: I'm made from strong stuff." I can relate to Jill Scott's character because I'm made from that same "stuff" and so are most of the people I know.

With this being my thirteenth novel in five years, writing each manuscript is more challenging than the next. As with all rewards, there's plenty of hard work and tears that go into each page. I can't tell you how many times I thought I wasn't going to make it to the end; how many times I would get two-thirds of the way through a novel and want to scream from physical pain and mental exhaustion. But it is also at that point that I see the other side of the mountain I've been climbing, and my spirit feels good. The tears turn into smiles, and I can see the last page in the horizon. Truly I've had many, many meltdowns, and each and every single time my mama, my children, and my faith bring me through. Thank you to the Creator for not only providing me with internal strength but also for surrounding me with people who love and support me through the entire journey.

~ Ashe ~

The Crew

Jayd

A sassy seventeen-year-old from Compton, California, who comes from a long line of Louisiana conjure women. She is the only one in her lineage born with brown eyes and a caul. Her grandmother appropriately named her "Jayd," which is also the name her grandmother took on in her days as a voodoo queen in New Orleans. Jayd now lives in her mother's apartment in Inglewood. She visits her grandmother on the weekends in Compton, her former home. Jayd is in all AP classes. She has a tense relationship with her father, whom she sees occasionally, and has never-ending drama in her life, whether at school or home.

Mama/Lynn Mae

When Jayd gets in over her head, her grandmother, Mama, is always there to help her. A full-time conjure woman with magical green eyes and a long list of both clients and haters, Mama also serves as Jayd's teacher, confidante, and protector.

Mom/Lynn Marie

At thirty-something years old, Lynn Marie would never be mistaken for a mother of a teenager. Jayd's mom is definitely all that and with her green eyes, she keeps the men guessing. Able to talk to Jayd telepathically, Lynn Marie is always there when Jayd needs her.

Netta

The owner of Netta's Never Nappy Beauty Shop, Netta is Mama's best friend, business partner, and godsister in their religion. She also serves as a godmother to Jayd, who works part-time at Netta's Shop.

Esmeralda

Mama's nemesis and Jayd's nightmare, this next-door neighbor is anything but friendly. She relocated to Compton from Louisiana around the same time Mama did and has been a thorn in Mama's side ever since. She continuously causes trouble for Mama and Jayd. Esmeralda's cold blue eyes have powers of their own, although not nearly as powerful as Mama's.

Rah

Rah is Jayd's first love from junior high school, who has come back into her life when a mutual friend, Nigel, transfers from Rah's high school (Westingle) to South Bay. He knows everything about her and is her spiritual confidant. Rah lives in Los Angeles but grew up with his grandparents in Compton like Jayd. He loves Jayd fiercely but has a baby-mama who refuses to go away. Rah is a hustler by necessity and a music producer by talent. He takes care of his younger brother, Kamal, and holds the house down while his dad is locked up and his mother strips at a local club.

Misty

The word "frenemies" was coined for this former best friend of Jayd's. Misty has made it her mission to sabotage Jayd any way she can. Living around the corner from Jayd, she has the unique advantage of being an original hater from the neighborhood and at school.

KJ

He's the most popular basketball player on campus, Jayd's ex-boyfriend, and Misty's current boyfriend. Ever since he and Jayd broke up, he's made it his personal mission to persecute her.

Nellie

One of Jayd's best friends, Nellie is the prissy princess of the crew. She is also dating Chance, even though it's Nigel she's really feeling. Nellie made history at South Bay by becoming the first black Homecoming princess and has let the crown go to her head.

Mickey

The gangster girl of Jayd's small crew, she and Nellie are best friends but often at odds with each other, mostly because Nellie secretly wishes she could be more like Mickey. A true hood girl, she loves being from Compton, and her ex-man with no name is a true gangster. Mickey and Nigel have quickly become South Bay High's newest couple.

Jeremy

A first for Jayd, Jeremy is her white on again, off again boyfriend who also happens to be the most popular cat at South Bay. Rich, tall, and extremely handsome, Jeremy's witty personality and good conversation keep Jayd on her toes and give Rah a run for his money—literally.

Mickey's Man

Never using his name, Mickey's original boyfriend is a troublemaker and always hot on Mickey's trail. Always in and out of jail, Mickey's man is notorious in her hood for being a coldhearted gangster, and loves to be in control. He also has a thing for Jayd, but Jayd can't stand to be anywhere near him.

Nigel

The quarterback on the block, Nigel is a friend of Jayd's from junior high and also Rah's best friend, making Jayd's world even smaller at South Bay High. Nigel dumped his ex-girlfriend at

Westingle (Tasha) to be with Mickey. Jayd is caught up in the mix as a friend to them both, but her loyalty lies with Nigel because she's known him longer and he's always had her back.

Chance

The rich, white hip-hop kid of the crew, Chance is Jayd's drama homie and Nellie's boyfriend, if you let him tell it. He used to have a crush on Jayd and now has turned his attention to Nellie for the time being. Chance's dreams of being black come true when he discovers he was adopted. His biological mother is half black, and his birth name is Chase.

Bryan

The youngest of Mama's children and Jayd's favorite uncle, Bryan is a DJ by night and works at the local grocery store during the day. He's also an acquaintance of both Rah and KJ from playing ball around the hood. Bryan often gives Jayd helpful advice about her problems with boys and hating girls alike. Out of all of Jayd's uncles, Bryan gives her grandparents the least amount of trouble.

Jay

Jay is more like an older brother to Jayd than her cousin. He lives with Mama, but his mother (Mama's youngest daughter, Anne) left him when he was a baby and never returned. He doesn't know his father and attends Compton High. He and Jayd often cook together and help Mama around the house.

Jayd's Journal

My mom always keeps an ink pen and pad in her glove compartment in case she needs to write something down while in the car. Now that I'm the main driver for her aging Mazda Protegé, I use the tools to write about anything significant that may have happened in my day before I forget, no matter where I am, which in this case is in the parking lot of Ralphs grocery store in the Ladera Center. We're not too far from Rah's house, which is also the scene of my latest chick fight with Rah's ex girlfriend, Sandy. I can't believe she let me inside of her mind—after she manhandled me—and that I got her to give up their daughter, Rahima, and finally move out of Rah's house. He owes me big-time for handling his baby mama drama for him.

I've been using my mom's powers like crazy, learning how to master them but still not able to control my dreams, which is where my true power lies. It's crazy, I know, but not crazier than Mama going off on the boys earlier this afternoon. Now, that was some serious drama. She and Netta left to cool Mama's head and on Mother's Day, too. It's bad enough she has to live with my trifling uncles every day of the week, but the one day of the year they should be grateful to her, one of them screwed it up instead.

Rah had to run inside the market for diapers on our way to pick up Nigel and he took Rahima with him. Nigel's going to spend the night at the hospital with Mickey, and his dad will pick him up in the morning. And since Rah's car is already there, I really just have to drop him and his daughter off, say hi to Mickey and my goddaughter, and call it a night. This has been one of the longest days of my life and as such calls for a good night's sleep. Even with school in the morning, it's the last month before summer and I couldn't be happier. We all need a break from the madness that is Drama High before I snap.

Prologue

When we finally arrive at Nigel's house, Mrs. Esop is enjoying the sunset from her garden view on the front porch. Great. Another tough broad to deal with, but I actually respect this one, even if I don't feel like socializing today. I just want to bless my godchild one more time and go home.

"Jayd, it's lovely to see you, my dear," Mrs. Esop says, rising from the patio chair to hug me. "And look at this little princess. Rahima looks more and more like you every day, Raheem." And she's right. Rah couldn't deny his namesake if he tried, not that he ever would. After all the hell he's been through, first trying to find his daughter the first time Sandy ran off and then again after he did find her. Rah loves his daughter with all he's got and then some.

Mrs. Esop squeezes Rahima's cheeks gently, making the little girl smile and hide behind her daddy. She can play that shy role all she wants, but I know Rahima's a natural-born ham and deserves all the attention she can get.

"Thank you and happy Mother's Day," Rah says, handing Mrs. Esop a box of Godiva chocolates he just purchased on our pit stop. From the look on her face, she's very pleased. What girl doesn't love chocolates?

"Oh, baby, you didn't have to do that, but I'm so glad you

did," Mrs. Esop says, taking the gold box and hugging her play-son. Since Rah's mom isn't around—even on her own holiday—Mrs. Esop's always here for him. "Rah, there are some fresh cookies on the counter. Why don't you give Rahima one while you wake up my son, who's asleep on the living room couch," Mrs. Esop says, reclaiming her seat. "Jayd, how are you enjoying this lovely Sunday?" She expertly excuses Rah from our conversation.

I'm too tired for this, but it doesn't look like I have much of a say in the matter.

"I'll be back in a minute, Jayd," Rah says, taking the not-so-subtle hint and heading through the front door hand in hand with his toddler.

"Jayd, aren't you glad that wasn't you in labor this morning?" Mrs. Esop asks, sipping her ice tea and gesturing for me to sit in the chair across from hers. It must be nice to pass the time in luxury. If she only knew I shared some of the pain with Mickey, she'd eat her words.

"Yes, ma'am. But Mickey handled it like a pro." I don't know why I just lied. But I feel obligated to stand up for my girl, because I know where this conversation is going. It can head in only one direction if Mrs. Esop's talking about her son's girlfriend.

"You look a little troubled, Jayd. Everything okay?"

I had checked myself in the visor mirror when I got in the car but haven't had a chance to fully recoup from my run-in at Rah's. I hate it when a trick pulls my hair. It messes up the entire flow of my usually smooth ponytail.

"Sandy moved back to her grandparents' house. I helped her pack," I say, still unable to process the thought. Is Sandy really gone for good? I know Mrs. Esop knows I'm lying about helping Sandy. Everyone knows we aren't friends, but I'm not going to tell Mrs. Esop I was in another fight. She thinks I'm growing into a nice young lady and I'm trying. But bitches are everywhere, and sometimes they have to be dealt with properly.

"Ah," Mrs. Esop says, taking one of the freshly cut pink roses from the clear vase on the table, bringing it to her nose and inhaling deeply. "Girls like Sandy are never gone for good, Jayd. Mark my words—that girl will be back." Mrs. Esop looks at me, her brown eyes narrowing at the truth in her words. I know she's not fully aware of my powers, but she knows Mama and our lineage, so I know she knows more than she's saying.

"Nigel will be out in a second," Rah says, stepping back onto the front porch with Rahima, who's happily munching on a cookie. "Jayd, you ready to roll?"

"Yes. It's getting late, and I know Mickey's wondering where we are," I say as I rise from my seat, suddenly feeling light-headed. I lean back and steady myself on the glass table before nearly falling back into my chair. What the hell?

"Jayd, are you okay?" Rah asks, letting go of his daughter's hand and grabbing me by the arm, helping me catch my balance. Mrs. Esop rises and takes my other arm with an equally concerned look on her face.

"Sit down," Mrs. Esop says, directing me to reclaim my seat, but I can't. The pounding in my head creeps from the back of my skull all the way to the front, dulling all other sounds around me. It feels like a brain freeze but much more painful. I look up at Mrs. Esop, who now appears to be Maman, my great-grandmother. I try to scream at the sudden visual transformation, with no success. Before I can let out a sound, Maman's gone and so is the pounding, but I still feel woozy. Between my lack of sleep, inadvertently sharing Mickey's labor, and dealing with Sandy's crazy ass, I'm completely wiped out.

"What's going on?" Nigel says, stepping out of the open front door looking as exhausted as I feel.

"Jayd's not feeling well. Nigel, get her some water," Mrs. Esops says, now forcing me to sit down.

I allow her to push me back into the chair. Maybe I do need to chill for a spell. Nigel walks back into the house, and Rahima follows, undoubtedly going back for another cookie, completely oblivious to my issues: if life were only that simple for us all.

"I'm fine, really. I probably just need some rest." What was that? I've never seen Maman so clearly outside of my dreams before. It was as if she took over Mrs. Esop's body for a moment, but I know that can't be.

"There's no probably about it, girl," Rah says, feeling my forehead like Mama does when she hears me make the slightest sniffle. "You need to chill."

"Maybe we should drop you off at home, Jayd. Mickey will understand," Nigel says, placing a cool glass of water down on the table in front of me. I pick up the crystal cup with both hands and bring it to my lips, sipping slowly at first and then swallowing the rest in two large gulps.

"Thirsty, baby?" Rah asks, smiling down at me.

But it's no joke. I feel like I ate a block of salt for dinner, and Mama doesn't cook with that much sodium. "Yes, I am." I hand Rah the glass, and he passes it to Nigel. "Can I have some more, please?" They all look at me, amazed. It was a tall glass, but, damn, can't a sistah quench her thirst?

"Okay, now I know something's wrong. I'm taking you home now." Rah uses both hands to check my temperature, annoying me. I gently swat his hands away from my face and attempt to again rise from the table. Mrs. Esop looks at me and then at Rah, and I know what she's thinking—literally. Without trying, I can hear her thoughts clearly.

"Mrs. Esop, I can assure you I'm not pregnant with Rah's baby—or anyone else's for that matter," I say, steadying myself before letting go of the glass table. "I'm a virgin and plan on staying that way for a long time."

"Jayd, how did you know that's what I was thinking?" Mrs. Esop's look of concern has turned into one of fear. She obviously knows I repeated her thoughts verbatim—all without focusing on her mind cooling and allowing me in like I usually do with my mom's powers. It was as if she threw the thought my way and I unintentionally caught it. I have to get my mom's powers on lock and fast before they get ahead of me, but I'll worry about that later.

"It was written all over your face," I say, taking the cool drink from Nigel's hands, swallowing it down quickly and returning the empty glass to him. Now that I'm hydrated, I feel like a new woman. "We should get going if we're going to make it before visiting hours are over. We only have an hour left," I say, glancing at Rah's wristwatch.

"The only place you're going is home," Rah says, helping me off the porch and down the driveway where we're parked. "Don't worry about the car situation. We'll work it out."

"Yeah, man. Drive her home. Mom, can I take your car?" Nigel asks.

I know his mom wants to say no, but under the circumstances, she reluctantly nods her head. I wouldn't want to give up the Jaguar, either.

"You guys don't have to do that. I can make it home," I say, and I can. "Thank you for the hospitality, Mrs. Esop. I'll see you next weekend for the debutante meeting. The water was just what I needed to feel better."

Nigel and Rah look at each other and reluctantly follow me to my car, retrieving Rahima's car seat and letting me go on my way.

"Feel better, Jayd," Mrs. Esop says, staring at me strangely.

I know she's tripping about sharing her thoughts with me, but what can I say? I didn't do it on purpose, and I doubt I can do it again—at least not voluntarily. I have a lot to learn about my mom's gift of sight and will read up on it more, but not tonight. I just want to wash Sandy's fingerprints out of my hair, watch my Sunday-night television shows, and pass out on my mom's couch—no scary visions or crazy broads.

~ 1 ~ Nicety

The men all pause / And they all sung the same old tune.
—KLYMAXX

Rah and Nigel must've texted and called me fifty times on the way from Nigel's hood in Lafayette Square to my mom's apartment in Inglewood. It's not a long drive because both areas are off of Crenshaw Boulevard, and it doesn't require much thought to get here. I understand their concern and sent them a message as soon as I pulled in a few minutes ago. I'm glad to have my mom's space to park in so I don't have to worry about walking down the block by myself late at night. Making it to the front door and up the stairs from the sunken carport is challenging enough.

"Hey, girl," my mom says, surprising me as I open the multi-locked front door. What's she doing here so late? Usually she'd be with her man, Karl, especially after spending the day with us at Mama's house. Maybe he had dinner plans with his mom for the special day.

"Hey, Mom," I say, closing the door behind me. From the looks of it, my mom came home to restock her clothes. She took the jar of quarters from her dresser and put them in one of the three laundry baskets on the living room floor. I guess she's finally run out of clean clothes. Although knowing my mom, she probably ran out weeks ago and just bought new ones to wear for the time being, which I'm sure got a little expensive.

I plop down next to my mom on the cozy couch, putting my purse on the coffee table and removing my sandals. I pick up my spirit notebook from the end table and flip through the pages. I should write down today's events, but I'm too tired to relive the drama. Besides, my notes are in the car, and there's no way I'm going back downstairs this evening.

"It's unprostitutional!" my mom says, shouting at the television in front of us. Tiger Woods and his hoes have been all over the news for months, and personally I'm tired of the shit. If his wife wants to deal with his trifling behavior, who am I to question who and what he does?

"Mom, is that even a word?" I ask, flipping through my spirit notes and trying to concentrate on the task at hand. I have a lot of work to catch up on, not to mention the personal things I want to focus on even if I still can't think straight. But with my mom yelling at the television and sitting on the small couch that doubles as my bed, I doubt I'll get to sleep anytime soon.

"It is if I say it is," my mom says, reaching for the pretty gift basket my cousin Jay gave her for Mother's Day and pulling out a bottle of lotion. I feel for him not having either of his parents around. Even if Jay's mom, my aunt Anne, did call earlier, it's rare for her to talk to Jay or Mama. Mama's always silent about what happened between her and her youngest daughter, but I know she thinks about Anne a lot and so does Jay.

"So," my mom says, lathering her ebony skin with the fragrant cream. "How long do you plan on hiding the truth from Mama?" Her gift sure does smell good. I wonder if she'll share.

"As long as I can. You know she's going to make me give your powers back, if there's even such a thing." Stripping them away is more like it. Mama doesn't believe in me having more than my fair share of our gift of sight right now, limiting me to my dreams. But I believe that the ancestors—mainly Maman Marie, my great-grandmother—are trying to tell me something different.

"You know it's not going to work for long, Jayd. The only reason she hasn't detected them yet is because she's so distracted with her initiations and my stupid-ass brothers. You know she does a ritual to keep other people's madness out of her head while she's involved in the process. But as soon as she takes a break, she's going to hone in on your new development, and when she does, God help you."

Why does my mom always have to be so theatrical with her shit? I guess that's where I get my acting skills.

I reach for the large, gold basket on the table and claim a small bottle of lemon oil to sample. All of the products look and smell delicious. Jay gave Mama the same thing plus flowers and a card. He sure can pick a nice gift.

"Mom, you worry too much. Like I said, I'll keep your sight in my head for as long as I can," I say, massaging my hands and feet with the intoxicating liquid. I know Mama and Netta have the baddest beauty line available, and my novice products aren't far behind theirs, but it's nice to try something different. "Once I master it, Mama will be so proud of me she'll have to let me hold on to your reclaimed powers."

"Are we talking about the same Mama?" my mom asks, snatching the tiny glass container away from me. "Mama doesn't have to do a damned thing. You know it and I know it. Hell, the whole damned world knows it, Jayd." My mom rises from the couch and walks toward her bedroom. "You're playing with fire, little girl, hiding this from your grandmother. She's not going to be happy at all when she finds out you've been sitting on this for so long."

Still massaging my silky hands, I get up from my comfy spot and follow her into her room. "I know, Mom. It'll be okay—you'll see," I say, claiming a corner at the foot of her queen-sized bed to sit on. I wish I felt comfortable sleeping in her room when she's gone, but I'd rather be in the living room in case someone tries to break in. That way I can hear them walk up the stairs and prepare myself ahead of time.

"I wish I could say the same thing for you, little one, but I can't." My mom looks at me, worried that I've bitten off more than I can chew. "Jayd, how come you didn't tell me about you retaining this power from one of your dreams, especially since the sight you now possess once belonged to me?"

I watch my mom sit down on her bed now and realize I've hurt her feelings. I didn't even know that was possible. She's usually so hard-core. My mom looks at me, her emerald eyes tearing up. Now I really feel bad.

"Mom, I just didn't think you were interested."

"Jayd, if it has anything to do with my baby, I'm interested. And besides, you can look in that book all you want. It's still not better than firsthand information when you can get it."

I never thought about it like that. My mom's got a good point, especially since there's limited information available in the spirit book on my mom's path because she stopped keeping up with her notes in high school. I jog back into the living room, retrieve my notebook and pen, and again make myself comfortable on her bed.

"Okay, what you got?" I ask, happy for the night tutorial session. I can study and sleep after she's gone.

"Memories and regret."

That's the first time I've ever heard my mom express regret about anything short of marrying my dad. I know how she feels: No matter how much they get on my nerves sometimes, I'd miss my dreams if I lost them.

"Exactly," she says in my mind. *"Had I not been so hot-*

headed in the first place, I would still have my powers. I was just getting good at them, too." My mom eyes the disheveled room around her. When she left my dad seventeen years ago, she also left the house and everything in it.

"I'll help you keep my sight under one condition, Jayd. The next time you need help, ask. The last thing I want is you having a meltdown like I did."

"It's a deal," I say, smiling at my mom. She can be real sweet when she wants to be. But like Mama and the rest of the women in our lineage, cross us and nice turns to nasty real quick. After disrespecting the stove my mom and I bought Mama for Mother's Day, my uncle Kurtis is learning that lesson the hard way now.

"And you have to tell Mama," my mom adds. "Now that I know, I'm an accomplice and I can't lie to Mama about this. Promise me that you'll tell her, Jayd."

"That's two things," I say, watching my mom get comfortable in the bed she rarely uses. She pulls back the black and gold comforter, revealing gold satin sheets, and slides her dainty feet underneath.

"They go together, Jayd. And telling Mama sooner rather than later is of the utmost importance. Mama's got all kinds of tricks up her sleeve you know nothing about. I hope you never have to find out what happens when one of her daughters crosses her."

"I know, right. I'd hate to be Uncle Kurtis right now," I say, getting under the oversized blanket from the opposite end of the bed and sliding back so that I'm up against the wall.

"Mama can be as sweet as honey or as lethal as a rattlesnake when she wants to be. Listen to what I'm telling you, girl," my mom says, fluffing one of the larger pillows behind her head. "Don't push Mama too far or she will hurt you. It may be out of love, but a bite is a bite just the same."

"Okay, okay. I'll tell her," I say, reaching for the decorative accent pillows on the other side of the bed and propping myself up, ready to learn. "Now, tell me everything you can remember about your ability to chill a person's mind out. And if I haven't told you before, it's a dope power to have."

My mom smiles at my enthusiasm, and I'm glad to spend some time with her. Finally, she chooses time with her daughter over her man, and I'm grateful for it.

"The first thing you need to learn is that everything has side effects, Jayd. Read the label carefully, which in our case is the spirit book. When you retained my vision from your dream, you should have looked for stories about things that happened to me after I started using my powers, not just the ways I used them. For example, the night I almost killed your father with my eyes when I tapped into his mind, witnessing his premarital infidelity firsthand," my mom says, as cool as ice, "I scared myself I was so angry. My powers almost drove me crazy."

"You never told me about that," I say, writing as fast as I can. I should've got a tape recorder for this lesson.

"Because you never asked. You should be much further along in your studies by now, Jayd. Even I know that." She sounds just like Mama and Netta. I know I'm not on my game if my mom agrees with them. My mom and Netta have a tense relationship, but it's improved over time.

"But you know what a full plate I have, Mom. With cheer practice, the spring play, the debutante ball, and being president of the African Student Union, I haven't had much time for my spirit studies lately, but I'm trying to catch up."

"Like I said, everything has side effects."

My mom's right. Luckily the ball and the play are temporary. I'll have to find a better way to juggle the rest of my school activities with my personal life. My spirit work can't remain the ultimate sacrifice.

"The second thing you need to know is that cold things

tend to be slippery, which can be both good and bad. When you want to easily access someone's mind and cool his or her thoughts immediately, it's a very good thing. But when the mind is too hot, it can make your cool boil, causing a mental meltdown of sorts, and that can be very dangerous," my mom says, pulling the comforter tighter. "I've literally almost drowned in someone else's negative thoughts before. I don't wish that feeling on anyone." She shudders at the memory.

I'm shaking and I don't even know what she's going through, nor do I want to. "Is that why women in our lineage are afraid of water?" I ask, continuing my fervent note taking. If I had known things would become this clear, I would've talked to my mom a long time ago.

"Partially, and also because we have a healthy respect for nature's power to build and destroy. Any type of drowning isn't fun," my mom says, yawning loudly. It's getting late for both of us.

"I hear that." I took swim lessons at the YMCA when I was ten years old and nearly drowned. Lifeguard or not, you won't catch my ass in deep water again.

"Those two lessons will go a long way when deciding whose thoughts to probe and who to stay away from. Be careful who you try to help and when because as with Mickey's labor, the experience can turn on you like a pit bull. If you had known then what you know now, you would've never jumped into your friend's mind when you did." My mom's right. I have a lot to learn about her powers and my own. And with a few more sessions like this between me and her, a sistah will be back on her A game in no time—good sleep included.

My mom left late last night after we stayed up talking most of the time away. I fell asleep soon after and am grateful for the dreamless rest. I never did get to wash my hair last night, so I woke up early this morning to get a quick wash and blow-dry in before my school day begins. I'll be damned if I go another moment with Sandy's handprint in my crown.

I turn the hot knob to the right and then turn the middle one to full blast, welcoming the steam. Showers wake me up every morning.

Stepping into the shower, I slide the glass doors shut behind me. I lather the shampoo, scrubbing my scalp good before massaging it through my hair. It always feels good getting a clean start in the morning. Rubbing the mango-scented lather up my tresses, my fingers suddenly feel like jelly and my head feels cold. Am I dreaming? My fingers continue moving up my hair until I can no longer feel anything. Instead, my hair is feeling me.

"Aaah!" I scream, opening my eyes, allowing the soap and water on my face to cloud my vision. The fingers in my hair continue to walk their way down my scalp and around my neck, stifling my scream. Without the use of my hands, I'm defenseless against my strangler. If this were a dream, I would try to wake up or at least have Mama somewhere around to help me out of this madness. But I'm wide awake, experiencing this nightmare—alone.

"Water, Jayd. Use the water to rinse your eyes," my mom says into my mind with panic in her voice. This shit feels too real to be a regular vision.

Near fainting, I turn around and rinse my face off in the water. As my sight clears, the feeling slowly returns to my hands. I push my hair back and feel around my neck to loosen the ghostly grip, but I can't. The steam seeps up my nostrils, clearing my airways and melting the fingers around my neck.

"That's it, Jayd. Inhale and then exhale. It's not real, baby. Mind over matter," my mom says, helping to calm my nerves.

Finally free, I reach for the metal knobs to turn off the water, ending this nightmare on Larch Street, but not before I lose my footing and fall flat on my ass, hitting my head on the back of the ceramic tub.

"Ouch!" I rub my head in the same spot where I hit it falling on black ice in one of my dreams a few weeks ago. It's already tender from that experience, and now I've reopened the wound. What the hell is really going on?

"It's like I told you last night, Jayd. You're holding on to the residual negative emotions from your clients. You have to get rid of it before it drives you crazy, and Mama's the only one who can tell you exactly what to do." I hate it when my mom's right, and I'm suffering the consequences in the midst of her revelation. *"You have to tell Mama, Jayd. Now get yourself up and shake it off, or you're going to be late for school."*

"Can a sistah get a little sympathy?" I ask aloud, picking myself up and grabbing the towel from the back of the shower door to dry off. I guess I'll be wearing my hair wet today with some leave-in conditioner since my shower was cut short.

"Hell no, you can't get any sympathy. You asked for it and here it is. I know it sounds mean, Jayd, but I'm telling you the truth. There's so much more to our visions you don't know about, and that ignorance alone can harm you. Tell Mama today. Bye," my mom says, checking out and leaving me to my Monday.

I'll tell Mama about this one as soon as possible, but I have to get through the rest of the school day first. I'll see Mama at Netta's shop this afternoon when I go to work. Until then, I'll have to deal with this madness on my own.

School has been pretty relaxed so far, except for drama class. It's fifth period and we're in full rehearsal mode. With both Nigel and Chance in the spring play, it's sure to be a lively production. Both of their girlfriends have been tripping about their men spending too much time with the Drama Club members lately—mainly me. Lucky for Nellie and Mickey, they're my girls and I know this routine all too well. Once the play is over, their jealousy will quiet down until the next time it rears its ugly green head.

I'm glad Chance is coming around, but he's still not answering to his common name. If we don't call him Chase, he gets extra sensitive about it. Personally, I'm over it. It's going to take some time for all of us to adjust to our friend's new identity. And if Chance is smart, he'll give it some time, too.

"Okay, from the top of the scene, please. Dim the lights!" Mrs. Sinclair shouts to Matt and Seth offstage. There are only fifteen minutes left in the period, and then I'm off to cheer practice. It's the guys' turn to get grilled this afternoon, leaving Alia and I free to study our lines outside. It's a breezy, sunny day, making me thankful I attend a school by the beach. I know it's sizzling in Compton where my cousin Jay's high school's located. There's no sea breeze that far inland, but knowing Jay and the majority of his classmates, they left campus hours ago. Most teenagers don't take the last month of school seriously.

"Jayd, do you know where Chance is?" Nellie asks, interrupting our flow.

I've got most of my lines down, and if I could stay in my head long enough to clearly hear the voice of my character, Suzy, I'd have the rest.

"He's inside rehearsing," I say, rolling my eyes.

Alia shakes her head at the rude intrusion and the fact that Nellie is completely ignoring her presence. If Nellie doesn't know Alia's name by now, she sure will when Alia finally makes a move on her man.

Before Nellie can walk through the open door, Chance emerges looking pissed. What did I miss?

"What's this about you not taking me shopping after school?" Nellie asks, shaking her cell phone up at her tall man. "You promised me a new summer wardrobe months ago."

"Nellie, calm down. It ain't that serious," Chance says, ignoring her outburst.

But my girl will be heard—damn the rehearsal. Ever since she wasn't chosen for the cheer squad, Nellie's been on one and she's doing her best to take everyone with her.

"Not that serious?" Nellie asks, her blond weave swinging in the wind. "I have to get new outfits for all of the end-of-year socials, and you don't seem to care."

"That's because I don't," Chance says, causing all our mouths to drop. "Besides, you can take yourself shopping. I'm not your servant boy anymore." Chance reenters the dark classroom, leaving our girl hanging.

"I've had it! Don't call me again until you get rid of the attitude," Nellie yells, storming back up the hill. Reappearing through the open door, Chance tilts his baseball cap back farther, revealing his crooked smile and red eyes. I know what he and the rest of my boys were up to at lunch.

"Don't hold your breath," Chance says to her back. I've never seen Chance so cold before. Looks like he found more than his long-lost relatives down South. "I'm back, people," Chance yells into the classroom in his best Tony Montana impersonation.

From the way Alia's eyes are shining, I can tell she wants to smile at the argument we just witnessed, but she holds in her joy. She's got Chance right where she wants him. If Nellie and Chance keep going at each other's throats like this, it's only a matter of time before Alia makes her move on our boy.

"You want to start from the top?" Alia asks, refocusing our attention to our work like nothing just happened. She can pretend to be unconcerned all she wants, but she can't fool me.

"Alia, how bad are you feeling my boy?" I ask her point-blank. If she's working her way into a permanent position into our crew, I need to get the preliminary interviews out of the way.

Without trying to hide her feelings, Alia looks up from her script and smiles at me, her silver braces shining bright. "Chance and I go way back to elementary school, Jayd. We were best friends," Alia says, playing with the booklet in her hands. "We were each other's first kiss."

This girl sounds eerily familiar, except I'm trying to get away from my first love, not waiting for him to be free of his crazy attachment. "That doesn't answer my question." I want the full confession. Alia's already secretary of the African Student Union and in Drama with us: If she's going to hang with our crew on the regular, I need to know she's down for the long haul.

"I've been in love with Chance for forever," Alia says, like she's Snow White and Chance is her Prince Charming. It's official: Nellie's got some serious competition vying for her man's attention, and Alia came first. If I know anything about puppy love, it's that it can become a full-grown bitch real quick. "Does he ever talk about me?" Alia asks, looking dreamy eyed.

"Not to me," I say. I don't want to hurt her feelings, but even Chance isn't that crazy. Alia looks at me, and we both acknowledge that although we may be cool, Nellie and I are girls. And some lines you don't cross, one of them being conspiring with the female trying to take my girl's man, no matter how I may feel about the issue. The bell for sixth period rings, and Alia jumps up to collect her things from the classroom without saying good-bye. That was awkward for both of us, but I hope she knows she can trust me. I'm not the one she should be worried about.

"What up, Jayd?" Nigel asks, placing his arm around my neck as he catches up with my quick stride. I'll be glad when this daily trek across campus is over. It's too hot for all of this every afternoon, and I know the other fifty or so students who have similar schedules feel me, too.

"Your boy Chance and his soon-to-be-ex-girl, that's what," I say, slowing down to match Nigel's pace. "You need to talk to him before it's too late."

"Unlike chicks, Jayd, we brothas don't get involved in another man's female problems," Nigel says, taking my backpack off my left shoulder and sliding it on his arm. He's such a good homeboy. "If Chance brings it up, we'll let him vent. Otherwise, it's like the shit isn't even happening in our world."

I guess Nigel's right. I'll have to go to the women for help with this one. Mama and Netta are the wisest women I know. Thank God I'll see them at work in a couple of hours. The occurrences in my life today alone will give us a lot to talk about. And I'm sure there's a lot going on in their worlds, too.

"Well, should he bring it up . . . ," I begin.

Nigel looks down at me, nodding his head. "I'll make sure to steer him in the right direction, Lady J," Nigel says, smiling. I know he's got our backs. Our crew can be a little crazy at times, but we're here for each other, no matter how out of hand things can get.

~ 2 ~
Mi Vida Loca

But I'm a rebel stressin' / To pull out of the heat no doubt.
—NAS

When I was a little girl, days home from school felt like a dream that lasted all day long. Mama would let me stay home whenever I asked—whether the request was verbal or not. At the slightest sniffle or bad dream, a phone call was made to the attendance office: No one at any of my schools ever questioned my grandmother's judgment. Once Mama's mind is made up, that's it—no discussion allowed, especially if it's about one of her own.

Keeping my mom's powers in spite of the crazy daydream I had in the shower this morning is my main priority this afternoon, even if Mama's adamantly against me doing so. Maybe with Netta there to have my back and the sweet spell I put on her and my mom a couple of months ago still in effect I can convince her to let me keep them a little while longer. Between hotheaded friends and crazy baby mamas, I need to maintain the ability to chill people's minds out now more than ever.

The sweet scent of strawberries and peaches leads me from the parking lot toward the front door of Netta's Never Nappy Beauty Shop, where Mama and Netta are already locking up for the day. They never close the salon early, so something must be wrong.

"Hi, Mama and Netta," I say, noticing their upbeat mood. At least I know whatever's going on isn't too serious.

"Little Jayd, you're just in time to help us," Netta says, passing me two large paper bags filled with supplies. There are several more on the ground in front of the door.

"How was your day, baby?" Mama asks, kissing me on the cheek and heading toward the parking lot.

Why are they acting like they're not messing with my money? I need to work this afternoon. "Where are all the clients?" I ask, turning around and following my grandmother and godmother. "And why are we leaving the shop?" Maybe there was an outbreak or something. I can't believe there's no work to do. These women always have a honey-do list at least two feet long.

"So many questions for a young queen in training," Netta says teasingly, going back for the rest of the items. I place the bags in the passenger seat and head back for the last one.

"We have a lot of work to do and need the family shrines to get it done," Mama says, loading the back of Netta's pickup with stuff of her own. She's still not comfortable riding in the car with me and probably never will be. I say she and Nellie need to get licenses. It's unimaginable to me that they would rather depend on others for a ride than to drive their own cars.

"We'll meet you back at the house," Netta says, getting behind the wheel and starting the massive truck's engine. Mama pulls herself into the passenger seat and shuts the heavy door. Netta's husband usually drives her around, but she's got the keys today. They still haven't explained how I'm supposed to make my money for the afternoon. Hopefully I'll pick up a few more personal clients to make up my weekly quota.

"There are some things more important than money,

chile," my grandmother says through the open window, wiping her brow. She's wearing her salt-and-pepper hair up in a white scarf this afternoon, showing off her dazzling green eyes and caramel complexion, making her look much younger than her fifty-plus years. "Especially doing work that can help us stay in the ancestors' and orishas' good favor."

Mama's right. Without them, none of the good in life would be possible. It's time to get my hands dirty and give thanks for all of my blessings, no matter how overwhelmed I may feel.

"Place the bags on your bed, Jayd," Mama says, unlocking the bedroom door and leading the way into her room. I haven't slept in here since I left Mama's house last month. I'm glad that insanity is over, but Mama's still not over me moving to my mom's apartment. We place the goods on the crowded bed now used as a storage space and remove our shoes, ready to work.

"Netta, you can start the libations. Jayd and I will get everything else ready," Mama says, moving to the side and letting Netta walk around her small bed and into the corner where the shrines are housed. This room is crowded for one person. How Mama and I shared it for sixteen years is something else. I miss Mama, but I wouldn't trade having my own space for anything in the world.

Netta kneels down and salutes the shrines before opening the sheer white fabric, revealing the three-tiered wooden shelves, each holding individual altars. I place my purse on the nightstand in between the two twin beds as Mama takes three cups from Netta to clean in the bathroom sink across the hall. My pink cell phone goes off, causing my purse to vibrate and Netta to look at me, cross. Nellie will have to wait. She doesn't want anything anyway except to yell at me about

Chance's behavior earlier today. I'll put her up in my prayers as soon as we get started. She and Chance need all the help they can get.

"Sorry," I say, turning the phone off and returning it to my bag where I can't help noticing two boarding passes with Mama's name on her side of the antique table. This can't be right.

"Going somewhere?" I ask, waving the colorful papers in the air before Netta has a chance to start the traditional prayers. Mama walks back into the room and shakes her head at me. I guess Nigel was right about us women being nosy.

"Your grandmother's finally going to Miami, and I'm going with her," Netta says, more excited than I've ever seen. She takes one of the fresh water glasses from Mama and places it on the floor in front of her knees. "One of her favorite clients moved there several years ago and recently opened a spiritual house. He wants Lynn Mae to come and bless it."

"Calm down, Netta," Mama says, replacing the clear glasses of water on the ancestor altar. Netta tosses back her shoulder-length brown curls and smiles at her friend. I can tell Mama's nervous even if she won't admit it. Mama hates to travel, especially if it has to do with a plane or a boat, and in this case, it's apparently both.

"I can't," Netta says, handing Mama the Florida water to sprinkle over the items that need blessing, including more belly balm for Mickey's stretch marks. I know Mickey will appreciate that. "It's been too long since we've traveled. She's agreed to the cruise to Puerto Rico and all. We're going to have so much fun."

Mama cuts her eyes at her friend, who's completely unfazed by her reservations. Netta's brown eyes are shining brighter than Mama's. If I didn't know any better, I'd say Netta's about to burst wide open she's so happy.

"The only traveling we're doing right now is to the spirit room," Mama says, helping Netta to her feet.

Netta smiles at Mama, who can't help but smile back at her best friend. Netta's slightly slimmer than Mama, but they're about the same height and build. They share clothes just like me and my girls used to do before their bodies changed: Mickey because of pregnancy and Nellie because of severe weight loss, trying to fit in with the rich-girl crew.

"For now. But soon we're going to be off on a real Legba adventure," Netta says, giggling as she picks up a few of the supplies and passes them to me to carry. She and Mama grab two bags and leave the rest on the bed. I step out into the hallway and Netta follows.

"I just pray that Legba blesses our journey and our homes while we're away," Mama says, calling on our father orisha to bless their travels. Legba's the orisha over movement of all kind, and he likes to play while doing it, which can be good or bad, depending on his inclination. That's why it's important for us to do the work that we do.

"Oh, Lynn Mae. I know you know Legba loves his children. We're going to have such a good time you won't want to come home."

Mama gives Netta a look that says she's not so sure what all the excitement's about. Once Mama gets away from all of the pressures of being a priestess and a housewife, hopefully she'll loosen up a bit.

"I'm going to leave it up to you to make sure the spirit room is not harmed while I'm gone, Jayd," Mama says, turning out the light in her bedroom before locking the door and walking toward the kitchen with Netta and me behind her. She looks at her stove and shakes her head in disgust. "Fools know no boundaries," Mama says, disturbed by the lack of respect her gift has been shown.

"Wise people know what's sacred," Netta says, touching Mama's shoulder with her free hand. Thank God Netta was here with us on Mother's Day. She's the only one who can calm Mama down when she goes completely off.

"My mom said the repair guy will be out by the end of the week," I say, wishing I could do more to help. My words provide little comfort to Mama, whose eyes turn red at the memory of her present being destroyed by my uncle Kurtis as we performed a ritual for the ancestral Mothers outside. Mama went way the hell off and will again if he's not out of her house soon.

"I hate that I lost my head that day, but sometimes it's the only way to bring about change," Mama says, wiping a single teardrop from beneath her right eye. "Don't be afraid to wear your crazy hat when need be, Jayd." Mama walks through the kitchen toward the back door.

"Yeah, girl. Crazy is where your power lies. And yielded properly, it can get the job done when nothing else can." Netta's crazy for saying that out loud, but it's the gospel. We all know that black women have an image of snapping at the drop of a hat, but Netta and Mama both have good points.

Before we can get out of the kitchen, a knock at the front door pulls us back inside. The hot summer weather and longer daylight hours keep the men in the streets longer, leaving us women at home alone this evening. We were enjoying the peace and quiet. In this house it's a luxury to get work done without any interruptions.

"Jayd, get the door please," Mama says, stepping onto the back porch and petting Lexi, who's always happy to see her owner.

"Yes, ma'am," I say, walking back up the steps and through the dining room. It's probably someone looking for one of my uncles. I should be able to get rid of them quickly. But when I open the front door, it's the last person I ever expected to see at Mama's house again.

"Alaafia, Princess Jayd," Hector, Emilio's godfather, says with my schoolmate Emilio by his side. Some people never learn. "Is your *abuela* home? We desperately need her assistance in an urgent matter."

This guy's a little heavy on the theatrics. Mama's not going to be happy about this pop-in visit at all.

"Alaafia, Baba. Emilio," I say, rolling my eyes at my schoolmate. After he tried to blackmail me into auditioning with him in exchange for me swaying Mama to become the head of their spiritual house with Hector, he has the nerve to step back onto my grandmother's front porch. "I'll see," I say, closing the door and walking back into the kitchen where Mama and Netta are waiting on the back porch. Lexi needs to take a bite out of our unexpected guests: Maybe that'll humble their asses.

"Mama, it's for you," I say, scratching Lexi behind her ears. "It's Hector and Emilio again."

Mama stops petting her German shepherd and looks up at Netta, who peers behind me at the front door. With enraged eyes, Mama marches through the dining room and opens the door, causing Emilio and the elder to jump in surprise. Netta charges behind her homegirl, signaling me to come, too.

"Alaafia, Iyalosha," Hector says, bowing at Mama's feet.

Emilio follows suit, but Mama's not amused.

"What can I do for you, Hector?" Mama asks without returning the false love. Rising without her blessing, Hector nervously answers her inquiry.

"We again have come to plead for the life of our ile, Queen Jayd," Hector says, again being overdramatic about the situation. "Would you please reconsider becoming the head of our little house?"

Netta and Mama exchange looks, knowing Mama's about to blow.

"I've tried to be nice about you showing up unannounced at my home, but you're pushing devotion to disrespect," Mama says, putting her right hand on her hip and looking Hector in the eye. "Get off my porch and don't step one foot back on it unless you're invited personally by me to do so." Mama steps back into the house and slams the door behind her. I know they got the message loud and clear this time.

"The nerve of some people," Netta says, heading back toward our original destination.

"Jayd, turn the porch light on and lock the door. We won't be back up here for a while," Mama says, taking a deep breath before following Netta into the kitchen.

"Lynn Mae, look." Netta points toward the living room window, through which we see Emilio and Hector walking across the narrow patch of grass separating our house from our evil neighbor Esmeralda's yard. She opens the gate for her guests, welcoming them into her encumbered animal fortress. Just the thought of stepping foot in her house gives me the chills. With all of the clutter Esmerelda's got going on over there, she could be on one of those hoarder shows.

"I don't care, Netta. As long as they're off my property, I'm happy." Mama turns around and heads back toward the kitchen and out the door. "Jayd, hurry up. We've got a lot of work to do," Mama says, closing the back door.

I guess we're going to be in the spirit room all night. So much for me practicing my lines for the spring play. Opening night's in two weeks, and I still have a lot to memorize, not to mention that I need to go over the notes from my mom's lessons on managing her powers in my head. If I don't review them soon, I might not be able to recognize some of the words. My handwriting's so challenged even I have a hard time reading it.

I step onto the front porch and flip the wall switch next to the door several times, realizing the light's out. You'd think that with all the men in this house, things like this would never go unnoticed. I bet it's been out for days. I quickly retrieve a new bulb from the hall closet and change the light. Before I can successfully retreat back inside, Esmeralda looks up at me from her porch, locking me in my place. Shit: When will I ever learn? Looking at Esmeralda is like looking into Medusa's eyes, except instead of turning her victim into cement, Esmeralda gives you a headache that makes you wish you were dead.

"Your grandmother should've joined us when she had the chance," Esmeralda hisses, grasping the iron bars of her porch railing with her pale hands. The veins running through her wrinkled fingers are as blue as her cold eyes. *"Then I might've shown her little prodigy more mercy,"* Esmeralda says, this time in my mind.

I'm not sure if that was intentional on her part, but that was her first mistake. The second was threatening my grandmother.

"I don't need your mercy, but you might want to ask for some of your own," I say as my mom's vision takes over. This time unafraid of Esmeralda's evil glare, I shoot her back a look of my own, instantly sending a cold front to her mind while releasing myself from her visual hold.

While inside Esmeralda's mind, I notice her emotions about Mama are going every which way. She's afraid of Mama, but at the same time she's hell-bent on destroying her. Esmeralda still has love for her former spiritual godsister, but she is also insanely jealous of my grandmother, fueling her revenge even more.

"You can't hurt me, girl," Esmeralda says, turning up her mental powers a couple of notches. Her hot head—usually ice cold—boils at my intrusion, eventually melting like ice

under my mom's even cooler sight. My mother warned about the danger of entering heads like Esmeralda's: If I stay in too long, I run the risk of drowning in the puddle of emotions swimming through her mind.

"I'm not trying to hurt you," I say into Esmeralda's head as I make my way out of her liquid web. *"You're forcing me to defend myself by any means necessary. If you get hurt in the process, then so be it."* Just when I think I've escaped her clutches, Esmeralda regains her strength and goes full throttle on my eyes.

"Ahhh," I say, moaning at the sheer thrust of her attack. I'm not prepared for all of this—or so I think. Unable to close my eyes, my mom's sight is pushed aside and I can feel my eyes glowing. Esmeralda continues to hold my gaze as my vision adjusts to Maman's presence taking over my mind. What the hell is really going on?

"What's happening?" Esmeralda asks, also noticing the change. "My head," she moans, sounding like I did a moment ago.

Maman's eyes hone in on the tiny veins in Esmeralda's forehead, controlling the blood as it pulsates through her body. I can feel every beat of her heart as Maman slows it down, causing excruciating pressure to build in Esmeralda's head. She attempts to retreat, but it's too late.

"I know how you feel," I say, noticing the jade reflection of my bright eyes against the glass light fixture. I completely surrender to Maman's will, allowing her to finish this battle for me. Once Esmeralda's begging ceases, Maman's presence fades as quickly as it appeared and my eyes return to their usual brown selves. I feel a little light-headed, but damned good about humbling Esmeralda's ass.

"You little wench!" Esmeralda yells, slamming the rusted porch gate shut and running inside. Good. That'll teach her to mess with me again. I may have been afraid of her before, but since rocking my mom's sight, I've got a little more gumption, and it's time to start using it more often.

Rather than going back through the house, I shut the door behind me, walk across the front lawn, and head through the back gate. Mama and Netta are already in the spirit room busy working. Before I can receive my directions for this evening's tasks, my head starts pounding. I can feel every drop of blood coursing through my veins, similar to what Esmeralda just experienced. I attempt to steady myself on the wooden table in the center of the small kitchen, but my hands are slippery with sweat, causing me to lose my grip.

"Is it hot in here to y'all?" I ask as I fan myself with my hands. I feel like I'm on fire. These must be the residual effects of using my mom's powers. She warned me about this. And I imagine Maman taking control of the situation has some drawbacks of its own: yet another thing to check out in the spirit book when I get a chance.

Noticing my ill demeanor from across the table, Mama drops the lemons she's holding and rushes to my aid.

"Jayd, you're burning up," Mama says, touching my forehead and receiving some of my heat. Thank God. I don't know how much more I can take.

"I'm thirsty," I say, smacking my dry tongue against the roof of my mouth. It feels like I ate sand for lunch. Netta takes a clean glass from the dish rack next to the sink where she's rinsing herbs and fills it with cold water.

"Have you had any water today?" Mama asks, still absorbing my discomfort. What would I do without Mama's healing touch?

"Not much," I say, taking the cool glass Netta offers and bringing it to my lips. I feel as parched as I did yesterday at Nigel's house when I felt Maman's presence. This can't be a coincidence.

"This always happens when you get dehydrated, girl. You

need your water." Mama takes a large yellow glass from the kitchen counter and fills it with spring water from a jar on the table, forcing me to drink it after finishing the first glass of tap. I welcome the sweet liquid home in five large gulps. I needed that.

"What happened to you that fast?" Netta asks, helping Mama clear the table of our work. Our clients will have to wait. I can't even think straight after that encounter of the cruel kind.

"Esmeralda," I say, barely whispering. My body's gradually cooling down, but the pounding's not going away so easily. If I speak any louder, it'll only make the pain worse.

"Esmeralda," Mama and Netta say simultaneously. They look toward her house, wishing they could blow it up through the wall, I'm sure. I wish I could have done more while I had Esmeralda's mind on lock: I bet she'll think twice before attacking me again, not that she'll ever stop. Esmeralda lives to make the Williams women suffer.

"I told you about looking that woman in the eye," Mama says, forcing my chin up as she works her visual magic on my head. Mama's green eyes continue to glow as she cools my mind down completely. I'm so grateful for her skills.

"She's so quick sometimes," I say, feeling the pounding soften with each fleck of Mama's vision.

"You have to be quicker," Mama says, probing my mind for damage. "It doesn't seem like she got a chance to do too much harm this time," Mama says quizzically. I know she's wondering what really happened out there. Maybe now's a good time to confess to Mama what she should've known about a couple of months ago when I first retained my gift from the dream world. Keeping something from Mama is the same thing as lying, and I know she's not going to take kindly to me being dishonest, no matter how much I try to justify my actions.

"I didn't let her keep me on lock for long," I say.

Both Mama and Netta look at me, surprised. If I didn't know better, I'd say they were impressed. That feeling may change once they know why I was such a badass with my skills this evening. I know I should tell Mama about it now like my mom suggested, but on second thought I'm in no mood for an ass whipping tonight. Esmeralda up in my head's enough punishment for one day, but I will tell Mama before she leaves for her trip.

"Your mama called to tell me there was something you needed to talk to me about," Mama says, returning to her duties, along with Netta, now that I'm better. I guess I should get on it, too, if I plan on getting back to Inglewood at a decent hour. I need to catch up on my sleep and my own work.

"It was a bad dream, but don't worry. My mom helped me work it out," I say, avoiding Mama's gaze. I wonder how long I can keep this dance up before Mama catches on. I know she senses something's up, but she can't quite put her finger on it because of her other spiritual distractions.

"Is that so?" Mama asks, smiling at her homegirl and sharing a secret I'm not privy to.

I can tell she wants details, but she's not going to push for full disclosure, and for that, I'm grateful. We can hear Emilio and his godfather in Esmeralda's backyard doing only God knows what. Mama and Netta glance out the door and over to her yard, shaking their heads. The last thing I want to do is add to Mama's already full plate. She needs to focus on shutting that madness down, not on the drama in my life.

"Maybe we should postpone the trip. There's so much work to be done here," Mama says, much to Netta's disapproval.

"Oh, Lynn Mae, there's always going to be something to pop up and distract us. It's nothing but the Devil trying get in our way," Netta says, chopping up fresh herbs and passing them to Mama to pound in her marble mortar, one of my favorite tools. "We need to ask Legba to clear this road and all obstacles in our way, including your excuses."

Mama glares at Netta, who in turn sticks her tongue out at her best friend, knowing she's right. I couldn't agree more. Mama needs to get the hell out of Compton. It's been too long since she traveled, mostly because she's always taking care of everyone else and not putting herself first. This Mother's Day was case in point that Mama deserves a break. I'm not going to be the one to stand in her way, and I'll be damned if anyone else tries to.

"Don't worry about anything, Mama," I say. "I'll be fine. Go on your trip and have some fun. You deserve it," I say. I pick up a broom to start the cleaning process. This is something I'll have to do before it's all said and done anyway. I might as well get it over with so there won't be as much for me to do later.

"You sure you can handle all of this on your own?" Mama asks, gesturing around us. The small room is packed from floor to ceiling with powders, potions, and other tools of our trade. She then places both hands on the huge, aged, leather-bound book holding the keys to our success and answers to any questions we might have. That is more important than any material item in this quaint house—shrines included.

"Yes, ma'am," I say. "You can trust me."

The look in Mama's eyes tells me she's not just talking about me taking charge of my own healing when it comes to bad dreams and wicked neighbors, but our clients' issues as well.

"Jayd, our clients depend on us. And you have a lot of social commitments to manage already," Mama says, alluding to the debutante ball, the play, and the cheer squad. She has always been against me overextending myself.

"I've got this, Mama." Mama and I exchange a look of trust, love, and fear. She's got to let me try.

"Okay, then; it's settled. Little Jayd will hold down the spiritual needs of our clients while we're gone, and you'll let her try, Big Jayd," Netta says, clapping her hands like she's really running things. We both know Mama has the final say in every major spiritual decision. There's only one queen in this house, and that's Mama. Even Esmeralda knows that, no matter how bad she might think she is.

Finally surrendering to our wills, Mama smiles and looks at me firmly.

"This is your chance to show us what you've got, girl. Most importantly, remember to ask for help when you need it," Mama says, checking my forehead with the back of her hand one more time before getting back to work. She said "us" but I know she meant her. There's a lot riding on my shoulders as the next queen in line to take charge of our lineage's responsibilities. I haven't been fully engrossed in the strenuous tasks involved in learning what I need to know for the next phase of my journey, but that's all about to change. I plan on being on my game this summer in more ways than one, starting with mastering my skills.

"Oh, Lynn Mae. Don't be so hard on the poor girl," Netta says, wrapping her right arm around my shoulders. She's such a good godmother. I can only hope I'm the same with Rahima and Nickey, Mickey's daughter. "Jayd, I can't wait to read about your learnings in the spirit book when we get back."

"Me neither," Mama says, half laughing.

I haven't done such a good job keeping up with my contributions to our family's history, but I plan on rectifying that situation, too. The next two weeks are going to be hectic both at home and at school. But if there's one thing I've learned about my crazy life, it's that as long as the ancestors are in my corner, I'm up for any challenge that comes my way.

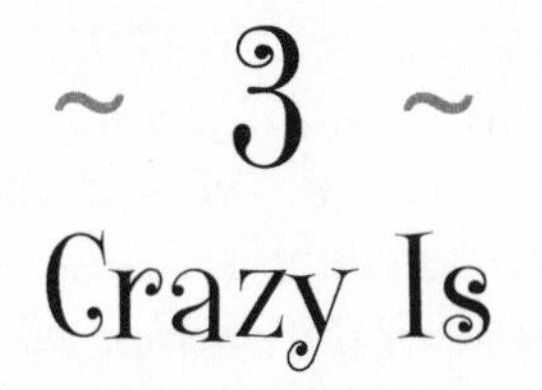

~ 3 ~ Crazy Is

My chick bad, my chick good /
My chick do stuff that your chick wish she could.

—LUDACRIS FEAT. DIAMOND, TRINA, AND EVE

The crisp air is refreshing on my cheeks, cooling my warm skin. I see white in every direction I look, and it's not just the sheer veil covering my eyes. I'm completely surrounded by a thick smoke blocking my vision and preventing any attempt to move for fear of stepping off into an abyss. The smoke thins slightly, allowing me to see that I'm standing on a theater stage alone, dressed in all white.

"Here comes the bride," Mama says from the audience. Netta and Mr. Adewale are also present, seated on either side of my grandmother. Not another dream where I'm getting married. And much like my last nuptial escapade, in which I was a young mother marrying Rah, this one is sure to end in disaster.

"Pray to our mother, Oshune, that she's always by your side," Netta says, gently blowing the air in front of her, dissipating the rest of the ivory haze around me. "Pray for her continued love and protection."

A silent Mr. Adewale begins pounding the ancient drum in his lap while Mama and Netta join in with songs to the orisha. Their melodic voices put me into a trance, and I sing along in the ancient tongue. I don't know what the words mean, but I can certainly feel their power.

"It's time," Mama says, now onstage behind me. She lifts the veil covering my face and urges me to walk forward. Mr. A's drumming grows more intense and Netta's singing louder with each beat. I reach the edge of the stage where I notice a thin gap between the audiences' seats and the stage steps. At the bottom of the long, narrow fall is the ocean crashing violently against the shore.

"I've got you, girl," Netta says, standing in front of her seat with her arms extended toward me. Oh, hell no. Dream or not, this is by far the craziest thing they've ever asked me to do.

"It's okay, baby," Mama says into my left ear, gently pushing me to keep going despite the looming danger below. She touches the five jade bracelets on my left arm, causing tiny bumps to form from the cool material against my skin. "Have faith that you will make it and you will." This isn't the Matrix and I'm not Neo. If I fall, I already know I'm not bouncing back up.

"Trust in your mothers, Jayd. We've always got your back, even when you don't know it." I look into Netta's eyes, and she smiles wide, stretching her arms out even farther. Mama touches the top of my shoulders, singing softly to the drumbeat taking over the vast theater. I take a deep breath, close my eyes, and jump.

"Mama!" I yell, waking out of my sleep drenched in sweat. Some of the salty liquid escapes through my fingers as I wipe my forehead. The perspiration trickles down to my lips, tasting like seawater. If I taste ocean water, then I must've landed in the sea and not into Netta's arms. What does that mean? Damn, that was a strange dream and I would know.

"Did the alarm go off?" Jeremy asks, rubbing his eyes open. I know he'll be glad when we don't have to wake up early for school anymore. However, if he continues spending the night at my mom's place, my crazy dreams will sometimes wake him up without warning.

"Not yet," I say, kicking the thin sheet off my body.

Jeremy looks at his cell on the floor next to his pillow and checks the time. I can tell by the darkness in the room that it's too early for most sane people to be up.

"Another bad dream?" Jeremy asks. I love that we're in sync. He touches my thigh, noticing the moist coating on my skin. "Damn, baby. Are you okay?"

"Yes, Jeremy. I'm fine," I say, rising from our self-made cot on the floor of my mother's apartment to dry off. "It's all a part of it."

Jeremy rises from his side and follows me toward the bathroom. "Isn't there something you can do to make them more pleasant?"

That's actually not a bad idea, but I don't think my gift of sight works like that. I take my towel off the rack on the wall and pat myself dry.

"I wish there were," I say, putting the towel back in its place and returning to the pile of blankets we use as a bed. The small couch can sleep only one. Jeremy joins me in the still room, readjusting himself to hold me in his arms.

"Baby, I've been dreaming like this all my life. I'm used to it," I say, only telling half the truth. Sometimes they scare the hell out of me, too.

"I don't see how you can ever get used to waking up from a dream screaming on a regular basis."

I grab Jeremy's forearms and tighten his grip around my waist, reassuring him that everything's okay. Jeremy's more shaken up than I am, and he didn't even have to risk his life.

"I promise it's not as bad as it seems." I stroke Jeremy's hands, feeling his breathing relax as we calm down. Before I can fully fall back to sleep, Jeremy turns me around and kisses my forehead. Face-to-face, he kisses me softly on the lips, bringing me back to life.

"I feel helpless when I see you uncomfortable," Jeremy says in between kisses.

How do I convey to him that his fear's unwarranted. "You shouldn't, baby," I say, taking over the early morning make-out session with a few kisses of my own. "Your presence alone makes me feel safe."

Jeremy kisses me passionately—damn sleeping. As far as we're concerned, this day has officially begun, and I for one am glad it's starting on the right foot. I can't predict how the rest of the school day will go, but if I can remember this feeling, nothing should be able to get under my skin.

No matter how different our cliques, hairstyles, and cultures may be, it's safe to say every student at South Bay High is glad the last two weeks of school are finally here. This year has been a whirlwind, and I'm ready to slow down for the next three months. I joined the summer reading circle for AP English, which includes studying for the SATs. That's all the schoolwork I have to do until the fall. It may take me a while to catch up to my privileged counterparts who've been groomed for all standardized tests from the womb, but I'm holding my own.

My mom and Mama agreeing that I need to get back on my spiritual game is enough for me to devote more time to my studies. They rarely agree on anything. And with my dreams and sight more off the chain than usual, I'm fully aware that I need to get on my spiritual p's & q's—not now, but right now. However, I have to make it through the rest of this short Tuesday before I can focus on anything else. I'm enjoying my part as the lead in the spring play and all the perks thereof, but it's a lot of work.

"Line," I say to my freshman understudy, Brenda, who is offstage. Laura, the Associated Student Body's queen bitch, was initially offered the spot but refused to work underneath me—her words, not mine. Brenda looks up from her script, irritated with my constant intrusion of her seeing how long she can stretch her Juicy Fruit gum before it snaps.

"Jayd, haven't you memorized the script yet?" Mrs. Sinclair asks, aggravated at my constant requests for help. I look to Brenda for my line, but she's lost her place. Some understudy she's turned out to be.

"Yes. I just got a little confused for a moment." My body may be in fifth-period drama class, but my mind is elsewhere. I've been thinking about Jeremy all day long. I'd rather be at the beach with him hugged up on a blanket than in this stuffy, dark room with Mrs. Sinclair on my ass any day.

"The star's confused. Fabulous. Just fabulous," Mrs. Sinclair says, taking a pencil out of her bushy red ponytail and tapping the clipboard on her lap. "Opening night is creeping upon us, and the star's confused." Mrs. Sinclair dramatically waves her hands around in the air. Maybe I am off my game a little bit, but it's not that serious. Mrs. Sinclair has never been so hard on me before.

The afternoon school announcements blare through the speakers, interrupting Mrs. Sinclair's rant. Usually I'm as annoyed by the rude interruption as our teacher visibly is, but I'm actually grateful for the save this afternoon. Reid's so annoying. Hopefully next year he'll be voted out of office as ASB president.

"It's okay, Jayd. She's always hardest on the star," Alia says, patting my shoulder. She's on point with her lines and stage cues and has the good fortune of having a competent alternate. How did I get all mixed up? Alia's attention is diverted to the door opening across the room. Nigel and Chance walk in from the main theater and smile our way. Alia's eyes brighten every time she sees Chance.

Every day there's something different about the new Chance. First it was his name, then his teeth and wardrobe. Today Chance has three wooden strings of rosary beads hanging around his neck. Unless something else has changed, I know he's not Catholic, so what's that all about?

"My ladies," Chance says, joining Alia and me in the center of the classroom. He hugs Alia, making her day even sweeter, and then me.

"What up, my peoples?" Nigel says, quickly hugging me and nodding to Alia. Reid can go on for ten minutes if the front office lets him. We might as well join Nigel and sit down.

"What's up with the beads?" I ask Chance, gently touching the largest crucifix out of respect. Mama wears a rosary sometimes with her elekes—beads for the orishas—in honor of our ancestors who hid voodoo behind Catholicism so that it could survive. She also says that even though Jesus may not be our ancestor, he's somebody's and should be honored as such.

"Everyone's wearing them in Hotlanta, shawty. Want me to get you one?" Chance asks, fingering the trio like it's platinum.

"Nah, I'm good. I've got all the bling I need right here," I say, stretching my arms out in front of me and shaking my wrists, allowing my bracelets to clink. My friends smile, but our teacher doesn't find me amusing at all.

"Jayd, what the hell is that noise?" Mrs. Sinclair asks over the speaker, eyeing my jade bracelets from her seat in front of the stage.

"My bracelets?" I ask, touching the ancient jewelry. "I've always had these on." I don't know which is more annoying: Reid's pompous ass or Mrs. Sinclair's other personality creeping out.

"You need to remove those cowbells at once. They're very distracting. Everyone, take five and be back on the set ready to impress me—no clinking allowed," she says, rolling her eyes. I guess she's had it with me.

"Mrs. Sinclair can be brutal when she wants to be," Chance says, feeling my pain.

"Damn, she didn't have to call you out like that," Nigel says, leading the way outside. It's a clear, hot day in Redondo Beach. Even the birds are chilling on the bus bench across the street, enjoying the warm sea breeze. The sun's shining brightly in the blue sky, again making me wish I were at the beach with Jeremy and his crew instead of stuck inside rehearsing. I asked for the lead role and got it, so I guess I shouldn't complain no matter how miserable I am.

"Ah, don't take it personally, Jayd. She always gets like that before opening night. You know that," Chance says, stepping off the sidewalk and out to the corner to light a cigarette. I noticed he changed from Marlboros to Newports. My uncles smoke Newports, and most of the white kids I know who smoke puff on Marlboros. I guess even Chance's choice of poison has to reflect his newfound blackness.

"Yeah, but I've never been in the lead before. I don't know what the hell I've gotten myself into," I say, gently fingering the five green bracelets dangling from my left arm. The bell sound the fragile jewelry makes is pleasant to my ears, but I know it can be loud, especially in a quiet room.

"You all right, Jayd? Usually this shit doesn't bother you so much," Chance says, noticing the concerned look on my face. I look up at Nigel standing over me and know he feels there's more behind what I'm saying.

"Yeah. I've just got a lot going on." And if I take these bracelets off, I have a feeling it's only going to get worse. Maybe I can keep them in my pocket or something. As long as they're on my body, I should be all right.

"Tell me about it," Chance says, tossing the lit butt into the gutter and rejoining us in front of our classroom. The rest of the students are inside enjoying the buffet the drama booster moms spread out for us during every production, and it's not your typical coffee and doughnuts. There's shrimp cocktail, several types of bread and butter, pasta, a large salad, and a fruit tray for the vegetarian cast and crew members. I wish I had some ziplock bags on me, because I would surely take some food to go. I haven't been grocery shopping in a week, and the little bit my mom provided is just about gone.

"What's up with you, girl?" Nigel asks, rubbing my shoulders hard like he used to do back in the day when Rah, Nigel, and I were inseparable. I miss junior high. There was still plenty of bull to deal with but nothing like we have in high school. I hope college takes it down a notch, because a sistah is tired of all the heat. The whole reason I'm overextending myself with all of my newfound extracurricular activities is to make my college applications well rounded. It had better be worth it in the end.

"Nothing new," I say, enjoying the massage. But something in Chance's pretty blue eyes tells me he's the one who needs to talk. "What's up with you, Chase?" I ask, finally remembering to respect my friend's wishes to be referred to by his birth name. I think "Chance" is more fitting, but it's not my choice to make.

"Shit, as usual," Chance says, shrugging his shoulders. "My dad's tripping hard because I'm proud of my black heritage, man. He thinks I'm rubbing it in his face, but I'm just being me—you know what I'm saying?"

Nigel and I look at Chance like the stranger he's becoming. I want to tell him he can't become black overnight, but he's trying his hardest to disprove that theory. I'm all for honoring our ancestors, but Chance has been a rich white boy from Palos Verdes for seventeen years. He can't become a brotha from the hood in a day no matter what he wears.

"How's your mom coping?" I ask, truly concerned about Mrs. Carmichael. Chance is her baby no matter whose body he actually came out of. I know she must be hitting the liquor cabinet hard these days.

"She's not," Chance says, and I know what that means. Escaping reality always seems easier when it's too much to bear. Chance actually looks concerned for a moment, but it doesn't last long.

"I'm sorry to hear that, Chase," I say, almost too relaxed from the massage to make the words audible. "Please be easy on her. She loves you, and y'all are so close. I'd hate to see that relationship ruined." Nigel's hands move from my shoulders up to my neck, damn near putting me to sleep. Whatever problems I had before are melting away.

I hope Mickey enjoys her man's kindness. When Rah and I were together, he never minded Nigel and I being close, because he knew it's a brother / sister thing with us. I've never been attracted to Nigel, and I don't think he's ever felt that way about me, either. But Mickey wouldn't be nearly as understanding if she saw us now. Luckily she's at home for a couple of more weeks healing from having the baby. Hopefully she'll be back for the last day of school. It won't be the same if the crew's incomplete.

"Whatever, man. I'm not worried about Lindsay and David right now," Chance says, calling his parents by their first names like they're strangers. "I've got to get my own shit together, especially since the first seventeen years of my life have been a lie. I've got a lot of catching up to do." Chance can't be serious. He's taking this adoption thing really hard. If I'd never dreamed about his birth parents, none of this would be happening, at least not now. Sometimes I feel like my dreams are more of a curse than a blessing, but I know better. The truth had to come out one way or another. I just wish my friend was handling it better.

"Did you just call your mom and dad by their first names?" Nigel asks, feeling my shock. If either of us tried that with our parents in a serious tone, we'd both be picking our faces up off the floor from having the sense slapped out of us.

"They're not my parents," Chance says. If I didn't know better, I'd think he was about to break down and cry. "My mom's name is Sylvia, and my dad's name is Bret."

"Wow," I say, unable to think of a proper response. What can I say? Chance has to process this new identity his way, and as his friend, I have to support him, even if I think he's going about it the wrong way.

"Your five minutes are up, people," Mrs. Sinclair says, interrupting our powwow. She's holding a large cup of coffee in one hand and her clipboard with the script in the other, ready to get back to business. Maybe if Mrs. Sinclair drank less coffee, she wouldn't be such a spaz.

"Yes, ma'am," Chance says, trying to make his favorite teacher laugh, which she does slightly.

But it's back to basics when she looks at me. Something about her eyes is a little off, and it's not the excessive caffeine. The three of us head back into the room, ready to finish our final scene for the day. There's no cheer practice after school for me today, because I have an optometrist appointment. Then it's me time since Jeremy has a family dinner tonight: I'm sure as hell not attending another one of those.

"And, Jayd, those bracelets have to go," Mrs. Sinclair says to me as I pass her petite frame by the door. "This isn't a night at the Apollo," she says, insulting the black in me. If I could slap her, I would, but I'll maintain my cool—for now. If she continues to push me, I'll eventually have to push back, and I guarantee she won't like the results.

"What's that supposed to mean?" Nigel asks, equally offended by the off-color comment.

Chance looks at us both, completely baffled. See what I mean about not turning black overnight? It's a lifetime of experiences, not just a change in cigarette choices and attire that makes us who we are.

"It means that this is a professional production, and all cast members are required to get into full character," Mrs. Sinclair says, defending her comment. She looks up at Nigel's tall stature and softens her stance a bit. She's never had to deal with another black student before, and I'm grateful for the support. "Suzy doesn't wear loud bangles, and as Suzy, you need to lose the noise, Jayd."

"Okay, I get it," I say, removing the jade bracelets one by one and sliding them into my jean pocket. Mama said I should never take them off, because they provide protection; this has to be a decent compromise. Patting the five delicate bracelets through my pants, I suddenly feel uncomfortable with my decision. There's physical contact in this scene, and they could easily break—then I'd really be in trouble. My purse might be a safer option to store them for the time being.

Finally I'm ready to continue rehearsing the final scene, in which my character darkens the room, putting everyone on her turf. Since Suzy's blind and her enemies aren't, she weakens their advantage over her by turning out the lights at night. Alia—playing an anxious ten-year-old girl named Gloria—is ready for the action to begin. Nigel, Chance, and Pete, another drama regular, are ready to play the bad guys.

"Places, everyone," Mrs. Sinclair yells. Matt and Seth get busy prepping the lighting and closing the doors, ready to start. Hopefully the Williams women's taboo of blindness—or completely losing our gift of sight—won't come back to haunt me for the time we have left in rehearsal. I glance at my purse across the room and silently pray for protection as the lights go off and the scene begins.

The remainder of the rehearsal went by without a hitch, thank goodness. I got so into character that I actually thought I was blind again, allowing my other senses to take over and guide me through until the very end.

"Good work, people," Mrs. Sinclair says, clapping loudly. The rest of the crew joins in the applause, making me feel good. I can't wait for Thursday to come. We have only two shows, with the last on Friday evening. I'm sure we'll be sold out both nights. "Lights, please. Chance, help me lock up the main stage," she yells, but they never come on. I'm still in darkness. What the hell?

"I can't see!" I exclaim, my blindness as real as a heart attack. I knew it was a bad idea to remove my bracelets. Shit. Now what do I do?

"Oh, Jayd, quit being so melodramatic. You did a good job. It's over now," Mrs. Sinclair says as she leaves the room, but I couldn't care less about her nonchalant ass right now. I literally cannot see, just like when I experienced my mom losing her vision, and this time it's not from a dream.

Taking a deep breath, I reach my hands out in front of me, feeling for whatever I can. I've got to find my bag.

"Jayd, what's up with you, girl?" Nigel asks, coming to my aid. I hold on tight to my friend and try not to panic.

"My bracelets are my protection, Nigel. I need my bracelets." I continue feeling around in front of me, reaching for my purse. Next time I'll have to figure out something else, because this shit ain't working for me at all. I feel like I'm going crazy, and I know I must look like it, too.

"Here's your purse, Jayd. I got you," Nigel says, handing me the bag as I frantically reach inside and claim my jewelry.

As I slide the cold circles onto my wrist one by one, reciting the chant for power Netta gave me to accompany the ancient birthday gift, my sight begins to clear. By the time the fifth one hits, I can see again, even if my vision's still a little blurry.

"Damn, that was scary," I say, rubbing my eyes clear. Mama wasn't kidding when she said never to take these off. Mama rarely jokes about anything. I don't know why I thought this time would be any different. I'm just glad the chant to Shango, one of the most powerful male orishas, worked. Come hell or high water, these bracelets have to stay in place for the play, damn what Mrs. Sinclair thinks. I'll figure something out, but this Suzy comes with bangles whether it's written into the script or not.

Chance and Mrs. Sinclair come back into the classroom, and we're ready to roll. Matt, Seth, and the rest of the stage crew buzz around, tearing down the set and performing other duties that come with their jobs. The rest of the class files outside with the ringing bell. Nigel and I head toward the gym while Alia and Chance walk toward the parking lot, exchanging knowing glances. They can try and be discreet all they want, but it's obvious they're sharing a secret. However, that can wait until later. I'm more concerned about the fact that I went blind for a moment. I knew I shouldn't have taken this part. It's too close to our lineage's taboo, and I walked right into the trap with my ego leading the way.

"And like every other challenge the women in our lineage have faced, you can't run from it or you'll be chased down until you face it head-on," my mom says, joining the trek.

Nigel's too busy texting to notice the warped look on my face that accompanies my mom's invasion.

"But, Mom, you saw what happened to me in the shower on Monday and now this, not to mention my meltdown yesterday, courtesy of Esmeralda." I think back. I really

need to write everything down before I forget it, although I don't see how that's possible. *"Something's wrong and I need to fix it."*

"Of course you do, but instead of telling Mama like I told you to, you decided to try and deal with it yourself. Way to go, Jayd."

Damn, my mom can be mean. I'm already having a bad day. I don't need her to make it any worse.

"If I told her, she would've chosen to stay behind instead of taking the vacation she needs and deserves," I say. Everyone has to make sacrifices sometimes. Regardless of my personal issues, I know I did the right thing. *"I can figure this out on my own."*

"If that's the case, then you need to get your big-girl panties on and get it done. Later, baby."

My mom's right. I can't afford any more mishaps, and they seem to be plentiful nowadays.

"Seems like you're in a world all of your own," Nigel says, now aware of my strange expression. The rest of the students walking during the passing period seem pretty laid-back at the end of the day while my day has been anything but easy.

"You were the one preoccupied," I say, glancing at his cell. It's too hot of a day for the long hike uphill, but neither of us slows down in spite of the sweat forming above our brows. If a cheerleader or an athlete is late to practice, that's more work and sweat.

"We're having a little dinner at Rah's house tonight for his birthday," Nigel says, but I'm not falling for it this time.

"Uh-uh," I say, shaking my head. "I am not giving him any more of my time, Nigel." We approach the boys' gym. "Especially not this week. I'm swamped."

"Come on, Jayd. You know he doesn't want to celebrate, but we can't have that, now, can we?" Nigel says, convincing me once and for all to make an appearance. With Rah's mom forever missing in action and his dad doing time in Georgia, his birthday's always bittersweet. His grandparents usually have a cake for him and cook something, but that's about the extent of it. I wasn't around the last two years to help him celebrate, and he is a good friend.

"Fine, I'll be there," I say, hugging Nigel.

"I'll let him know. And all he wants from you is a free braid," Nigel says.

"I think I can handle that."

"Bet, Jayd. See you then." Nigel disappears into the boys' locker room leaving me to head toward the main parking lot. After the two days I've had, all I really want to do is get some uninterrupted sleep. It'll have to wait until after the party. We all deserve a happy birthday, including Rah.

After a grueling two-hour drive from Long Beach to Inglewood down the 405 freeway, I manage to stop by Mom's apartment, shower, and grab my hair bag, ready to grant Rah's sole birthday wish from me. I spoke to Jeremy briefly, and he teased me about needing glasses, or so the good doctor said during my short visit. But I'm not taking his word for it. Other than my insane episodes every now and then, my vision is just fine; I don't care how many degrees he has.

It's already six-thirty, and I'm apparently the first one of our friends here. Nigel's probably getting home from practice, and who knows where the rest of the crew is, not that Chance and Nellie are necessarily expected to come with all of the drama they've got going on. As long as Nigel and Mickey make it, we should be able to have a good time.

I walk up the driveway and ring the doorbell, half-expecting Sandy to answer. Even after I mentally convinced her it was time to move on, there's no telling how long the peace will last. Sandy's about as unstable as they come.

"What up, girl?" Rah says, letting me in through the front door.

I step into the small foyer and notice the house is immaculate. Nope, Sandy's definitely not here.

"Happy birthday," I say, handing him the heavy hair bag with all of my tools inside before giving him a hug.

"Thank you," he says, returning the affection and closing the door. "You want to hook a brotha up now? I'm in desperate need of a touch-up," he says, taking off his cap and revealing the mess on top of his head. How did he mess it up so quickly?

"What happened?" I ask, reaching up to touch his dilapidated braids. "It looks like a woodpecker invaded your hair."

"I know. It's a long story," he says, leading me into the garage-turned-studio where he and Nigel spend most of their free time. The crew used to assemble here on the regular before he let his crazy baby mama move in. Now that Sandy's gone, maybe we can get back to kickin' it here. I miss being a witness to the musical genius of Rah and Nigel.

"I don't need the details," I say, opening the bag of supplies Rah placed on his desk and retrieving my personal line of hair-care products. "Let's begin with the basics. In the bathroom and on your knees," I say, pointing toward the open door on the far side of the spacious room. It's hard to believe Rah and Nigel did all of this by themselves, with a little help from some of their homeboys. If the music thing doesn't work out, they can always go into construction.

"Yes, Miss Jackson," he says, smiling.

His well-defined cheekbones are set deep into his ebony skin, revealing his perfectly straight teeth. I thought Rah would always have braces he wore them for so many years. They were well worth the wait.

I hope our friends have a good reason for keeping us waiting. At least I have my work to keep me busy. That way when they finally do arrive, we can be freed up to chill.

In the hour that I've been here, I've washed, conditioned, blow-dried, and braided half of Rah's thick hair—a true testament of my professionalism. And Rah has been completely compliant under my command, as usual. The stress I felt in his body when I first started has all but disappeared.

The doorbell rings, and I'm glad Nigel and Mickey have finally showed up. Now we can get this party started right. They called a little while ago and said they were bringing dinner once Mickey's mom was home from work to watch Nickey. The reality of having a baby has set in for Mickey, and Nigel's there with her all the way, like a good man should be. Rah and I both rise from our comfortable positions to help our friends with the food.

"Happy birthday, punk," Sandy says, surprising us both. What the hell is she doing here? "I should've known," Sandy says, glaring at me. I would return the evil greeting, but Rah jumps in before I have the chance.

"Sandy, I thought we had an agreement that you would stay with your grandparents and I wouldn't have to see you on my front porch anymore," Rah says angrily.

"Fool, that was then. This is now," Sandy says, barely able to stand up straight. Something's not right with this broad—more than the usual.

"You've got that Sybil syndrome going on, huh, Sandy?" Rah asks.

"Whatever, nigga," Sandy says, pushing her way through the front door. "Where's my daughter? I want to see her."

I step out of the way into the living room, knowing where this is headed.

"She's not here, Sandy. Does your parole officer know you left Pomona?"

"No, because I never went. And don't tell him you saw me, either. You got that, Jayd? I was never here." Sandy looks around the house, stumbling like a drunk.

"Sandy, how did you get here?" Rah asks, closing the door and following her into the kitchen.

I'm glad Rahima's at Rah's grandparents' house with his younger brother, Kamal. They can shelter her from seeing her mother completely lose it.

"The bus, fool. You know that big-ass thing on wheels that rolls up and down the street, stopping every five minutes to let some punk out at the corner? I had to get a bus pass since somebody won't let me drive their car anymore."

"Sandy, have you been smoking crack?"

Usually Rah would be joking about anyone we know smoking crack, but this broad is definitely high on something and it ain't life. This chick's having a rough day, and she's got the look to prove it.

"Didn't you hear? Crack is whack," Sandy says in her best Whitney Houston impression. "I don't shoot up, Rah."

"Okay, then what is it, because you're acting very strange."

I'm with my boy. Sandy's tripping hard, even for her.

"I slipped a little E at this party last night, that's all. It was some good shit, too, because I'm still feeling it," she says, eyeing the box of cereal on top of the refrigerator like it's gold. She reaches above Rah's head and snatches the box down, tearing into the crispy treats. I can't believe what I just heard.

"Damn, Sandy, are you serious?" Rah asks, snatching the box away from her. He looks just as crazy as she does with his hair half braided. I need to finish my work and get out of here. As usual, his baby mama can clear a room. "What if Rahima were here? Do you really want our two-year-old daughter seeing you like this?"

"She don't know nothing," Sandy says, reclaiming the box.

This is too much.

"Rah, I've got to get going," I say, wanting to leave the kitchen and return to the studio to get my tools and purse. Birthday dinner or not, I have too much work to do to get caught up with their madness. And I damned sure don't want to accidentally jump into Sandy's mind again. Her thoughts are more confusing than Esmeralda's, and that is almost too much to bear. And because she's under the influence of some man-made poison, I know her mind will be extra clouded this afternoon.

"What about my braids?" he asks, looking sad.

Before I can respond, Sandy leaves the kitchen, heading for the living room.

"You can come over and get them finished when you handle your situation," I say.

Rah gives me his signature puppy-dog eyes, pleading with me to stay, but they have little effect on me when there's a dangerous bitch in our midst.

"Hey, what do you think you're doing?" Rah asks his estranged baby mama, following her.

"I can't move," Sandy says, laid out on the couch. Whatever dignity she was born with has long since left the building. Her black pleather, thigh-high boots are holding on by a string. The three-inch heels are worn to the nail, and she's darkened the faded spots with a Sharpie one too many times. Rah covers her with a blanket—not because he wants her to be comfortable, now completely passed out in his house, but because she neglected to wear a skirt long enough to cover her bare ass when she's lying down.

"I'm sorry, Jayd," Rah says, looking at the ugly scene in disbelief.

"Happy birthday, Rah. Holla when you're ready to finish." I go claim my bag and purse from the studio, walk through the kitchen, and out the front door. Mickey and Nigel can take over from here. I'm so glad I'm not Rah's girlfriend anymore. I can't even imagine feeling like I had to stick around with all of that drama going on in his life. I feel for my boy, but him cheating on me with Sandy, my former best friend, and subsequently lying to me about having a baby was a good thing in retrospect. I'm not his girlfriend anymore, which means I can leave when it gets too hot for me.

~ 4 ~
Birds of a Feather

There is a house in New Orleans called the rising sun /
It's been the ruin of many men and Lord knows I'm one.

—Gregory Isaacs

It's been a long, long week. Thank God I don't have any more homework to deal with. Otherwise, I'd really be out of it. Mrs. Sinclair made us rehearse late into the night Wednesday, and after a successful opening night last night, she's chilled out for our final performance this evening. She even brought doughnuts to class last period, giving us the entire hour to relax—just what I needed to deal with cheer practice this afternoon.

Because of Wednesday's blind episode during the play rehearsal, I ended up telling Mama about Mrs. Sinclair requesting I remove my bracelets for the show. Before I could finish my story, Mama knew I'd lost my sight again and that I hadn't been diligent in saying my protection prayer five times a day. When Mama gave the bracelets to me to wear permanently, the prayers from Netta came with the birthday gift. Mama says that losing our sight is a warning from the Mothers to remember that what they give they can also take. I admit I've been slacking in the prayer department lately, but I will make it a point to remember from now on.

Tuesday's visit to the optometrist was purely to silence my father's nagging about not using his medical insurance, yet I ended up with a pair of glasses. I don't care what that eye doctor thinks. I don't really need them, which is why I left the specs on my mom's coffee table. I refuse to wear those things every day. What's the point of having the gift of sight if I need help seeing? None of the women in my family has needed outside assistance before.

My mom's become overly concerned about my recent hot flashes: She thinks they are a sign of me holding on to residual energy from my vision quests both in and out of my dreams. My mom also strongly suggested that I give Dr. Whitmore—Mama's trusted family doctor and loyal friend—a visit since I refuse to tell Mama my problem until she returns from her vacation. I agreed to check out the good doctor after school's out next Friday. Too bad we have cheer practice all summer. I could use a break from those tricks, too.

"I want you all to welcome our newest addition to the varsity cheer squad—Ellen," Ms. Carter says, clapping as the boisterous blonde comes jogging out of the girls' locker room like she's a celebrity. Where'd this chick come from? She's obviously not from around here, wearing a fluorescent green scrunchy in her hair.

"Hi, y'all," Ellen says, waving excitedly at the rest of the squad. "I'm from a little high school in Houston, Texas, home of the second-best cheer squad in the entire country. Now I'm a member of the number-one cheer squad. Isn't that right, Lady Hawks?"

Texas: that explains it. She's got *privileged Southern girl* written all over her flushed face.

The rest of the squad cheers loudly, jumping on the Southern bandwagon. Ellen puts her arms straight up in the air and flips backward, not once or twice, but across the entire length of the basketball court without stopping. Even my mouth drops at the sight.

"Damn," KJ says from the sidelines, much to the disapproval of Misty, who's seated next to her man with the rest of their crew. She refuses to take those tacky-looking blue contacts out of her eyes, but they can't hide her jealousy. Basketball players love to date cheerleaders, and girlfriend or not, KJ's no exception.

"That white girl's got skills," Del says, with Money nodding his head in approval.

I guess they all like what they see. I'm not hatin' on Ellen's talent, either, but something about her instant presence makes me uncomfortable.

"Okay, ladies. Let's get started. We have only a few days to get our routine for the final assembly tight. Ellen's going to show us a few moves like that to really impress the crowd and show them our talent for next year," Ms. Carter says. Ellen's even got Ms. Carter on one, and she's never moved to a state of jubilance by a student's performance. "This is going to be the best cheer season ever. Get to it," Ms. Carter says as she; the captain, Shauna; and the cocaptain, Alicia, head toward the bleachers. You'd think Ellen invented cheerleading the way everyone's acting.

"That's right," Ellen says, picking up the red and white pom-poms and shaking them in the air. "Let's see what you can do. We'll start with a basic cartwheel and blackflip combination, then move on to the hard stuff."

The hard stuff? Is she insane? I've never flipped straight a day in my life—side to side or backward—and today's not the day to try any new tricks. The two routines we've been practicing are challenging enough for me, and I can't afford to be sore for my final play performance tonight. I want to make it memorable because of my talent, not my stiffness.

"Hi. I'm Jayd," I say, introducing myself to the perky chick. Maybe I can talk some sense into her. "Are we all supposed to learn to flip like that?"

"Nice to meet you, Jayd. And yup, you are." Noticing my

disbelief, she walks up to me and pats my shoulder. Now I'm really not feeling her. "It's easy, girl. Watch this," Ellen says, bending backward like a human pretzel. Now she's just showing off. "Trust me, Jayd. Your body can do whatever you want it to, no matter how much you weigh." Was that a crack at my weight? Oh, no, this little pencil didn't just go there with me. I don't need any more help disliking her ass.

"You're tripping if you think I'm doing all that," I say, my neck in full roll. Before I introduced myself, I was just irritated. Now I'm pissed as all get-out. "Call me crazy, but I could've sworn this was the cheer squad, not the gymnastics team."

"Oh, Jayd. Cheer is more than dancing and pepping the crowd with boring routines. You've got to work for championship trophies, girl." She repeats the same combination, expecting me to follow suit. Is she deaf or just plain stupid? The other squad members practice their flips, none as perfect as Little Miss Texas.

"Come on, girl. Let me see what you've got," Ellen says, stepping behind me and putting her hands around my waist in an attempt to flip me backward. She's stronger than she looks.

"Hey, back up off me," I say, pushing her nimble fingers away from my body. I stand up straight, turning around to face her.

"Jayd, you can't be afraid to jump or you'll never fly," Ellen says, not getting the message. She touches my waist, again attempting to force me into submission. We don't get down like that where I'm from. What the hell is wrong with this girl?

"Don't push it, Ellen," I say, grabbing her hands before she can clasp them around my stomach. She stares at me, shocked at my reaction. "I don't need a drill sergeant." Snatching her hands out of my strong grip, Ellen narrows her piercing gray eyes at me. I know she thinks of herself as the cheer czar of the South, but no one has that kind of power over me.

"Jayd, you're at a ten and I need you at a two," Ellen says, putting up two fingers, tempting me to break them both. The other forty girls gather around us, making it obvious to Ms. Carter, Shauna, and Alicia that something else is going on other than basic flip lessons. A few of them snicker at this broad's attempt to clown me, but not everyone finds her amusing. There are now two teams on the squad this afternoon: team Ellen and team Jayd. I need to check her once and for all, or she'll never get off my ass.

"You're about to see me at a twenty if you don't move your fingers out of my face." Ellen backs up, realizing I'm not playing. "I don't know how it works in Houston, but in Cali we don't go around touching people without their permission. That's just asking for a beat-down." I look into Ellen's gray eyes and leap into her mind without any warning.

I understand she's intimidated by me and that she's not used to working with black girls—Ellen should fit in perfectly here. While I'm in here, I'll cool her down a bit. Then we'll both get what we want.

"Is everything all right here?" Ms. Carter asks, walking to the middle of the gym floor and breaking our bonding session. Ellen shakes her head, trying to gather her thoughts.

"Yes, Ms. Carter. Everything's fine," Ellen says, confused. "I need to take five."

She needs to take more than that. I hope she learned her lesson the first time around. I don't want to have to jump back into her head. It was a little too cool for me.

"Everyone take a break," Ms. Carter says, following Ellen toward the locker room.

Alicia and Shauna join us, assessing the scene before following Ms. Carter into the locker room. They look at me, and

I can tell they're thinking that what they've heard about me has some truth to it. No doubt Misty and Nellie shared what they could when they were trying out for the squad in an attempt to get in good with the veteran cheerleaders. Shauna and Alicia took a liking to me the first day of tryouts and never once questioned me about the rumors. Like most people with good sense, they just leave me alone, because, really, if I were a witch, I'd be the last person to mess with.

The thought of my haters calling me anything but the young priestess-in-training I am makes my blood boil. Trouble seems to seek me out—not the other way around—but somehow I always get blamed for the drama in my life. Even the only two other sistahs on varsity jump to Ellen's defense before mine because of what they've heard. I can't wait to get to the shop tomorrow afternoon to talk with Mama and Netta about this. If any women know how to deal with vicious rumors and haters alike, it's my grandmother and godmother. Until then, I'll have to deal with it on my own.

The thirty-minute drive from Inglewood to Compton isn't enough time to cool my head. I'm still upset about my argument with the Texas cheer princess yesterday. Even a standing ovation after last night's performance and two new clients this morning don't improve my disposition for long. And with Mama and Netta pretending like they're Thelma and Louise, I think I'm going to go completely insane.

Initially their getaway was only supposed to be for a couple of weeks, but now they're considering extending it until they feel like coming back. Netta's sisters, Rita and Celia, are flying in from New Orleans this afternoon to take over the salon in their absence and should be at the shop by the time I arrive. I can't wait to meet the other two women in their sibling threesome.

"There's our girl now," Netta says, buzzing me through

the front door. I stop at the threshold momentarily, taking in the thick, sweet-scented air before closing the door. They must be making something real special, because it's a scent I'm not all that familiar with, but it's sure working to set my hostile mood straight.

"Hey, baby," Mama says from her post in the washroom. Three clients are under the driers reading their gossip magazines and romance novels, giving Mama and Netta a chance to get some other things done around the shop. From the looks of it, they had a busy morning.

"Did your grandmother tell you about our change in plans?" Netta asks, clinking several hot combs and curlers together before wiping the instruments on a white towel. "We're driving. First we're stopping in New Orleans, and then it's on to Miami. The cruise ship to Puerto Rico leaves from there."

"New Orleans?" I ask, opening the cabinet door along the wall to secure my belongings. I claim my work apron, also noticing the cabinets need dusting—yet another task for me to do that can wait another day. There's much more pressing business to handle this afternoon. "Why are y'all stopping there?" Not that they need a reason to go home, but I'm surprised by the detour. How long are they planning on being gone anyway?

"Because we need to visit folks and make sure our family plots and shrines are being well taken care of," Netta says, placing the iron hair tools in a basket. We clean everything in this shop to a sparkle daily. I guess I know what my first duty of the afternoon will be. "My sisters aren't into our line of worship anymore, so who knows what's happened to them."

I head to the back to say my prayers and give myself a quick head cleansing before beginning my work. The calm office in the rear of the shop where Netta's shrines are housed could clear the most confused head. I immediately bow to her ancestors and our orishas and pay the proper respect for our blessings before walking into the bathroom across the hall for my mini prework cleansing ritual.

"I miss our cemetery shrines. Who knows what they look like post-Katrina," Mama says, folding the clean towels for me to put away next. Luckily Netta's family was spared most of the damage from the hurricane, but others weren't so fortunate. "We need to lay eyes on our birthplace for ourselves and do what we can to help while we're there."

"And besides, how can we go through the South and not stop at home? That's just plain disrespectful," Netta says, clamping the last curling iron and placing it on top of the pile before heading to the back. I look from Netta to Mama with tears in my eyes. I already miss them both, and they're not even gone yet. I don't know what I'm going to do without them here to make sense of the world for me.

"That's why driving is better than flying. Birds fly, not people," Mama says, continuing her folding. Netta emerges from the back porch, directing me to collect the rest of the hair tools at her station.

"Says the passenger," Netta says, causing Mama to roll her jade eyes and sigh deeply. Netta can't help but laugh at her friend. Mama doesn't drive—period—yet it was probably her idea to drive across country rather than fly. Poor Netta.

"Why are you giving me such a hard time? You love driving, Netta," Mama says, unremorseful. "Besides, you were the one who said we needed a road trip, so we're hitting the road." Mama pats the stack of towels for emphasis, packing them firmly in the laundry basket before moving on to the next pile of clean laundry to fold. The clients are happily chatting away under the driers in the front of the shop, unconcerned with our conversation.

"Lynn Mae, there are several ways to get to where we're going," Netta says, claiming a spray bottle and cloth to wipe down her station after I finish gathering all of the hair tools to clean. I need to do the same with my own collection when I get home.

"Yes, there are, Netta. And driving is the best way. That way we can take everything we need and be on our own time." Mama smiles at Netta, knowing her best friend's just giving her a hard time out of fun. Netta and Mama are down for each other no matter what and have proven that very thing on more than one occasion.

"Did your sisters make it?" I ask, anxious to meet Celia and Rita. I've heard so much about them I feel like I know them.

"Not yet but soon come," Netta says in a convincing Jamaican accent.

While Mama lived in South Carolina before she married Daddy, Netta lived in Jamaica for a couple of years.

"Jayd, bring the two large buckets sitting in front of the shrine please," Mama says, looking around for the next item on her never-ending to-do list.

I place the basket full of combs, brushes, and hair clips down on the table and do as I'm told. Sometimes I feel like Cinderella. But unlike the character, I get paid for my work. I retrieve the requested items, carrying the heavy liquid-filled buckets by their metal handles and walking carefully across the floor. The scent coming from the covered vessels is the same one I noticed a few minutes ago.

"We're going to give you a little cleansing before we leave to make sure you stay strong," Netta says, checking the clients' timers, adding another twenty minutes to the automatic hair driers. Sometimes I wish I had the luxury of escaping through my hairdresser, but it's not the same feeling when you do your own hair. Her clients continue gossiping, happy for a few extra moments of relaxation before returning to their real worlds of cooking and cleaning for the church and their families. It's funny how Mama has so much in common with these women, yet she's their polar opposite.

"I do need some help staying on point. I've been feeling a little off lately," I say, shifting my weight to balance the load. Netta takes one of the heavy containers out of my hand and guides me toward the back porch. She lives for this stuff. I like doing our spirit work, too, even if it is a lot of work. The three of us wash our hands in the basins and walk out the back door.

"A quick *rogación de cabeza* will also cool your head. I can feel your heat under my skin," Mama says. Having a head cleansing is as close as I get to having my hair done—allowing anyone else to touch my head is taboo unless it's one of my mothers.

"Get comfortable," Netta says, pointing to one of three wooden stools in the corner of the roomy deck. Mama claims the one to my right while Netta takes a white lapa from a stack of clean laundry on top of the drier and wraps it around my body. She and Netta also cover themselves with the large cloths, ready to hook me up.

"You've been sweating so much you can't even keep your press in," Mama says, touching my hair and taking it all in. I didn't tell her about the confrontation I had with Ellen's flexible ass, but I have a feeling she's already in the know about it all.

The alley behind the salon is quiet this afternoon. Usually there's a steady flow of pedestrians who like to use it as a shortcut to the gas station in the lot next to the shop. Netta's husband made sure to secure the porch while Netta and Mama added the finishing touch of draping it in white cloth—keeping our business private from spying eyes.

"It's been a rough week," I say, allowing Mama's soft

touch to ease my thoughts. "Everyone's got an opinion about what I should do and how I should do it."

"You know what they say about opinions," Netta says, gathering the grated shea and cocoa butter to mix with the other ingredients. Mama will handle the actual application. "Everybody's got one and they all stink."

"That's the truth," I say. "Especially when they don't know what they're talking about, like Misty always spreading rumors about me being a witch when she's the one up to no good."

"Shhh, child. I'm working back here," Mama says, concentrating on my healing and probably still worried about traveling. She really dreads too much movement, even if it's local.

"People will always talk, but you have to find a way to honor your lineage, obey your readings, and live in this world. It's a hard balance, but you've got more than what it takes to get the job done." Mama places a white cover over my eyes and begins the ritual.

"Honor your ancestors no matter what," Netta says, opening the containers and letting the scent take over the intimate space. It's the same intoxicating smell that welcomed me to work. Mama and Netta begin singing softly in Yoruban, reminiscent of my dream a few nights ago when I jumped.

The front doorbell rings through the peaceful area, interrupting our healing ceremony.

"Nettie!" a loud woman's voice calls from the front of the shop.

Mama and Netta stop singing and uncover my eyes.

"They're here," Netta shouts excitedly. She leaps to her feet and dashes through the shop to greet her sisters.

"We'll have to finish this later," Mama says, slightly annoyed at the untimely intrusion.

If I didn't know any better, I'd say Mama isn't as happy to

see Netta's sisters as I'd assumed she'd be. It wouldn't surprise me if Mama's got beef with Celia and Rita. I don't think she has too many drama-free associations. It must be a Williams women trait because I can testify to that fact of life myself.

"Let's greet our guests," I say, undraping my cloth. I return the lapa to its place and head toward the back door. I can hear Netta and her sisters laughing, happy to be reunited.

"I'll be up in a minute," Mama says, prepping the ingredients Netta left behind. Mama's energy has gone from one of intense calming to sadness. What gives?

"Mama, are you all right?" I ask, concerned for my grandmother's well-being. She's always going above and beyond her duties as a mother and a priestess. She needs to take a break now more than ever.

"Yes, baby. I'm fine," Mama says, looking me in the eye and smiling, but I can tell there are tears under her mask. "Go on and say hi to the Bell sisters so we can get back here and finish our work," Mama says with plenty of salt.

I forgot Netta's maiden name, which her unmarried sisters still carry. At least she's allowing me to greet them. Depending on the enemy, Mama strongly suggests when I should speak and when I shouldn't.

"Jayd, come on up here and meet my sisters," Netta says, conveniently leaving out an invitation for my grandmother.

Now I know there's something to my suspicions. I'll have to get the real story later.

"Hi, I'm Jayd," I say, walking up to the trio and putting my right hand out, but they're not having such a formal greeting.

"Girl, come here and give us a hug," says the tallest of the two women. They're both about the same height, towering over their little sister.

"Oh, shug. You didn't tell me she was such a pretty little thing," the other sister says, squeezing my cheeks like I'm five years old.

I don't know what Mama's problem is, but mine is manifesting itself through my sore face.

"Oh, now, Rita. That's enough," Netta says, freeing me from the double embrace. Now I know how Nigel feels when he gets tackled. "And, Jayd, this here is the eldest, Celia."

"It's nice to meet you both," I say, rubbing the pain out of my jaw.

"And such a lady, too," Rita says, still impressed with me. "My sister told me you're going to be in a cotillion soon." Damn, Netta's been running her mouth. That's not exactly my claim to fame. "You should come to Nawlins sometime. We have the best and most traditional coming-out parties for our young ladies."

"You know there are some places in New Orleans where people should never visit unless they're wearing proper spiritual protection," Mama says, scaring both our visitors and the clients alike. Mama has that effect on people when she wants to.

"Lynn Mae. We didn't know you were here," Celia says, eyeing her sisters nervously. The three of them look uncomfortable as Mama steps fully into the front of the intimate shop.

"That's true of some places, but there's something very special about the ancestral energy in Nawlins," Netta says, showing pride in her hometown in an attempt to break the ice, but it's too thick.

"True indeed. I'm glad y'all made it safely," Mama says, glaring at Netta before returning to the back porch. The buzzers on the hair driers ring loudly in the tense air.

"Thank God," Rita says, holding her chest like she's recovering from a heart attack. I don't know if she's referring to Netta silencing the alarm or Mama leaving, but she's obviously relieved.

"Netta, I don't see how you can stand it," Celia begins, but one harsh look from Netta tells her to be quiet.

That was definitely about Mama.

"Why don't we help out, Netta? After all, that's why we're here," Rita says, putting her car keys in her purse and looping her arm through Celia's.

Netta nods in agreement, and both sisters go into the back to wash up before joining the work flow.

"We can finish the cleansing at home," Mama says, walking across the floor with two bags in each hand, including her purse. Why is she in such a hurry all of a sudden?

"Lynn Mae, we still have clients in the shop and orders to fill," Netta says, but there's no use in her pleading. Mama's ready to roll.

Celia and Rita walk back into the room, scared to walk past Mama, who's in their path. Mama rolls her eyes at the women and walks out of the shop without another word. Damn, it's like that?

"We're leaving, y'all," Netta says to her sisters, who look more than content to man the shop alone. They've already put a Bible in the corner by the door across from Legba's shrine, giving me a clue as to why the energy's so putrid between Mama and Netta's sisters.

"We love you, honey, and will be home as soon as we finish up here. I can't wait to see that nephew of mine," Celia says, clapping the curlers like her sister.

"Who dat, shug?" Rita says, smacking her gum loudly much like Netta does when she's excited.

"Who dat?" Netta says to her sister, laughing as the traditional New Orleans greeting rings in the air.

When the Saints finally won a Super Bowl, I thought Mama and Netta would pass out from pride, and normally they couldn't care less about football. Netta introduces her sisters to the three clients who only need their rollers removed and their hair combed out—a simple task that would have been mine, including the resulting tips. They've really been messing with a sistah's bottom line lately.

"Thank you, loves, and I'll see you back at the house," Netta says, grabbing her purse from the coat rack and directing me to get my things and come on. She blows a kiss to her sisters before heading out.

"It was nice meeting you both," I say, removing my apron and placing it back in my locker. I look inside my purse and see two missed calls from Jeremy on my cell. I'll call him back in the car. Once I get to Mama's, I know I won't have a chance to talk.

"You, too, Jayd. We'll have a chance to talk next time," Celia says to my back.

"What took y'all so long?" Mama asks from the passenger seat of Netta's truck. Netta and I look at each other and shake our heads. Mama's a trip when she's in a good mood, which this is anything but.

"Look at that girl," Netta says, opening the car door. Eva waves at us on her way to the gas station with her boyfriend, and we return the gesture in awe. "Eva doesn't even know her true worth. If she did, she wouldn't give that little fool the time of day." Eva and Jesse—Compton's own Whitney and Bobby—have been together for about a year, only after Jesse wore Eva completely down. He must've caught her on an off day, because if she was in her right mind, there's no way in hell a scrub like him could've pulled a diva like herself.

"We lose a lot of our young queens to less than worthy

people," Mama says, looking back toward the shop. I know she's not worried about Netta's sisters having a bad influence on me, is she? "We'll see you at home, Jayd."

I get in my mom's car and start the engine. I have only a minute to chat, but it's better than nothing.

"Hey, baby," I say into the speakerphone on my lap. "What's up?"

"Shit. How's work?" Jeremy asks, sounding distracted. Something in his voice is off. I shift into second gear, expertly balancing the cell phone between my thighs. I would get a Bluetooth, but I'm afraid of wearing the small gadget in my ear. Something about the blue light scares me.

"It's going okay, but you don't sound so good," I say, relieved that Netta and I are separated by the red light. Jeremy sighs and says nothing for a moment. I'm only a block away from Gunlock, so I'd better make this quick.

"Tania had the baby," Jeremy says, sounding more sullen than ever. "It's a boy."

"How are they?" I ask, parking in front of Mama's house where Netta and my grandmother have already arrived. Some of the neighbors are out mowing their lawns, and others are smoking on their porches enjoying a typical Saturday afternoon in our hood.

"I guess they're okay. My brother told me about it," Jeremy says. "Tania couldn't even bother to call me. I could've been there."

"I didn't know you wanted to be there, especially since her family's surely present." I wouldn't want to be anywhere near the people who tried to hide my child from me. If Tania's parents had it their way, Jeremy wouldn't be an issue at all. But Tania's still feeling my man no matter how married she is. I watch Mama and Netta disappear behind the gate. If I'm not right behind them, I'm afraid I'll become the unintentional target of Mama's wrath.

"I didn't think I wanted to, either—until it happened and I wasn't there. I don't know how to feel about it."

All I can think about is how Chance is dealing with finding out about his birth parents and that his adopted mom kept the secret from him. What if Jeremy's son grows up with the same resentment? I don't wish Chance's identity crisis on anyone, especially not on Jeremy's son.

"If you want me to come with you this evening after I get off, I can," I offer. I don't want to see Tania and her rich-bitch crew, but I'll endure the fire for my man. "Which hospital are they in?"

"I don't even know." Jeremy sounds like he wants to cry he's so hurt. "How am I supposed to enjoy my vacation when I have a son in the world I don't even know? And how can I look my dad in the eye when it's because of his stupid hatred I can't be a father to my own child?" This is a new side of Jeremy. Maybe being around me and all of my baby-bearing friends is rubbing off on him.

"We'll still have a great summer," I say, turning off the ignition. Jeremy pauses and I know there's something more he's not saying. "Jeremy, are you there?"

"Yeah, Jayd. I also found out this morning that our family trip to Europe is back on," he says, dropping his second bomb for the afternoon. "My dad didn't think he'd be able to leave work, but I guess he's going to take it with him."

"Europe? What the hell for?" I ask, attempting to catch my breath, but my head's heating up the longer I stay on the phone.

"We go somewhere every summer, Jayd. Doesn't your family travel during the break?" Jeremy asks.

Is he serious? Hasn't this boy known me long enough to understand my hustle? I don't work because I love juggling two jobs. I work because I need the money, but I doubt he truly knows what being broke is like.

"Not really. Every other year we might go to Texas for a family reunion, but I haven't been since I was ten." And I don't plan on going again anytime soon. It was hotter than hell in Texas that July. As a matter of fact, I would probably have been better off in hell the way I was burning up.

"Candace's family goes to the same resorts and so does half the block. It's a Palos Verdes tradition. Otherwise, I'd rather be here with my favorite girl any day."

I know he's trying to be sweet, but it sounds like the same shit Rah used to say when we were dating before he'd go sneaking off with Sandy.

"Jeremy, this is all so sudden. I thought we'd have the entire summer to chill together," I whine. "And isn't it convenient that Cameron will be there in my absence?" I'm pissed. I know she's feeling my man, and Jeremy's stupid if he doesn't feel it, too. Jeremy's a nice-looking guy and he's loaded, so I expect to deal with females sniffing around him on the regular. But I can't do anything about it if he's on another continent.

"Jayd, what else can I say but I love you. I want to be with you and only you. No matter what goes down with Tania and the baby or who's going to be at the resort, you have to know that I love you."

Lexi pokes her head through the open gate, letting me know Mama's summoning me. I'd better get going.

"I know that." I close the car door and arm the alarm. It may be daylight, but thieves have a way of copping shit no matter what time it is.

"Do you? Because I think you're still insecure about us, and that's got to stop. I'm not Rah, and you can't treat me like I am. You have to learn to trust me, baby."

"You're right," I say, smiling at Jeremy's logic. His cool head is what keeps me sane on the craziest days. "I need to put my big-girl panties on and deal with reality."

"What does the size of your panties have to do with anything?" Jeremy is so clueless sometimes it's unbelievable.

"Never mind, baby," I say, giggling at my boyfriend. "I'll call you when I'm on my way home."

"I look forward to it, Lady J."

At least we're ending the conversation on a good note. I don't know if he had a smile on his face, but he definitely sounded better than he did when he first answered the phone.

I walk up the driveway and through the back gate with Lexi by my side. Reaching down to greet my four-legged friend, I notice her eyes are a brighter hazel than usual.

"Jayd, you've got to get on it, little girl," Lexi says, talking to me telepathically.

I think I'm going crazy now, for real. I notice that Lexi's eyes are now a shade of light green. How come even she has the jade eyes present through my bloodline and I'm the only one with brown ones? I know I'm tripping off the wrong thing, but it isn't fair even if my eyes are playing tricks on me.

"Your eyes are fine, Jayd," Lexi says, walking to the threshold of the backhouse and claiming her customary stance across it. *"You've just borrowed Esmeralda's powers from the last time she invaded your thoughts. Now you know what her power feels like."* No matter the origin of our pet-psychic session, the shit's still freaking me out. The dog's not really doing anything unusual; the only difference is that I can hear Lexi talking as if she's an old woman and not the German shepherd she is.

"Everything okay, Jayd?" Mama asks, breaking my communication with her dog.

I hope that's the end of the remnants of Esmeralda's sight. She's the last person I want to borrow from.

"Yes, Mama. I'm fine," I say, stepping into the spirit room. Netta's already back to work on the head-cleansing ingredients as well as other spirit work to be completed this afternoon.

"When we're finished with your *rogación,* we're going to make special elekes for traveling," Mama says, taking out multiple colored beads from one of the dozens of clear jars lining the counters, each filled with different tools necessary for our line of work.

Netta passes me a fresh lapa, and I cover myself before washing my hands in the kitchen sink. I instinctively take out the unwaxed dental floss to thread the beads for the traditional bracelets. We also have to consecrate them once they're finished. With the three of us working on them it shouldn't take too long. Out of all the tasks we do, this is one of my favorite activities.

"There are about twenty orders like this that you'll need to fill while we're gone, Jayd," Mama says.

Damn, I don't like doing it that much.

"There are so many initiations this summer. When we return, we'll have about ten to assist in before it's all said and done," Netta says with a smile on her face as if nothing just went down between her sisters and Mama.

This isn't the right time to bring it up, but I'm not letting that confrontation go. Celia and Rita definitely have something against Mama and vice versa.

"We're making these for Ogun and Legba, the main orishas we petition to for safe and prosperous travels."

Maybe I should make one for Jeremy since he's leaving me, too. I'll also add some beads for Oshune so she can keep my man sweet and faithful while he's gone. I know Jeremy's a good guy, but there's nothing wrong with a little extra protection.

"What time are y'all leaving Thursday morning? I can be late to school since it's the last week." No one's really counting attendance next week even though I probably won't take advantage of the unofficial end-of-the-year custom. The last thing I need is for my government teacher, Mrs. Peterson, to mark me tardy out of spite. She'd love to end my year on a miserable note.

"With the sunrise, baby," Mama says, ushering me away from the kitchen table and into the small open room where the shrines are housed. I kneel down on the bamboo mat while Mama lights the tall, white seven-day candles along the windowsills.

"Yes, little Jayd. Anytime you travel, go with nature," Netta says, joining us with a wooden mortar full of the fragrant elements for my crown. "You rise with the morning sun and rest when it sets."

"Don't worry about seeing us off, baby. Just wake up at that time and pray for a safe and open road."

I'm glad Mama said it because I'm not feeling waking up that early. "I'm going to miss you both," I say, becoming teary-eyed. The three people I depend on daily are leaving me at the same time. What am I going to do without them?

"We'll miss you, too, Jayd. But just because we aren't here in the physical doesn't mean you can't call on us when you need our help."

Netta's right. I don't care where they go; I know they'll always be within earshot of my prayers.

"And that also doesn't mean we're not watching you, little girl, so be good and handle your business."

"Yes, ma'am," I say, laughing at Mama keeping it real.

"And most importantly, be careful of your associations. Birds of a feather flock together, Jayd. Remember that."

She's right about that. I witnessed firsthand how crows operate when Little Miss Texas arrived at cheer practice yesterday. Mama places her hands on my head, ready to restart the ancient ceremony. Netta passes the mortar to her friend and retrieves a glass of water from the shrines to open with a prayer.

"We'll always be within reach, Jayd. Always."

I know Mama can never be that far away no matter where her travels take her. And for that I'm grateful. I hate saying good-bye, but like Jeremy said, I have to have faith that it'll all be all right no matter how painful it may be.

You can't make it feel right when you know that it's wrong / I'm already gone.

—Kelly Clarkson

It's been a quiet day at South Bay High with the entire senior population missing in action for Senior Ditch Day. Ever since Mama and Netta cleansed my head Saturday, I've felt completely refreshed. It's amazing what one simple ritual can accomplish. The remnants of Esmeralda's sight seem to be gone as well as most of the heat in my head. It's probably temporary, but I'm grateful for the break from the insanity that's plagued me lately. Yesterday's cheer performance at the final assembly went well, and I didn't even snap at Ellen's country-bumpkin ass nor did she try touching me again.

I can't believe we've finally made it to the last day of school. It's been a long, tough year, but we made it through. Summer couldn't have come sooner, even if it's not going to be as much fun as I initially thought it would. Mama and Netta left yesterday morning right on schedule. They've already made it to Arizona and will call when they reach Louisiana. It's bad enough that Jeremy's leaving for the first half of the extended vacation, but with Mama and Netta also gone, it's going to be an unbearable break. At least I'll have my other commitments and work to keep me occupied.

"Hola, Yeyekeke," Emilio says, creeping up behind me in the nearly vacant main hall. No one's called me *little mama*

in Yoruban in a long time, nor did I give this punk permission to do so. Emilio's like a fly: annoying and unnecessary, yet he refuses to go away.

"It's Jayd to you," I say, shutting my empty locker. I've been systematically cleaning out the year's worth of paper and other trash so I wouldn't have to spend today doing it, unlike the rest of my friends who are all perpetual procrastinators when it comes to this kind of thing.

"Pardon, Jayd," Emilio says in his thick Venezuelan accent with an air of false humility. "Maybe I should refer to you as Madam President, since I did have a hand in giving you that title."

I turn around and face Emilio's smug ass. He's only a couple of inches taller than my five-foot frame. I know I could take him down if I had to.

"What do you want, Emilio?" I ask impatiently. Where's a flyswatter when I need one? We have only a couple of minutes to get to third period, and I'm not willing to be late for this fool.

"The same thing we all want, Jayd. For your grandmother to join our spiritual family." Emilio's smile grows more sinister as he takes a step closer to me, nearly pinning my back against the long row of lockers. I need to join our fellow students in their mid-morning exodus to class before I end up kneeing this boy in his family jewels.

"Who's this elusive 'everybody,' because no one I know wants that," I say, maneuvering my way around him and charging toward the history corridor attached to the large hall.

"You know me, and I do," Emilio says, keeping up with my fast pace. "Besides, you owe me a favor."

I stop in midstride, almost causing a collision behind me, and look this punk dead in the eye. If I could conjure my great-grandmother's powers, I would. Emilio would be crippled by my thoughts, and that would suit me just fine.

"Let's get this straight, Emilio, once and for all. I don't owe you a damned thing." My head's getting hot and right after I had a cleansing, too. Damn this boy and his pushy godfather.

"Of course you do, Madam President. If I'd voted for myself instead of you, I'd be president of the African Student Union and you would be vice president. You and I both know that we were neck and neck, Jayd." Emilio touches my shoulders, his touch cool against my skin. If I'd known he was going to lay his hands on me again, I wouldn't have worn a tank top.

We stare each other down, neither of us relenting in our stance. My head begins to boil at the thought of Emilio threatening my grandmother or having the audacity to think I needed his help to win the election for the club I founded. As if. Before I can escape Emilio's grasp without acting violent, his fingers coil around my neck like the snakes in my shower nightmare a couple of weeks ago. Emilio's eyes glow at my entrance into his mind, but the trick's on me: My head's too hot, and his cool thoughts are causing my vision to blur.

"Let go of me," I say, grabbing both his wrists in my hands and forcing them away from my body, ending our mental quest. I may not be at a hundred percent, but my fifty percent beats Emilio's weak ass any day. The tardy bell rings, and Emilio walks away as defeated as he was when he first approached my locker. I vigorously shake my head and enter the barren classroom where Jeremy's waiting at his desk next to mine. I'm not letting Emilio ruin our last day of school, even if he does need to be dealt with in a serious way.

* * *

After third period, Jeremy decided to ditch fourth but promised he'd return for lunch. We have to sign yearbooks, take photos, and say our good-byes to folks we won't see until September, like my homegirl Maggie and her crew hanging in their customary spot in the quad, El Barrio. KJ, Misty, and the rest of South Central were missing from Mr. Adewale's speech and debate class, and I for one was grateful for the peace. It seems the rest of my crew decided to stick around for lunch, too, but will probably leave right after. I might do the same since Mrs. Sinclair officially ended drama class after the play last week, and there's no cheer practice this afternoon.

"What up, senior?" Mickey asks, walking up to the lunch bench I've claimed for us.

"I like the sound of that, senior," I say, exchanging yearbooks with my girl. "I'm glad you made it, Mickey. It wouldn't be the same without you. How's Nickey adjusting to not being with you during the day?"

"I don't know and I don't care," Mickey says, propping herself up on the table and opening her Diet Coke. "I'm just glad to be out of the damned house."

"Mickey, you're too much," I say, stating the obvious. I think I'll put that fact of life in her book, too.

"Whatever," she says. "I need to ask Misty how she lost all that weight," Mickey says, eyeing Misty and KJ walking across the lunch quad with the rest of their crew in tow. As usual, Misty's red outfit leaves little to the imagination. Mickey's right about one thing: Misty's swag is completely different from our sophomore year. Not only did she shed a good thirty pounds, but she also adjusted her wardrobe and her height by wearing high heels every day. From the outside looking in, Misty's entire junior year was all about social change. Too bad her metamorphosis didn't carry over to her academics. Rumor has it she barely passed the eleventh grade.

"Are you kidding? Misty's always up in someone's business. That alone can burn a thousand calories a day," I say, making my girl giggle. "It's a wonder the chick has all that ass left."

"Yeah, she is rocking the J.Lo, but KJ seems to love it," Mickey says.

I never thought I'd see the day Mickey was envious of Misty. I can't believe it.

"Of course he does," I say, trying not to talk with my mouth full, but this turkey sandwich is banging and I'm hungry. "It's all his, even if he's not returning the same loyalty to Misty." KJ couldn't turn down an available broad to save his life. Most might say that KJ's the man for running game, but I say it's a sign of how deep his insecurities lie.

"Why should he? KJ's got game and he's fine."

Mickey can be so shallow sometimes, I swear. We both wave to the rest of our crew exiting the main hall and heading our way. They had to clean out their lockers or risk staying after school to get the job done. South Bay High doesn't play about school beautification and will gladly charge a fee to anyone who doesn't follow the rules.

"All I'm saying is if a girl talked to every dude who looked good, she would be seen as having daddy issues. Therefore, I think it's safe to say that KJ has mama issues. His love of booty is his way of compensating for attention he missed during childhood."

Mickey looks up at me in midsip and smiles.

"Somebody's been watching too much *Dr. Phil,*" Mickey says, checking her shirt and making sure her breasts aren't leaking.

I had to go to three different stores to find the perfect

breast-feeding bra. After all the trouble I went through, of course Mickey's ready to throw in the towel and bottle-feed my goddaughter.

"Whatever, Mickey," I say, stuffing the last Frito into my mouth, along with my sub. Damn, these things are good. It must be that time of the month. I always crave salt and chocolate when Mother Nature's ready to make her grand appearance. "I don't see where you need to lose weight. You're wearing the same jeans you wore on the first day of school."

"You're right," Mickey says, looking down at her Express pants and poking at her belly roll. Granted, her pudge is new, but what did she expect after having a baby? "I need to go shopping."

As usual, Mickey misses the point completely.

Jeremy, Chance, Nigel, and Nellie finally reach our table with their yearbooks and lunch in hand, ready to chill.

"What up, my peeps?" Chance says, claiming a spot on the bench.

Nigel hands Mickey her lunch and everyone couples up—even Chance and Nellie. I guess they're speaking again for the time being. Looking at my friends, I become misty-eyed knowing we won't be able to chill like this again for a while. Man, my hormones and my sight have got me tripping hard.

"What's harshing your mellow?" Jeremy asks, noticing my mood shift and putting his arm around me.

Sometimes I swear we speak a different language. "I'm going to miss you. My grandmother left yesterday, and I already miss her, too," I say, attempting to hold it together. It's all too much for me to handle this afternoon. And besides, I'm supposed to be happy on my last day. At least I'm not anticipating any end-of-the-year fights, which is the usual mode of operation in my hood for the last day.

"I've got something that'll make you smile," Jeremy says, pulling a tightly rolled plastic bag from his back pocket.

I open the black bag and unfold the T-shirt and tank top inside.

"This one's for you," Jeremy says, taking the pale blue tank and holding it up to my chest. "South Bay Surfer," he says, reading the white words aloud.

"You are crazy, Jeremy," I say, holding up the extra-large yellow shirt. "And this is supposed to be yours, I assume."

"You know it, baby," he says, pointing to the word *Gold-digger* printed across the front in bold, black letters. He must've been high when he bought these, but I don't care. I needed to laugh.

"Y'all are nuts," Nigel says, laughing at us.

The rest of our crew shake their heads and continue eating and signing. The other excited students around us are all pretty much doing the same thing.

"I love my gift, baby," I say, kissing my man. "Thank you." I return the shirt to the generic bag and bring the last bite of my sandwich to my lips. "When do you leave?"

"Early tomorrow morning, Jayd. It's an eight-hour flight to London," Jeremy says, shocking me. I knew it was soon but not less than twenty-four hours from now. Against my best effort, tears well up in my eyes, instantly eliminating my remaining appetite. I try to hold them back, but they fall to my cheeks anyway.

"I'm going to miss you," I say, replacing Mickey's yearbook with Jeremy's and turning to my spot. I reserved pages in each of my friends' books when we received them Wednesday: We all did the same thing.

"I'm going to miss you, too," Jeremy says, signing my book. "But you'll see. Six weeks will fly by and I'll be right back here with you, Lady J."

"Yeah, we'll see about that." Mama's gone indefinitely having big fun in New Orleans and Puerto Rico, and now my boyfriend's leaving for half the summer, too. This isn't fair.

"Hey, Jayd and Jeremy," Cameron says, smiling too big at my man. She doesn't know the rest of our crew, and they choose not to greet her, either. I guess it's too late in the year to make new friends. "Want to sign my yearbook?" she asks, placing her book on top of mine as if it's not even there. If Cameron wasn't one of the cool white girls on my AP track, I'd probably be more jealous than I already am. She'd better not push her luck, because I don't like her that much.

"Sure, C," Jeremy says, rubbing my exposed thigh while simultaneously signing his name and adding the infamous "K.I.T." before getting back to mine: I get way more than three letters.

I love wearing shorts, especially since I joined the cheer squad. My legs have never been this fit, and they'll only get better with our summer practice schedule. It's not so bad because we have practice only three times a week. I can handle that, and I could use the distraction since my boo will be traveling.

"Is your family going to make it to Europe this summer?" she asks. Cameron passes her book to me, which I quickly sign.

"Yeah, unfortunately," Jeremy says, looking into my sad eyes.

I can't believe we're finally in a good space and being forced to spend time apart. Life isn't fair in the least bit.

"It should be fun, unlike last year," Cameron says, piquing my interest and that of my friends. Last year? What the hell am I missing here?

Sensing my irritation, Jeremy rubs my thigh harder to reassure me it's not what he knows I'm thinking. Cameron eyes Jeremy's book in my lap like she wants to snatch it up, and I wish she would. Then I'll be justified in slapping that bright smile off her face.

"I just want to go and get it over with. Last year I didn't want to be in Redondo for the summer. This year I can't think of anywhere else I'd rather be," Jeremy says, kissing my nose.

"Oh my God, you're one whipped nigga," Mickey says, ruining the sweet moment and serving it to Cameron, who looks more than ready to roll: It's too much color over here for her.

"Well, okay, then. Bye," Cameron says, replastering her fake smile and bidding us farewell without signing a damn thing. I should've signed her book "So long, trick, and stay away from my man while you're at it" instead of "Have a good summer." She might get too literal with that shit.

"Who the hell was that, and why is she vacationing with your man?" Mickey asks, digging into her food and my raw emotions.

It's hard to believe she gave birth a little over a month ago. I wish I could eat whatever I wanted and still fit into a size four, even if she does have new handles to hold on to.

"She's not going anywhere with me," Jeremy says, shutting down Mickey's hating. "Our families vacation at the same resort, just like Chance and his folks, right, man?"

"It's Chase, man. Chase," Chance says passionately while at the same time ignoring Jeremy's question. "Session at my house after school—I insist," Chance says, leaning on Nellie. Their on again / off again relationship is working my nerves, not to mention I'm still hurt that he flaked on the lead role even if Nigel rocked it. I wonder if Nigel will take Mrs. Sinclair up on her recommendation for him to join the drama class next year. It'll be nice to have another brother in class.

"I'm down," Nigel says, devouring the last of his chili Fritos. He hasn't said much, and I can see why. All of his food is gone.

"I'll have to see if my mom can watch the baby," Mickey says.

The sad look in her eyes isn't from missing Nickey but rather from missing her life before motherhood, envying our seemingly carefree schedules. I'm the only one who can feel her sense of responsibility, because I'm usually the one with all of the work to do. But now that Netta's sisters have taken over the shop while she and Mama are out of town, my time at the shop has dramatically decreased per Mama's insistence, allowing me more time to get my side hustle on.

"Let's make it a good one with everyone in attendance," Chance says, eyeing Jeremy and me.

He knows we'll want to spend the night alone, being that my man's leaving in the morning. But I guess we have to make time for our friends, too.

"Is that Tania?" Nellie asks, pointing toward the front parking lot, way too excited to see the head bitch in charge on campus. I guess she wanted to spend the last day with her graduating class even if she already took the GED. Maybe the administration's letting her walk in tonight's graduation.

"Yeah, it is," Jeremy says, looking at his ex-girlfriend hard like he can see his son through her even if the baby's not here. If he didn't want to get away before, I'm sure he's looking for an escape route now.

"I have to say hi to her and get the latest dish. Her baby's probably too cute," Nellie says, leaving us at the table to run off and join the other groupies. What's so damned special about that chick? She's an evil broad at her nicest and a mean, rich bitch every other day of the year. What gives?

"You can go say hi if you want," I say to Jeremy, who hasn't taken his eyes off her—not even to blink. I know his disdain for his baby's mama runs deep, but I don't mind if he wants to check on the status of his newborn son.

"Why would I want to do that?" Jeremy asks, looking down at me and exhaling deeply. "Forget her and her parents." What he's not saying is forget his dad, too. Because Tania's Persian and therefore has brown skin, Mr. Weiner wouldn't allow Jeremy to claim the baby. If he tried, Jeremy would be disowned and cut out of the family inheritance and probably kicked out of the house even if he's only seventeen.

"There's the bell," Chance says, and I'm thankful for the diversion. "My house, after school. No exceptions."

"We'll be there," Nigel says, giving his boys dap.

"Us too," I say, hugging my man, who's still in shock. Tania looks a little sore from here but good. I can't believe she and Mickey bounced back in a week after giving birth. Mama says as long as women are healthy, they should give birth naturally for the very same reason. There's no quick recovery time with a C-section, which is what Mickey initially wanted.

We claim our trash and head off to complete our final day as juniors, although I'm positive we'll all take it easy for the rest of the day. Maybe if Jeremy and Tania had been in love when they made their baby, they would've fought harder to stay together. Whatever the case, her loss is my gain and I'm not going anywhere anytime soon without my man in my pocket. And if Cameron knows what's good for her, she'll back up off mine, too. Jeremy knows I'm all the girl he needs, and the feeling's definitely mutual.

~ 6 ~
If I Was Your Girlfriend

If I was your one and only friend, would you run to me if somebody hurt you / Even if that somebody was me?

—PRINCE

Before I left campus for the day, I had to say good-bye to Ms. Toni, who was overwhelmed with graduation duties. As the activities director, her job never ends and she informed me that she'd be on campus over the summer. Some of us just can't get enough of Drama High. Ms. Toni also gave me free access to her personal library, and I took advantage of it, this time picking out a novel, *The Hand I Fan With,* about this sistah Lena who has an affair with a ghost she wished up. I can't wait to dig into it. The soft texture of the cover's already got me wishing for more.

We've been at Chance's house for over three hours, and the rest of my friends are already lit—minus Nellie's prude ass, of course. She's been unusually quiet lately, constantly texting in private. I came into the kitchen thinking Nellie would be here, but she's nowhere to be found. I'm sure Nellie would rather be with her rich-girl crew, but they're slowly eliminating her from their group now that the year's over. The whole homecoming-princess thing can only last so long. I feel sorry for my girl, but not that bad. Once Nellie's ass is completely humbled, maybe we'll finally get the Nellie back we all know and love.

I might as well get something to drink while I'm here. I

open the stainless-steel mega refrigerator, eyeing the collection of cold beverages lining the door. At Mama's house, they only have family-sized containers of milk and Sunny Delight. I can buy whatever groceries I can afford at my mom's house, and so far other than water, Kool-Aid is my best friend. But at Chance's crib, there are single servings of the good stuff: cranberry juice, ginger ale, and raspberry lemonade—my favorite.

"Jayd. It's always a pleasure to see you, love," Mrs. Carmichael says, entering the massive Spanish-style kitchen and scaring the hell out of me. I thought Chance's parents weren't home. His mom must've snuck in on the sly.

"Hello, Mrs. Carmichael," I say, returning the hug she's got me engulfed in. I claim my drink and close the door. Mrs. Carmichael's been trying to get me back in her home ever since we had dinner a couple of months ago, when she let it be known that she knew all about my gift of sight.

"Oh, please, stop with all that 'Mrs. Carmichael' stuff. Just, call me Lindsay."

"I can't do that without feeling like I'm disrespecting my elders," I say, swallowing the cool lemonade. I needed that.

"I wouldn't expect anything less from you, Jayd. It's rare to meet a girl with Southern manners. I like that," Mrs. Carmichael says, obviously still hopeful that her son and I will take our friendship to the next level, but that'll never happen. Like Nigel, Chance and I are the best of friends for life—nothing more. Why can't she and Nellie both get that through their thick skulls? The kitchen phone rings, interrupting our chat and allowing me to make my escape. All I wanted was something to drink, not a full-blown conversation.

"Yes, this is the home of Lindsay and David Carmichael," Mrs. Carmichael says, looking concerned at the voice on the other end of the receiver. She reaches her hand out, holding on to my wrist, momentarily preventing my disappearing act. Damn, she's quick. Mrs. Carmichael finishes her conversation and returns the phone to its wall charger, looking shocked.

"That was Chance's grandfather," she says, releasing her hold on me. "He wants Chance to spend the summer with him in Atlanta, and apparently Chance already accepted his invitation without ever mentioning it to me." Mrs. Carmichael looks like she's going to pass out she's so disturbed by the news. "He just wanted to clear it with me first and to have Chance call him back to make the final arrangements."

I know part of her wants to forget to give her son the message, but she can't risk violating Chance's trust again. "That's not so bad, is it?" I ask, unable to walk away from a suffering person no matter how bad I want to go back to the den and hang with my friends. Why do I always get caught up in other folks' drama?

"You don't understand, Jayd," Mrs. Carmichael yells, now showing her true drunken colors. I can smell the expensive liquor all over her. "I'm losing my son. He's already calling himself Chase instead of the befitting name I gave him, and now he's going to spend the summer in Atlanta instead of traveling with me like he usually does. What am I going to do without my baby?" She breaks down in ugly sobs, holding her chest like her heart's going to fall out if she lets go. I can't take this for too much longer without spiritually intervening on one of my best friend's behalf. Helping Chance's mother is also helping him, and she's begging for my assistance.

"Mrs. Carmichael, Chance isn't a baby anymore," I say, wrapping one arm around her shoulders, trying my best to comfort her. "He's almost a grown man."

"I know that, Jayd," she says, taking a paper towel from the stand on the marble counter and blowing her nose. "That's why this time is so important. We don't have many summers left. And his father's barely been home since

Chance found out about his birth family," she says angrily. "I'm sure his secretary is more than pleased with our family meltdown."

And that's what I call too much information. I think Mrs. Carmichael would be better off without her arrogant husband, but we're not homegirls, and I have no right to give anyone relationship advice.

"I need your help."

"What do you think I can do to help your situation? Chance won't listen to anyone right now because he's so confused."

Mrs. Carmichael's tears return full force, causing her bloodshot blue eyes to become even more red. She can't force her son to do anything he doesn't want to, especially not when it comes to Chance exploring his true identity.

I look into Mrs. Carmichael's eyes, wishing I could ease her pain. I can at least cool her mind, hopefully calming her down and allowing her to think clearly about the situation. I jump into Mrs. Carmichael's mind, feeling the hurt she's not so quietly bearing. I truly feel sorry for her. I can see her regret for not being able to have her own children, and I wish I could heal her womb, but that's not why I'm in her head this evening. I can also see her memories of going to Mama back in New Orleans for help getting pregnant, which Mama did assist with successfully. But Mrs. Carmichael lost three babies in one year, and Mr. Carmichael kept her from trying again, forcing her to cease contact with Mama. Eventually, she had to have a full hysterectomy, and that was the end of her trying. She's always resented her husband for that.

"Your grandmother was my only hope of salvation, and my husband was the one who destroyed everything," Mrs. Carmichael murmurs, further explaining the memory we're sharing. I focus on her eyes, drying her tears and calming her down. With all of this heat, she's liable to try and kill Mr.

Carmichael if he walked through the door within the next two minutes, and I can't have that on my conscience. Instead of her head becoming cool, mine does. My brain freeze is crippling me like Esmeralda's eyes do.

"Oh shit," I say, rubbing my temples and trying to hold on to the vision for as long as I can. Mrs. Carmichael's carrying a lot of pain, and I want to help, but not at my own expense. I look down, ending the sorrowful vision quest, but the discomfort in my head doesn't leave so easily.

"Hey, Mrs. C," Jeremy says, coming into the kitchen and causing us both to jump. "Jayd, we'd better get going. It's getting late and I still have to pack," Jeremy says, reminding me once again of his impending departure.

"Okay, baby," I say, shaking my head clear. I've decided to stop fighting the inevitable and enjoy our last night together. And I have to give him the special bracelet I made for him to wear for protection during his travels. It'll also keep me on his mind and the broads at bay.

"Jayd, please don't leave yet. I need a favor from you," Mrs. Carmichael says, again staring into my tired eyes. I look down, avoiding her look until I can get my own shit under control. It's been easier to unlock my eyes once I'm inside someone's mind, but not without some level of uneasiness, always. I wish I could have done the same thing when Mickey was in labor. I'll never forget sharing that pain as long as I live.

"Good. You shouldn't," my mom says, all up in my business. *"It's the best birth control I've ever heard of."*

"Mom, can I help you?" I say, still avoiding Mrs. Carmichael's glance. Jeremy looks from Chance's mom and back to me, wondering what's really going on. I'll fill him in later. Right now I have to get out of this uncomfortable space.

"Oh, no, you don't, little girl," my mom says. *"She's made*

a request, and you have to honor it. You've been all up in that lady's head and that makes her a client."

"Are you serious?" I say. I smile at Jeremy and glance at the watch on his arm. It's already after seven. If we don't leave soon, we won't have any time to ourselves. This special spirit session will have to wait.

"Very serious, Jayd. Had you followed my directions and told Mama about your little souvenir, this wouldn't be your sacrifice to make. But Mama left you in charge, and I'm here to help you. So, get to it. I don't have all day."

"Jeremy, can you give us a minute?" I say, holding my baby's hand and rubbing his gray knuckles. I didn't think white folks got ashy like we do, but dry is dry, and my man could use some lotion.

"Okay. I'll check the movie times at the dollar theater," Jeremy says, bringing my hand to his lips and kissing it gently before leaving us ladies alone.

"Thank you, Jeremy," Mrs. Carmichael says, smiling for the first time this evening. "Jayd, I wanted to tell you about my history with your family sooner, but I figured you'd eventually see it for yourself and I was right: you did." Mrs. Carmichael takes my hand, happy I've agreed to help. I can feel my mom's presence focus in my thoughts and then into our client's head. What am I getting myself into?

"The business of healing, also known as your destiny," my mom says, answering my unspoken question. *"Now, ask her what she wants."*

"What is it that I can do for you, Mrs. Carmichael?" I ask while reentering her mind.

"Slow down, little girl," my mom says before we lock onto Mrs. Carmichael's vision. *"Pace yourself, Jayd. It's not a race."*

Instead of jumping right in, I ease into her mind, careful

not to overdo it. I don't want to repeat the sensation I felt a few minutes ago. Much like drinking a cold drink too fast, a head freeze comes on suddenly and can't leave quick enough.

"That's it. Sense her true desires, urging her to ask for them out loud so that the power of her request is made clear."

I think my mom's enjoying her powers through me. I witness the formation of Mrs. Carmichael's thoughts unfold like blankets of various tapestries to voice what she wants without her desires hurting her son. If Chance has any doubts about his mother's true feelings for him, I can reassure him that she couldn't love him any more if he were her biological child. And that seems to be all she wants from me: to get through to her son in a way that she can't.

"Okay, Jayd. You can see what I see," my mom says. "Now help her hold on to that vision and work it out."

"I just want my baby back," Mrs. Carmichael says, breaking down in convulsive sobs before I let her completely go, inadvertently absorbing some of her sorrow.

"Babe, we've got to get going if we want to make the show," Jeremy says, again interrupting our session. "Is everything okay?" he asks, noticing Mrs. Carmichael crying like a baby. I could cry, too, but I'm not shedding any more tears today.

"Yes, I'm fine, thanks to your girlfriend," Mrs. Carmichael says, hugging me tightly before heading upstairs with a full bottle of wine. Next time I'll work on cooling her love of liquor. "Thank you again, Jayd. I hope to see you sooner than later. Good night, Jeremy, and tell your mother to call me once you all arrive at the resort. We won't be able to make it this year."

"All right, Mrs. C," Jeremy says, holding my hand tightly

and wondering what the hell just went down. "Let's say good-bye and get going, Jayd. I'm done sharing you for the night." I couldn't agree more.

On our way down the hill from Palos Verdes to the pier in Manhattan Beach, we dropped Jeremy's car off at his house around the corner from Chance's. There's no need to take two cars, and with the way my man's been smoking, I feel safer being the designated driver tonight.

"So which old movie do you want to see? *Avatar*'s playing," I say, hoping he's as anxious as I am to see the science-fiction thriller for the third time. It has such a great following it'll probably be out forever.

"That sounds good," Jeremy says, leading the way toward the ticket counter. "Where's the polka necklace I bought you?" Jeremy asks, flicking my gold charm again like he's picking bird crap off my neck.

"In a safe place," I say, fingering my neck and recalling the night Rah presented me with the extravagant birthday gift.

"Even aliens know you're supposed to remain faithful to one person, and that includes wearing someone else's jewelry and using the phone they gave you," Jeremy says, taking a mental inventory of what possessions of mine he provided and which ones Rah purchased. Jeremy knows he's winning by a landslide, but this male territorial shit is taking its toll on my man. Love makes us all act strange, but I still don't think I should have to give up my bling to make my man feel better.

"And you're right, little girl," my mom says, again adding her telepathic two cents. She's on a roll today. When it comes to boyfriend jewelry, my mom's the expert on proper protocol. *"His insecurities are just that—his. And it's not your job to make Jeremy feel more secure. He has to deal with that mess on his own."*

"But as his girlfriend, aren't I partially obligated to compromise something?" I ask, knowing I'm talking to the wrong woman about compromise. My mom doesn't believe in giving up shit if she doesn't absolutely have to.

"Hell no, Jayd. This isn't compromise. This is sacrifice and you don't have to give up a damned thing to make him feel better. Trust me, Jayd. If the shoe were on the other foot, best believe Jeremy wouldn't be giving up a thing. Heed my words, little girl. The minute you start giving in to his wishes is the exact same moment you begin losing yourself."

And on that note, my mom's out and we're in the movie. I hope Jeremy and I can have the type of relationship where trust is never an issue. After all, he's the one leaving me. I'm the one stuck here with the same people and all the madness thereof. If we can't have faith in each other, then we have nothing. I for one believe Jeremy and I have something special no matter the distance between us. I just hope he feels the same way.

It was a bittersweet night, but Jeremy and I managed to finally let go of each other for the next few weeks. He called early this morning to say good-bye again. Our date didn't end until almost two, and he woke me up at seven, which wasn't a bad thing. Luckily I had clients booked back-to-back today, starting with my neighbor Shawntrese, to keep me distracted from the pain I'm already experiencing from Jeremy's absence.

Jeremy and I made out for as long as we could before finally catching a few hours of sleep. I hate that I have to spend the first several weeks of the summer break without my man. That's just wrong. It even feels weird being at the coffeehouse without him, but I needed a break from the norm in order to get some reading done.

I love summertime even with the writing group starting

next week. It's pleasant because of the nice weather and because I don't have to go to school every day, and I'm making hella ends braiding hair. I'm grateful to be done early enough for some me time. Since Netta's sisters like running the shop their way, my services aren't needed as much, nor do I want to be there without my grandmother and godmother having my back. As instructed, I will make sure all the clients' orders and boxes are filled as well as my other housekeeping duties, which can all be performed in small doses, leaving me more time to chill and study until Netta and Mama return.

So far, I'm loving my summer reading collection. The first book on my school list is by some white lady writing about black women in the South and a little white girl with bees in her wall. I hope it's worth the read. We have a new title each week and have to write a three-to-five-page paper on whatever pops into our heads. It's similar to English class minus the exams. I'm looking forward to sharpening my writing skills. And with Alia, Charlotte, and the other usual AP suspects in attendance, I'm sure there'll be some healthy debate to keep it interesting.

With my green tea in hand, I find a spot next to one of the only black girls in the chill space, forcing her to move all the shit she's got spread across the small corner table we have to share. Her laptop cord is spread across the empty oversized chair, and she's forced to move that, too, much to her dislike. Too bad. If she wanted to spread out in the living room, she should've stayed her ass at home. Finally seated, I settle in for some good reading time, but not before her cell rings, disturbing the serene energy throughout the quaint space.

"Hello," she says loudly into her phone.

It might as well be on speaker as loud as both she and her mother are talking. I can hear their conversation, and it's ruining my concentration. Black people, I tell you.

I roll my eyes at my neighbor, hoping she gets the message without me having to say anything directly to her. When two sistahs go at it in public, it's anything but pretty, and I'm really not in the mood to give these white folks in here the pleasure of showing my ass. They would be all too happy to witness what they already think they know about black people going down right in front of them. I'm sure they thought by putting the coffeehouse in the middle of West LA, no black people would frequent the spot, but there are a few of us willing to drive a few miles out of our comfort zones for some peace and a good cup of fancy caffeine. I would have gone to one of the spots Jeremy and I frequent by the beach, but I have to stay out this way to be at Rah's in a little while and need to conserve all the gas I can.

I'm still wondering why I agreed to attend Westingle's grad night with Nigel and Rah. It's not my school, nor do I have any friends who go there outside of my boys. And with the way I've been feeling lately, the last place I want to be if I have another mental meltdown is around a bunch of bougie-ass folks. I'm liable to go off if Nigel's and Rah's ex-girlfriends say a word to me. Tasha and Trish roll deep like me and my girls usually do: Where there's one, the other isn't far behind. Maybe I can feign illness or something to get out of it. It won't be too much of a lie since just the thought of those heffas makes me sick to my stomach, but I'm trying to be sweeter these days no matter how difficult it may be. Unfortunately, this chick next to me is really testing my patience.

"Mama, please. I'm just chilling at the coffeehouse, ain't doing shit," the girl says, louder than ever.

The other patrons eye her, afraid to say something, but I'm not. I've had it with being an unwilling witness to her public conversation.

"Excuse me," I say, interrupting her in midsentence. "Would you mind toning it down a bit? I'm trying to read."

"Ain't nobody stopping you from reading," she says, not getting the clue. Why is this trick going to make me come outside of myself and on such a nice day, too?

"Actually, you and your mama are," I say, causing her to again pause in midsentence. "I know way too much about you and your issues already, and I need to focus on what's in front of me, not the results of your latest pap smear." At first she looks offended and hot that I would even dare say something to her. But after glancing around the shop, pure embarrassment comes over her. The other patrons look away, embarrassed themselves but still awaiting the next move.

"Mama, let me call you back when I get in the car," she says, hurriedly gathering her things and leaving the establishment. The other customers breathe a sigh of relief at the rude girl's departure. Now we can all enjoy the rest of our Saturday afternoon in peace . . . or maybe not. A gorgeous brotha just stepped through the door, instantly warming the over-air-conditioned venue and permanently distracting my thoughts.

After paying for his drink, he scans the place and his eyes land on the recently vacated chair next to mine.

"Is anyone sitting here?" he asks, making me completely forget what the proper answer would be.

"I'm sorry. I didn't hear you," I say, trying to focus on the words forming in my head, but his deep brown eyes, chiseled cheekbones, and extra-white teeth are distracting a sistah's good sense. Damn, where did he come from, and can I go back there with him?

"Is this seat taken?" he repeats with a grin.

"Oh, no. Not at all," I say, smiling big as I move my pastry and tea over to make room for my new neighbor. If I wasn't a faithful girlfriend, I'd definitely try to get this dude's number, but he looks too old for me anyway.

"Thanks," he says, taking his backpack off and setting it

down on the floor next to the oversized chair. He takes his seat and places his coffee down on the table, getting comfortable. I read the UCLA monogram on his shirt, trying not to stare directly at him. I don't want the dude to think I'm a stalker.

"Good read?" he asks, pointing to the novel in my hand. I forgot all about the main reason I'm here.

"Yes. It's okay," I say, flipping through the barely touched text. "I'm a little tired of reading about black women from white folks' perspectives, though," I say, obviously impressing my new neighbor. He takes out his laptop and headphones, ready to get his work on, too.

"I felt the same way when I read it for my American literature class last quarter. The second book about the mermaid was the same way, but what can you say? At least we can't forget where we are and whose country we're living in."

Damn, who is this brotha, and where can I find more like him?

"My sentiments exactly," I say, smiling as big as all outside and temporarily forgetting about my boyfriend, who's probably flying over an ocean by now. It's just an innocent conversation with a little subtle flirting and nothing more.

"My name's Keenan," he says, extending his right hand, and I return the polite gesture. "And you might be?"

"Jayd," I say, blushing at the smile in his eyes. He is too cute to be single and so am I. But we can chat it up—no guilt necessary.

"Well, it's certainly nice to meet an intelligent black woman around here, Jayd."

Me, a woman? Really? I wonder how old he thinks I am. I'm going to hold off on telling him I'm barely seventeen until after the wedding in my imagination.

"Thank you, Keenan. It's refreshing to meet you, too."

Before we can get better acquainted, my phone vibrates in

my purse. I take out the pink cell and reluctantly answer Nigel's call.

"Jayd, what up?" Nigel asks. "Hey, can you hook me up with some braids when you get here? I want to look like the baller I am tonight." Nigel's more excited about the party than the actual graduates. I know he misses his alma mater.

"Whatever, fool. I got you," I say in a low voice, smiling at my silly friend. It's been nice hanging out with Nigel during our cotillion rehearsals, especially since we can't stand the rest of the participants. Having him in the play was cool, too. I almost forgot how good it is hanging with Nigel without Mickey always in his lap. Like Chance, Nigel was my boy first, and even if I'm not their girlfriends or a dude, I'm still the best homie my boys could ask for, if I do say so myself. And they've always got my best interest at heart. "You know I raised my rates, right?" I say, looking at Keenan, who's absorbed in the computer screen in front of him. He's working on a Mac, so I know he's got cheddar.

"Girl, please. You know I got you right back. Holla at your boy," Nigel says, ending the quick call. I have to get a move on if I'm going to do my own hair and Nigel's braids. He usually likes to rock his afro out, but I guess he wants to change his style up a bit for his old homies at Westingle High.

"What was that all about?" Keenan asks, all up in my business like he's my man.

Why are dudes so nosy? "I don't think we know each other well enough to keep tabs on one another's phone calls, do we?" Keenan smiles at my sass, but I'm serious. I can't have my folks that curious about my associations.

"Not yet, but we will soon," he says, sipping his coffee.

I love a confident man. "Well, it was nice talking to you," I say, reluctantly rising from the comfortable chair with my book. I've been here for two hours and am still not ready to go, but duty calls and so do my friends.

"Likewise," Keenan says. "I hope we run into each other again soon." He extends his hand, and I take it into mine, holding it one second too long. I hope I run into Keenan again sooner than later. Just because my man is traveling doesn't mean I can't enjoy the company of an intelligent companion. And it doesn't hurt if he's fine, too. All I can say is that I'm thankful for the quick intellectual session. Jeremy's soft lips and fresh scent aren't the only things I miss about my man. His mind has always been his most attractive quality, and that's true for all of the dudes I've liked—excluding KJ. And from the brief interaction Keenan and I just shared, so far so good.

~ 7 ~
Too Hot to Trot

My prince is gone / Far, far away.
—Jah Mason

Once I returned to my mom's apartment, I gave my head a much-needed wash and conditioning with my new mango-honey hair products. I'm still perfecting the combination, but I like the early results. Even Nigel's neglected ebony hair's shining because of the new blend.

Mickey's in rare form this afternoon, getting ready for the party tonight like it's all about her. I guess since Nigel's mom chose me to be in the cotillion and Nigel to be my partner, Mickey's taking this opportunity to firmly cement her place in Nigel's life as his one and only girl. So there's no confusion, Mickey even made Nigel buy her a fake diamond to pass off as an engagement ring. My mom says that promise rings are bad luck, but I'm not going to bother Mickey with my logic, not that she'd listen anyway.

I'm putting the finishing touches on Nigel's braids, giving him exactly seventeen to match his football number. I think it's sweet that South Bay gave him the same number he wore at Westingle, even if it did belong to another player. Fortunately the other player was on junior varsity and understood the significance of a senior varsity player maintaining his lucky number at the time of his transfer.

"I love it, girl," Nigel says, looking at his reflection in the hand mirror. "You've got mad skills, Jayd."

Mickey can't help but slit her heavily shadowed eyes at me. "She ain't got nothing until she can hook up my hair," Mickey says, slicking down the edges of her extensions. The gold and brown weave is loosely braided all over her head, giving me a headache just thinking about dealing with all of that shit.

"I told you, Mickey. I'm all natural with my skills," I say, taking out the last sample of braid-sheen spray, putting the finishing touches on Nigel's do. Next to the business cards I'm working on, a satisfied customer is the best advertisement there is.

"I gotta change into my fresh gear to match my clean braids. Thank you, girl." Nigel hands me a fifty-dollar bill and smiles, knowing it's double my usual friends' rate. A simple cornrow is forty dollars plus tip for my regular clients. But for my boys and my girl, Shawntrese, I charge only twenty dollars, but they usually give me twenty-five for a job well done.

Mickey, eyeing the generous exchange, gets red at her man's appreciation for my excellent work. "How the hell are you going to pay Jayd fifty dollars to do a twenty-dollar job when you didn't even want to spend that much on my ring?" Mickey asks, waving her nonengagement ring in the air. It's a nice knockoff, but she's right. It couldn't have cost more than Nigel's hair, and we all know Nigel can afford it, but I'm staying out of this one. Something else is obviously going on here, and it's between Mickey and Nigel.

"Because I can," Nigel says. "And Jayd deserves it. She didn't have to fit me into her work schedule on such short notice, and I know she was already tired from braiding all day, but she did it anyway." Nigel takes his outfit off the hanger on the back of the door. "When you work, you get paid. It's that simple."

Mickey looks at Nigel like she wants to kill him; obviously he's hit a sore spot. They've been arguing about money lately, and I'm with Nigel: Mickey needs to get her ass a job, especially now that she's got another person to be responsible for and not depend solely on the county for relief, although it is a necessary supplement.

"So, what are you saying?" Mickey asks, becoming overly emotional. "That I don't deserve a nice ring? That I don't work for mine? Because I do." Mickey places her hands on her hips. Nigel rolls his eyes at his girl's customary outburst. "And don't act like you don't like the way I work it, because that's not what you said last night or this morning."

"Okay, that was way too much information," I say, packing up my hair tools in the black bag, ready to leave this uncomfortable scene and join the rest of our friends in the living room next door. We're in the den because the baby's taking a nap in here. Mickey has to drop Nickey off in Compton before meeting us back here to go to the party in downtown Los Angeles. They've been here all day, and I'm sure Nigel's feeling a bit smothered by his instant family.

"I agree," Nigel says, irritated by Mickey's crassness. "Damn, Mickey. Some shit's just between us—know what I'm saying?" Nigel leaves the room, slamming the door and waking Nickey. I pick up my goddaughter and kiss her chubby cheeks in an attempt to calm her fussing.

"Damn him for waking her up," Mickey says. "All that baby does is shit, cry, eat, and sleep."

"Here, Mickey. I thought this might help," I say, passing the medium-sized vial to her. "It's a tincture for new moms my grandmother helped me make just for you."

"Does a new apartment and a nanny pop out?" Mickey asks, looking at the blue vile suspiciously.

"No, but it will help with your emotions, uncomfortable digestive issues, and milk production."

"Damn, Jayd. You make me sound like a factory cow. I'm a girl, not a machine," Mickey says, plumping her larger-than-usual breasts in her revealing top.

"I didn't mean it like that, but you are producing for two now. Mama says the ingredients in this tincture will make you feel a whole lot better, and it'll pass on to Nickey. She needs her nutrients, too."

Mickey looks at the bottle and sucks her teeth before putting it down on the bed where Nickey's lying down on her baby blanket.

"Mickey, be careful. Nickey could get into this," I say, moving the bottle away from the curious baby girl.

"I thought you said it was good for her, too. She might as well get it like that because I'm not taking that shit." Mickey continues her primping.

"Why do you have to be so rude, Mickey? Damn, I'm just trying to help you adjust to your new role."

"I'm not taking on a new role, Jayd. Now that the baby's out, I'm going back to the old me," Mickey says, picking up a crying Nickey and walking over to the diaper bag hanging on the back of the door.

"You're only feeding her formula?" I ask when Mickey takes a bottle out of the bag, surprised that Mickey's not breast-feeding anymore. Last week she had enough milk to feed a couple of babies. "What happened?"

"What happened is that I realized my breasts and my body are finally mine again, and I'm over it. Similac works just as good, and it's free through the county. It's a win-win situation," Mickey says, vigorously shaking the bottle. My goddaughter looks at me, her brown eyes wiser than her six weeks of age. If I were her mother, I'd do it differently. But this is out of my hands. Ultimately it's Mickey's responsibility, and I have to stay out of this decision.

"Okay, Mickey. I've tried to be the best homegirl I can be to you, but you're not making it easy, as usual." I take Nickey and feed her the thick concoction.

"Whatever, Jayd. This ain't got shit to do with you. Why do you care?"

I stare into Mickey's brown eyes, automatically jumping into her mind and reliving the memory of her labor where I took over for her while she rested. That pain was so intense it made me question having babies of my own. If I weren't a virgin, that experience would have made me close my legs for good.

"I thought I was dreaming when I fell asleep during Nickey's birth," Mickey says, her eyes turning from a curious look to an angry glare. "How dare you invade my mind like that!"

"Mickey, do you really think I wanted to experience your labor pains for you, for real?" Finished with Nickey's evening meal, I put the empty bottle down and place Nickey on my shoulder to burp. Mickey looks at us like she wants to smack us both. Why does she have to be so damned evil sometimes?

"I don't know what to think, but I know that it's obvious you want my life. You're trying your best to take Nigel from me and be his baby mama. But this is my life, Jayd. Get your own."

Oh, no, this heffa didn't go off on me for trying to help her after all that I've done for her. What a wench.

"I was just trying to help," I say, tired of defending myself. I place Nickey belly down on the futon while her mama slips out of her tight jeans and into a short skirt, completing the ho look she's going for.

"Mickey, are you ready to go?" Nigel asks, interrupting us.

"We have to leave here in an hour, so you'd better get Nickey home." Nigel steps into the den and eyes Mickey's sexy outfit. His reaction mirrors my own, much to his girlfriend's disappointment.

"What's wrong with your face?" Mickey asks, looking at her man in the mirror. She barely looks away from her own image to catch Nigel's glare. At least I'm not the only one who thinks Mickey should slow her roll. After all, she is a new mom, and showing all her goods may not be the best idea. Even if Westingle isn't our school, we're still going to be under the watchful eye of teachers and parents who know Nigel and Rah, and more importantly, they know Nigel's parents. If it gets back to Mrs. Esop that Nigel showed up to Westingle's grad night with a tramp on his arm, it might not be good for our boy.

"The same thing that's wrong with your eyes if you think you're going anywhere with me like that," Nigel says, looking around the room for something to drape over his girlfriend.

"You're tripping. I look good, man," Mickey says, running her fingers through her loosely curled gold-streaked hair. Has Mickey forgotten Nigel's ex-girlfriend Tasha will probably be there? And where there's Tasha, there's also her best friend, Trish—another one of Rah's former chicks. She's calmed down a bit since I put a little something on Trish to make her back up off Rah for his own sake. But Trish continues to linger around, using the fact that her older brother is Rah's major supplier to keep associating with him even if Rah's told her in no uncertain terms that he's no longer interested in her plain ass.

"Baby, I didn't say that you don't look sexy as hell. It's just a bit much for a high school party, don't you think?" Nigel asks, approaching Mickey from behind as he places his letterman jacket from South Bay around her shoulders. He's sporting his other one from Westingle out of respect to his former team. I know he misses attending school with his Westchester and Inglewood homies, like Rah. Although Nigel's made new friends at South Bay and having me there has helped, it's not the same as kicking it with his crew on a daily basis.

"Nigel, it's eighty degrees outside. I'm not wearing this thick-ass thing anywhere," Mickey says, tossing the leather jacket off her body and onto the floor. Does she know how many females would line up at the chance to wear one of her man's prized athletic possessions? "Besides, why would I want to hide all of this fineness?" Still admiring her postpartum figure, Mickey readjusts the black tube top, shocking Nigel.

"Damn, girl. You just had a baby. Act like it," Nigel says, picking up his jacket from the floor and throwing it on the futon against the wall.

Rah walks in, and Nigel storms out the back door with a blunt in his hand. Why does Mickey have to be such a bitch sometimes? I guess that's like asking why do dogs bite: It's simply in her nature.

"What was that all about?" Rah asks, oblivious to the drama unfolding in his studio. He stops in the doorway, taking me in. I know I look good, and it doesn't hurt that I'm sporting Lakers colors—his favorite basketball team.

"You don't want to know," I say, smiling at Rah. I can smell the fresh herbal essence Rah's wearing, which explains his bloodshot eyes.

"Are we ready to roll, people?" Nigel asks, returning much more mellow than when he walked out two minutes ago.

Mickey rolls her eyes at her man, and he couldn't care less, or so I think.

"Yeah, man. Just let me get another quick hit and we'll be on our way." Rah claims the lighter and blunt from Nigel, ready to step back outside.

"I'll get in on that rotation, too," Mickey says, finally stepping away from the mirror and attempting to follow Rah outside. He stops in his tracks, noticing her attire, and almost chokes on his own spit. If it were me instead of Mickey, he'd have a heart attack.

"What the hell are you wearing?" Rah asks, looking at Nigel but talking to Mickey, now recognizing the source of the tension in the air.

"I'm wearing exactly what the hell I want to," Mickey says, taking the tightly rolled cigar from a distracted Rah. Nigel walks out and Rah follows like the true homeboy he is, and he'd better move fast. Otherwise there might be holes present in the studio wall that weren't there before. I've seen a brotha enraged, and that's the kind of heat I'm feeling from Nigel. Maybe I can help defuse the situation before it gets out of control.

"Girl, what the hell is wrong with you?" I ask, taking Mickey by the arm. "Have you completely lost your mind?"

Mickey snatches her bare arm away from me and narrows her eyes. I understand she's trying to get her sexy back, but at what cost?

"No, but you have, grabbing on me like that," Mickey says. "Nigel knew what he was getting when he started seeing me: The shit ain't changed."

"Hell yeah, shit's changed," I say, attempting to lock onto Mickey's sight, but she's not making it easy. "You had a baby."

"So what? Mamas can't be sexy?"

Mickey's beyond all reasoning and rationale this evening. "You're not Kendra, and Nigel's not Hank Baskett, Mickey," I say. Hank knew he was getting a professional stripper when he married his wife, so he can't say shit about what she wears and around whom. But this is completely different, starting with the fact that we're minors attending a high school graduation party, not former Playmates spending a day at the

Playboy mansion, which is exactly where Mickey looks like she belongs. "This isn't a reality show, girl. It's real life, and you're making it more difficult than it needs to be."

"Whatever, Jayd. You've never been sexy. I wouldn't expect you to understand," Mickey says, leaving me speechless.

What a bitch and then some. Switching her ornery ass as she walks out of the room, Mickey rolls her eyes at me and I return the rude gesture. Before I can go completely off, Jeremy calls. He must've made it to London: They've been flying all day long.

"Jeremy," I say, smiling into my cell.

"Hey, baby," he says, sounding groggy. "We finally made it."

"I'm glad," I say, stepping into the hallway for more privacy—or so I think. Nigel and Mickey are at war. I'll let them continue their arguing and step back into the den where my goddaughter's resting peacefully. At least she's immune to the bull going on around her. "It's good to hear your voice, even if it is on another continent." Rah walks in and notices my demeanor. Anyone can tell I'm talking to my man, and I couldn't care less. I wish Jeremy were here in the flesh. His ever-chilled attitude always helps me relax.

"Jeremy, your mom wants us downstairs for breakfast," a female voice says, reigniting my fire. Jeremy doesn't have any sisters, and I know his brothers didn't bring their women along—his mom made it very clear it's a Weiner-only event, even if the oldest one is married. But because his wife hasn't spawned any new progeny, she's out of the family loop. Their parents are no joke when it comes to the whole family-unit thing. How do they deal with such jerks for parents?

"Who the hell was that?" I ask in full neck-roll mode. Mickey and Nigel are still at it, and now Rah's jealous. Maybe I should chill alone tonight, unlike my man's apparently doing.

"Cameron," Jeremy says reluctantly. Oh, hell no, that trick's not part of the trip like that.

"Okay. So why is she in your room?"

Mickey storms into the den, picks up her daughter and diaper bag, and heads back out. I guess they're finally going to drop the baby off.

"She's not. I'm in the front lobby of the hotel. I was looking for some privacy, but I guess I'm not safe even all the way out here," he says. I can hear Jeremy's smile through the phone automatically forcing one of my own. "I miss you, Jayd. I can't wait to come home."

"I miss you, too, Jeremy." And I trust you as far as I can throw Cameron, but I'll keep that part to myself. "Call me tomorrow, okay?" I need to look up a chant or something that works across miles to keep that girl away from my boyfriend in a real way. Cameron's not even trying to play coy and neither am I.

"What up, my peeps?" Chance says, walking up the stairs with his grill gleaming. His new platinum and gold chain matches his mouthpiece. This boy's got too much money and time on his hands.

"Tell my boy I said what up," Jeremy says before officially ending the call. That was too short, but it'll have to do. We both have other people to tend to.

"Jeremy sends his greetings," I say, closing my phone and putting it in the small purse on my shoulder. Rather than my large Lucky hobo, I opted for the petite New York & Company demi bag, another accessory courtesy of my mom's dwindling closet.

"Cool. Tell him I said to holla at me. I'm going to be traveling myself tomorrow," Chance says, engulfing me in his thin yet firm embrace.

"Tomorrow?" I ask, already knowing he's headed back

down South and his mother back to the bottle, not that she ever left.

"Yeah, babe. I'm out on the first flight in the morning. Tomorrow's Father's Day, and I want to be with my real grandfather and his family," Chance says, releasing me as we proceed downstairs to where the rest of our crew's waiting, ready to go.

"Chase, please listen to me," I say, touching his shoulder when we reach the foyer. I've decided to call him by his preferred name, even if I still call him Chance in my mind. Maybe the acknowledgment will cool him down a bit. "Your mom's grieving, too. She feels like she's lost the most important person in her life. You need to let her know she still has you." I look into Chance's pretty blues, unable to lock on good enough to have any real influence.

"She hasn't lost anything she already had," Chance says sorrowfully. I know he's torn between two worlds and it's difficult for him, but he still needs to be considerate of his mother's feelings. "I just want to get to know my real family. Is that so bad?"

"Not at all, Chance," I say, accepting his hand in mine. I squeeze tightly, letting him know I'm here for him and always will be.

Nellie comes inside and glares at us both. Oh hell, here we go: first Mickey's foul attitude, now Nellie. They're like the homegirl hater tag team, I swear.

"What are you two talking about?" she asks, folding her arms across her barely there chest, attempting to look badass, but sassy is as close as she'll get.

"Nothing. Just shit," Chance says, not ready to have this conversation with his girlfriend. Even if I think he should, I completely understand why Chance doesn't want to talk with Nellie in depth about his family issues. She's been less than sympathetic about it all lately and fights him about it every opportunity she gets. I hope Nellie soon realizes Chance needs a shoulder, not a fist.

"As thick as it is up in here, it must be something heavy, so spit it out." Nellie's the bossiest bitch I know. Rather than hang with her man earlier today, she chose to hang out with Laura and the rest of their bitch clique, including Jeremy's prodigal baby mama, Tania. I'm not happy about that at all, but I've ceased arguing with my girls about their trifling behavior. As usual, I'll be here when the shit hits the fan, as it always does.

"Nellie, it's nothing. Damn." Chance lets go of my hand and heads toward the open front door. "Now let it go, please," he says, tiring of her forceful behavior. He told her about going to Atlanta for a couple of weeks, and she was less than pleased, which is why he left everything else out. Nellie can't stand being out of the know even if it's something she doesn't care about. Just the thought of Chance sharing something with me and not her makes Nellie's ass itch.

"Am I your girlfriend or is Jayd your girlfriend, because I'm confused," Nellie says.

I roll my eyes as high as I can, secretly hoping I'll be carried away from this all-too-familiar scene. I wish they'd never gotten together—and Mickey and Nigel, too. It was better when my boys were my boys and my girls were my girls. All this mixing and mingling is too much for our stressed-out crew to handle.

"All right, folks. Nigel and Mickey will meet us downtown," Rah says from the driveway. "Are we ready to roll, people?"

Chance and Nellie glare at each other, and Rah instinctively knows he's interrupting another arguing couple.

"I am," I say, stepping past Nellie and Chance and heading toward my car parked on the street.

Rah looks at our friends still posted and gets impatient with the drama. "Hey, tonight's all about Nigel," he says, having his boy's back when he can't be here to speak for himself. "Get over it and come on or not: I don't really care. But if you're coming, let's get a move on. It's Saturday night and the streets are packed."

"We're coming, man," Chance says, pulling the door shut behind him as he and Nellie walk to his Chevy parked in the driveway.

I'm with Rah. Tonight's all about Nigel, and as his friends, we need to put our egos aside and support him. I still wish my man were here to make it all better, but I'm going to enjoy the party tonight regardless of the madness we're all experiencing.

~ 8 ~
Daddy's Day

I keep forgetting we're not in love anymore /
I keep forgetting things will never be the same again.

—Michael McDonald

As expected, the traffic from Nigel's house to downtown Los Angeles is brutal. I don't know if there is an accident or what, but it takes twice as long to get here as it usually does. Nigel texted Rah a few minutes ago and told him to have us wait for him and Mickey before walking in so we make his grand entrance together. We might be unstable at the moment, but we're still a good-looking crew, no doubt. What's a star football player without his entourage?

"They're here," Rah says, opening my car door.

There weren't four spaces next to each other, so Chance and Nellie parked on one level while Rah and I parked on the lower deck. Who knows where Nigel and Mickey ended up.

"Thank you," I say, stepping out and arming the alarm. We both check the number of our parking spots before stepping into the elevator. Nellie and Chance are already in the hotel lobby not talking to one another when we walk inside. Mickey and Nigel step through the front door of the snazzy hotel looking like high school royalty.

"All right, people. Let's do this," Nigel says, leading the way to the grand ballroom for the festivities. He's so hyped, and I'm happy for my boy. He deserves all the good he can get.

When we step inside the massive banquet hall of the W Hotel, black and gold streamers hang from everywhere. It's packed inside, resembling a nightclub more than a high school graduation party—minus the liquor, of course. There are teacher and parent chaperones lining the walls with students everywhere the eye can see. I bet their prom was off the chain.

"Wow," Nellie says, expressing all our sentiments exactly.

Westingle went way out for their senior class. Even Chance's wealthy ass looks impressed with the eloquent décor.

"Daddy's home," Nigel says, smiling at the warm welcome he's feeling from the school colors and familiar faces.

Rah looks pleased with his boy's reaction but not with the unofficial welcome committee heading our way.

"Nigel, Rah, I'm so glad you all could make it," Tasha says with Trish beside her.

Out of the hundreds of people present, they would be the first two broads we run into. Mickey grabs her man's hand and holds on tight with her ring finger proudly on display.

"I didn't think you'd be here," Trish says, eyeing me like shit on the bottom of a shoe. As usual, she and Tasha are dressed top to bottom in black Prada, showing off their money and boring personalities all in one outfit.

"It's nice to see you," Tasha says, eyeing her ex-man like candy. She looks at Mickey, who looks as uncomfortable as she ought to feel. We all tried to tell her this wasn't the time or the place to wear that outfit, but who are we? Maybe she'll listen the next time we try and save her ass from embarrassment.

"Okay, ladies, move it along. We've got business to tend," Rah says, fanning the hoes away and leading us through the crowd. We find a standing table and post up, ready to have some fun. There's enough food to feed an army, and I'm ready to dig in.

"Nigel, glad you could make it," one of the football coaches from his former school says, walking over to greet us. "There are some people here from UCLA I want you to meet." He nods his bald head as a greeting to the rest of us. Unlike at South Bay High, most of the staff at Westingle is black, including the coaches. "I took the liberty of inviting a few of our alumni to meet the new first-draft pick," he says excitedly. Noticing Nigel's arm candy, he does a double take at Mickey's attire, further solidifying my girl's shame.

"Coach Johnson, we don't even know about that yet," Nigel says, trying to be modest, but everyone knows he'll get into whatever school he chooses.

Mickey reluctantly lets go of her man's arm as the coach pulls him away. She'd better get used to that part of being a star athlete's girl if she plans on sticking around.

As the coach waves some guys over, I recognize one of the familiar faces from the coffeehouse earlier. What the hell is Keenan doing here?

"You know what your problem is, Esop?" the coach says, referring to Nigel by his last name. "You're too humble about your talent. No one likes a meek quarterback, or one who doubles as a basketball player during the off season," Coach Johnson says, getting a kick out of his own joke. He smacks Nigel hard on the back, making my boy smile. If I didn't know better, I'd say Nigel was blushing through his dark brown complexion.

As the three college men approach our table, the heat rises in my cheeks. I catch my girls also checking out the two fine brothas and a white dude. Rah and Chance greet them with Nigel like they're a part of the team.

"This is Keenan, Bruce, and Will—all first-draft picks from the South Bay region and all attending UCLA. This is Nigel Esop, your soon-to-be new teammate," the coach says.

"Nice to finally meet the legendary high school wonder

boy," Will says, running his fingers through his blond tresses, making Nellie melt. He's damn good-looking, making me miss Jeremy even more.

"Welcome to the team," Bruce says, shaking Nigel's hand while checking Mickey out. She's hard to ignore with her business out for all to see.

Keenan smiles my way, and I can tell he's pleased by our unplanned reunion.

"We're always in need of a good arm," Keenan says, shifting his attention to Nigel. I'm grateful the heat's off me. But it doesn't look like he's going to let the chance meeting slide by.

"Yeah, man. Thanks," Nigel says. "And these are my friends Rah, Chance, Jayd, and Nellie. This is my girlfriend, Mickey."

We all exchange friendly hellos, but Keenan's greeting is more personal than the rest.

"Small world, isn't it?" Keenan says, extending his hand like he did earlier, again causing my face to turn red.

My friends look at me and smile, knowing I'm busted even if I didn't do anything.

"It's a small world, indeed," I say, returning the handshake. I quickly let go and try to squelch my bright smile.

"Come on. Let's get something to eat and talk about your future," Coach Johnson says, leading the boys toward the buffet, except for Chance, who's busy texting.

"Shit. I'm hungry, too," Mickey says, tugging at her clothes. "Come on, Nellie. Let's see what they've got up in this fancy place to munch on."

Nellie dutifully follows Mickey, although I doubt she'll have more than a carrot stick. She needs to fill her plate with chicken wings and gain some weight.

"So, who's the pretty nigga?" Chance asks, taking his newfound blackness too far, too soon.

"No one," I say, uncomfortable with his line of questioning. I have nothing to feel guilty about, but I'm feeling something I can't quite name.

"You can't lie to me, Jayd," Chance says, looking me in the eye. "I hope you don't forget you're in a relationship while your boy's away."

"I am well aware of my relationship, thank you very much," I say, moving to a quiet corner for Chance and I to talk. The last thing I need is more heat from my girls. "I met him earlier today at a coffeehouse, and he struck up a conversation about reading and whatnot. That's all."

"Oh, really?"

"Yes, really. There's nothing else to the story, man," I say, tapping Chance on the shoulder. "And how dare you think I'd cheat on my man no matter how far away he is or how long he's going to be gone. I'm truly insulted by your accusation."

"Just checking," Chance says. "If you were my girlfriend, I wouldn't have left you alone for that long, especially not in the summer." Chance is right. Jeremy should be here, but I'm trying not to think about that right now. "You're showing off them legs, ain't you?" Chance says, making me blush and laugh, momentarily easing my loneliness.

"Shut up, Chance," I say, slapping his hand and causing Nellie to resume her jealous status from across the room where Mickey has struck culinary gold. When will Nellie ever learn? My girls charge across the dimly lit floor, ignoring the dancing couples in their path.

"I'll be right back," Chance says, looking down at his buzzing cell while walking toward the front door. I'll see what that's all about later.

"I'm ready to go," Mickey says, trying to extend her ultraminiskirt and cover her cleavage with one hand. She looks uncomfortable, and I feel for my girl. Around these rich, snooty folks, Mickey's hood ass sticks out like a sore thumb.

"Jayd, can you take me back to Nigel's so I can get my car? I'm over this tired-ass scene," she says, smacking on the chips and salsa on her full plate.

Nellie's munching on hummus and veggies, ever concerned about her size 2 figure. I still say she needs to put some meat on her plate and thicken up a bit.

"Are you serious, Mickey? We've only been here for a half hour," I say, looking around. I could actually enjoy myself if they'd shut up and let me. The deejay's cool, the food looks good, and I couldn't care less about the hating females, because all I see are potential clients. There's too much black hair around for me to get my hands into to leave now.

"Yes. Very," Mickey says, downing her food and glaring Nigel's way. Surrounded by his people, Nigel completely ignores Mickey, who's an embarrassment. Damn, this is going to get ugly if Mickey gets any hotter. Maybe I should get her out of here before she makes a scene, humiliating us all.

"But what about Nigel?" I ask, looking at our boy enjoying his old crew. "Don't you think we should stay and support him?"

"He's not concerned with me and my feelings, so why should I care about his needs?"

Leave it to Mickey to make herself the victim no matter the circumstance.

"This night is about your man and his future, Mickey. Last I checked, that included you and Nickey."

Mickey looks at me, pissed at my logic, but she has to know I'm right. "I'm ready to go," Mickey repeats, dead set on leaving and finishing her plate.

"Me too," Nellie says, rubbing her flat tummy like she's six months pregnant. "I think I ate too much."

Mickey and I look at our girl, realizing she's got more serious food issues than we thought. Nellie gestures for Chance to wrap up his phone conversation and join us.

"Chance, let's get out of here. This isn't our type of party anyway," Nellie says, grabbing her man by the arm, making me miss Jeremy even more than I already do. I'd rather hang with him than deal with my emotional friends any day. Keenan catches my attention from across the room, causing the temperature in my body to again rise to the surface. I can't stop staring at him staring at me.

"Speak for yourself," Chance says, grooving to Drake's latest song blaring through the speakers. "I'm not going anywhere."

I feel that. If I'm not too tired, I might just drop these heckling heffas off and come back. With Keenan's fine ass present, this is indeed the place to be tonight.

"Fine, then. I'll leave with Jayd and Mickey," Nellie says.

I look at my girls, realizing they're serious about bouncing and I'm the chosen designated driver. Shit. Out of all the nights they choose to trip on their men, this had to be it.

Noticing the commotion, Keenan walks over to us. Butterflies flutter in my empty stomach with every step he takes. Rah follows Keenan, watching him watch me. This isn't going to be good.

"You guys are welcome to join us," Keenan says, speaking to the four of us but focused on me. Rah stands beside Keenan, observing the energy between us.

"Yeah, come on over and get something to eat," Rah says, holding his hand out for me to take. Keenan looks from Rah to me, thinking he's got it all figured out. As far as I'm concerned, the Rah and Jayd ship sailed a long time ago.

"We're actually not staying," Mickey says, taking my hand and unknowingly saving me from another awkward moment.

"Yeah. It's a girl thing," Nellie adds, holding herself by the waist. The boys look at us, bewildered, but don't protest. These broads are going to pay for this one in a real way.

"Let's go," I say, pissed as all get-out. "Next time you need to bring your own car, Mickey. I'm not a chauffeur, here at your beck and call. And, Nellie, get a license." Nellie looks at me like she wants to spit she's so mad, and I dare her. She'll be walking her blond ass back to Nigel's neck of the woods. "Tell Nigel we said bye, please." Chance nods in agreement. He, Rah, and Keenan rejoin their friends to officially get the all-boys night started. It's going to be a long drive back to Nigel's house.

"So, who the hell was that fine-ass dude trying to holla at you?" Mickey asks, getting right into my business before I can even get the car started. I press on the clutch, shift the gear into neutral, and turn the key. The sooner I get them back to Lafayette Square, the sooner I can get back to the W and enjoy the gratis evening. It's almost eleven now, and the lateness is beginning to set in. Lucky for me, tomorrow's Father's Day and I don't have any clients lined up as of yet, but that could change and I don't mind if it does. Money is money no matter the holiday.

"His name is Keenan, and I don't know who he is," I say, pulling out of the packed lot. Nellie's sulking quietly in the backseat, pissed that Chance isn't her yes-man anymore. It must be weird for her sitting in the back since she's used to riding shotgun with the three of us. Before I started driving a few months ago, Mickey was the designated driver and I always rode in the back of her classic ride. Now I'm rolling my mom's Mazda, Mickey's a mama, and Nellie's in limbo between her original homegirls and the bitch brigade. The tables have turned on our little crew and will never be the same. I just hope we survive the evolution.

"Well, he sure did seem to know you," Nellie says, joining the conversation.

It's been a long time since me and my girls had some "us" time to talk. For the past several months, it's been all about the baby and Nellie's goddamn crown. I'm glad for the girlfriend chat, even if I'm the one under fire at the moment.

"It's all innocent," I say, turning on the congested one-way street leading to the 110 freeway. It's a hot Saturday night, and the people are out enjoying it. "I met him at a coffeehouse this afternoon, and we got into a conversation about books and whatnot," I say, basically repeating the same spiel I gave Chance earlier.

"Books and whatnot?" Mickey asks, disgusted. "Who the hell talks about school shit with a fine-ass nigga like that hollering?"

"You see, Mickey. That's your damn problem right there," I say, laughing at my girl. Nellie nods her head in approval, but I'm not sure who she's agreeing with. "Everybody's not like you, girl."

"Not everybody, but most people are, Jayd," Mickey says, checking her ringing cell.

Who's calling her this time of night? I know it's not Nigel because he has a special ringtone, unlike this caller.

"Mickey, please tell me you're not up to your old tricks again," I say, already dreading the answer. Mickey ignores my comment and quickly returns the text.

"Again?" Nellie adds. "Did she ever stop?"

I didn't even consider the possibility that once the pregnancy was over Mickey would resume her pimping. She's always got a dude or two on the side.

We cruise down the highway smoothly. The traffic has died down, and we should reach Nigel's neck of the woods soon. The air smells of night-blooming jasmines, one of my favorite flowers.

"Shut up, Nellie," Mickey says, a little too defensively for me. "Anyway, we're not talking about me. We're talking about Jayd and her new sugar daddy."

"I don't have a sugar daddy, and I don't want one," I say, turning on my left blinker.

"Sometimes they come to you anyway. You need to learn how to work your magic, girl," Mickey says, pulling down the passenger's visor and looking in the small lit mirror. "You're not bad-looking, and you've got that whole smart thing going for you. All you need is someone to teach you how to work it, and Keenan looks like he might want to give you some private lessons."

Mickey's so nasty sometimes it's ridiculous. It's no wonder her ass was pregnant at sixteen. If she's not careful, she's going to find herself pregnant at seventeen, too.

"She's not going to ruin her relationship with Jeremy for that fool, even if he is gorgeous and in college," Nellie says. I can see her smiling in the rearview mirror. My girls are really tripping this evening.

"Whatever," Mickey says, reapplying her red lipstick. "Jeremy ain't thinking about her ass, over there high-profiling in Arabia or wherever the hell he is with that white girl."

Mickey's words sting; she knows she hit a sore spot. "You're like a little devil on my shoulder poking my ears with a hot pitchfork, Mickey. You know that?" I ask, stopping at the last red light before the turn into Nigel's hood. I'll be glad to get them out of my car so I can get on with my night.

"And I'm the angel, right?" Nellie asks excitedly. I know she can't be serious. "I'm even wearing all white like Lisa-Raye McCoy."

Nellie's got all kinds of diva role models and none of them are angels.

"Looks can be deceiving, Nellie," I say, making both of my girls laugh. They know who they are, and that's one thing I love about my girls. If nothing else, we keep it one hundred all day, every day.

I park in front of Nigel's crib and pull up the emergency brake without turning off the engine.

"Seriously, Jayd. Jeremy's not here and even if he was, you're your own person," Mickey says, removing her seat belt and taking her purse from the floor. "If Keenan wants to be your daddy, let him. You ain't married." Mickey smiles as she exits my car. Nellie pats me on my right shoulder before opening the back door and following our girl to her ride parked in front of mine.

"I'm not looking for another daddy, Mickey," I say out of my open window. "I've already got one and he's quite enough, thank you." I reach into the glove compartment for my iPod and travel speaker. I want to go back to the party, but I think it's best if I go home and work on my own shit, not go flirt with Keenan. He's liable to get me into some serious trouble, and I'm not trying to go there. I've got enough to deal with without adding more to my plate.

"You're welcome," Mickey says, shutting the passenger door. "We'll talk about it later." Yeah, we'll talk about it all right. Mickey will try to convince me to cheat on my man while I attempt to block her unwanted ill advice. We need to get down to the root of her sugar-daddy issues.

"I'm so looking forward to the conversation," I say, making sure my girls get in Mickey's classic ride okay. It looks like Nigel's parents are home, and I don't want to run into them tonight. I've had it with Mrs. Esop and the debutante ball talk this week. Between that and cheer, I can't take any more bitchy broads in my world. Luckily, my girls and I always find our way back to the middle.

"You're such a smart-ass sometimes, you know that?" Mickey says, starting her car and waking up the quiet neighborhood with Lil Wayne bumping loudly through her speakers. If Nigel's parents didn't know we were here before, they sure as hell know now.

"So I've been told," I say, pulling away from the curb. "Bye, Nellie. Later, Mickey, and please give my goddaughter a kiss for me."

"Our goddaughter," Nellie says, checking her text messages for the umpteenth time this evening. Apparently she's taking Mickey's advice to heart and not her own.

"Semantics," I say, driving out of Nigel's neighborhood and back toward Inglewood. It'll only take me about fifteen minutes to get home, which should put me in the house by midnight. Tomorrow I have to perform the obligatory Father's Day duties, then the rest of the day belongs to me. Rah mentioned something about a session at his crib tomorrow evening for Father's Day, and that might be cool, especially if the babies are there. But first I'll have to get through greeting my daddies, and then I can have fun with my crew.

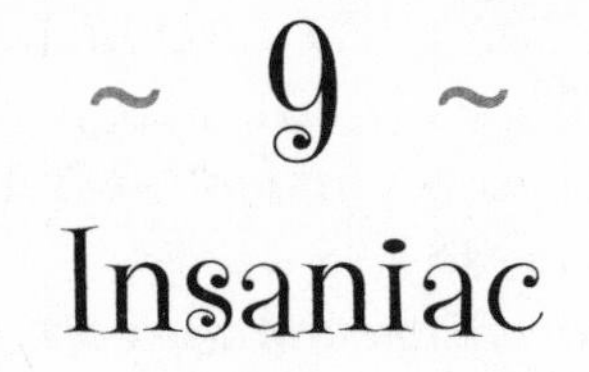

~ 9 ~ Insaniac

Insane in the membrane / Insane in the brain.
—Cypress Hill

"Madame, Madame. Regarder," the young woman says.

I'm standing in the front parlor of an old house dressed in all white. I pick up my skirt and rush into the kitchen next to me, following after the excited girl. "Flamme! Flamme!" *the girl shouts, pointing at the antique stove in flames.*

"Get back," I say, unable to process my thoughts quickly enough to translate into the French Creole my companion is speaking. I look around the large room for a fire extinguisher, but something tells me the invention wasn't readily available in this time period. "Arroser," I say, directing her to hand me the bucket of water used for dishes to quench the scorching flames.

We pour the water, but the growing fire seems to thrive from the liquid.

"Madame!" she shouts, pointing to my shirt, which is also on fire.

I try to pat the flames and then remember to stop, drop, and roll like they taught us in elementary school, but it's not helping.

"Sir! Appelar, à l'aide, s'il vous plaît!" the girl shouts, running out of the kitchen toward the front door.

Just then, Keenan walks in and takes quick action. What the hell is he doing here?

"Are you okay, love?" Keenan asks after putting out both fires.

Who's he calling "love"?

"Madame?" the young girl asks, kneeling by my side. She takes my left hand and helps me sit up on the cool floor. From the frightened look in her eyes, I can tell she's worried about my silence and so am I.

"Marie, are you hurt?" Keenan asks, kneeling by my right side and checking me out. I'm walking through my dream as Maman again. Keenan must be my great-grandfather, Jean Paul.

"No. I'm fine," I say, still confused. The girl rubs my hand, smiling at me. Her brown eyes are sad but sweet, hiding years of pain and abuse; she can't be more than nine years old. I know it was hard being a black girl in the antebellum South.

"Tina, go and fetch your mother to help Madame Marie change her clothes," Jean Paul says, helping me regain my footing. "I told you a woman in your condition shouldn't be on her feet, especially not my wife," he says to me. Maman must be pregnant with Mama: This is too weird.

"Sir Jean Paul," the woman says, slightly bowing as she enters the kitchen. She looks about the same age as my mom. I touch my stomach, grateful it's too early in the pregnancy to show. I don't know if I can handle feeling Mama kick inside of me. That would be a little too freaky for even my strangest dreams.

"Help my wife get out of these burned clothes and into bed. I can't have the great Voodoo Queen of New Orleans looking like a common cook who doesn't know how to use a

stove," Jean Paul says. He's the only one present who finds any humor in his insensitive statement.

"Oui, *monsieur," the mother and daughter team say in unison.*

They guide me to the back of the spacious single-story house, where we enter a bathroom adjacent to what I assume to be Maman's room. It's painted yellow with a huge wall altar dedicated entirely to Oshune next to the largest of three windows in the massive space. I feel like I've walked into a living shrine.

"You're going to make me the happiest father alive, Marie, starting by staying out of the kitchen. That's what the help is for," Jean Paul says from the hall. We look at each other and sigh. Jean Paul was a jackass, and we have the spirit book stories to prove it.

"You're going to be fine, madame. You just need a bath to calm your nerves," Tina's mother says, helping me out of my dress and into the ceramic tub. Tina begins passing her mother cupfuls of cold water. "Lean forward," she says in a commanding voice. I bend forward and grab my knees, allowing the frigid water to pour from the nape of my neck down my back. She pours it again, this time over my head, causing me to wake up in a cold sweat.

"It's too cold!" I shout, now fully awake. I look around the dark apartment, adjusting to my surroundings.

"I'm not pregnant," I say aloud, feeling my stomach. My dreams are getting more confused with reality every day. Dreaming about Keenan as my husband is the same kind of fantasy as my dreams of being Mrs. Adewale, and they both come from my strong attraction to these men, but I can't keep getting this hot and bothered. My top is soaking wet, and I feel like I'm on fire. Maybe after I change and dry off I can get some more sleep. It's way too early to be up on a

Sunday morning, especially when I have no clients scheduled. I'm going to rest for as long as I can. Hopefully, the realistic dreams are over for today.

After my crazy dream, I slept for a few more hours and woke up feeling refreshed and a little lazy. It's strange having the morning to myself, which I've taken full advantage of. After studying my spirit lessons and my schoolwork, I decided to chill for a little while before getting dressed by watching *Las Vegas* reruns and eating microwave popcorn for brunch. I take a handful of the salty snack and stuff my mouth. This is an episode I've never seen before, where they're in New Orleans visiting a voodoo queen. I wonder if Mama's got it on her DVR. She loves this show. Speak of the angel, my cell rings with Mama's special tone. She must've felt me thinking about her.

"Hola," I say, singing along with the words of the Cuban music that accompanies Mama's call. She's the only one who used to get that type of favoritism until Jeremy came along. Now they both have their own distinctive soundtracks. Mama only uses her cell in case of emergencies or when she's traveling, which is rare, but this is one of those times.

"Jayd, it's so good to hear your voice. How are you, baby?" Mama asks. It's good to hear her voice, too, even if it sounds distant through her outdated equipment.

"I'm good, Mama," I say, taking a swig of water from my cup on the dining room table to clear my throat. My mouth's so dry I can barely speak. "How's Miami?" I think that's where they are. The last time Mama called, she and Netta were living it up in New Orleans. I almost didn't recognize Mama's voice she was so happy. I sit up on the couch, throwing the sheets off my legs, half expecting them to be on fire like my skirt in my nightmare. Maybe Mama felt that one all the way across the country.

"Hot, girl. But it's beautiful. You'll have to come with us next time." I plan to take her up on that. "By the way, Netta wants you to drop by the shop and make sure the clients' boxes are in order as well as all of the other necessary duties her sisters might forget to check on before tomorrow." Lucky for Netta, she and her two sisters know the hair business inside and out. While her older siblings are still holding it down in New Orleans, Netta started her own shop in Compton over thirty years ago and hasn't looked back, although she misses her hometown.

"I'm melting," Netta says in the background, giving her best imitation of the wicked witch from *The Wizard of Oz.* I miss Netta's funny spirit.

"I would love to visit there and Puerto Rico," I say, envious of my grandmother's travel itinerary. I've only been to New Orleans in my dreams. I'd love to touch the holy place one day with my own hands. "So when do you leave for the island?"

"Not until the middle of next week," Mama says. "How's the spirit room? Any news about my clients?"

"Everything's fine, Mama. And don't worry, all of your clients are surviving in your absence, although they do miss you." I stretch my arms above my head, fully feeling my aching body. Cheer camp's no joke. I even feel the burn when I'm not working out, but it's all good. This week I'll be on it like no other.

"Good," Mama says, coughing slightly. "It's healthy to allow people to feel your absence every once in a while. It reminds them of your uniqueness next time they decide to act a fool."

"Well said," and I agree. When I stopped talking to Rah two years ago, he never forgot how valuable a friend I am and never will. It's the same thing with Jeremy. Although I miss him terribly, it's good for couples to take a break from one another. We both could use the space to miss each other—but not too much. My mom's apartment feels lonely without my boo.

"You got that right, Lynn Mae," Netta says. "We're about to go through a tunnel, ladies. Say your good-byes and love you, Little Jayd."

I can just see her brown, shoulder-length hair blowing in the wind as the truck speeds down the road.

"I love you, Jayd, and I'll check in with you later," Mama says, almost shouting because of the bad connection. "By the way, I want a full report about your spirit work and your dreams next time we talk, little girl."

A full report? I don't know about that, but I'll do my best.

"Yes, ma'am. And I love you, too. Y'all be safe out there," I say, closing the phone. I'm glad Mama and Netta are enjoying life, but the hater in me is slightly jealous. I neglected to take notes on my reading this morning. Maybe I should review the pages and jot something down so I'll have something coherent to chat about next time Mama calls, which I hope will be soon. I miss her hugs, the smell of lavender and cocoa butter on her skin, and most of all, her warm smile. The last thing I want is to disappoint her while she's gone.

As instructed, I study a bit more and learn more about Maman's path before she married Jean Paul. It says that her powers were weakened the moment she became his wife because of a spell he put on her wedding ring. Once she figured it out, she took it off and never wore it again, which is what eventually led to my great-grandfather killing Maman. The more I read about our lineage, the more amazed I am by the Williams women's strength. Individually and collectively, we are a force to be reckoned with.

After working for about an hour, I touch up a few of my loose braids before heading to my grandmother's house in Compton. I love wearing my hair with the ends out and curly from the cornrows I put in yesterday. I need to drop by Mama's house and check on things as well as drop off Daddy's card. I usually call my father for his special day since it's too uncomfortable for us to be in the same room for long. But before I can dial my daddy's number, my phone rings with an odd number in the display.

"Hello," I say into the phone in my gruffest voice. I have a lot of new clients, but I still want people to know it's not okay to call me out of the blue unless someone has referred them. Otherwise, I'm giving them hella attitude for both taking up my cell minutes and wasting my time.

"Hello," the male voice says nervously. "I'm looking for Jayd." Whoever this is had better make it quick. I'm ready to walk out the door and have only a few seconds to talk.

"You found her," I say, going into my mother's room to check out my outfit one last time. It's only noon and already ninety degrees outside, or so the weatherman said. My pink sundress should keep me cool and comfortable for the day's events.

"Hi, Jayd," he says, this time sounding more secure. "This is Keenan from the coffeehouse."

Keenan. This dude has moved from my dreams to my cell. How did he get my number? And more importantly, why am I suddenly more concerned with how I look even if he can't see me through the phone? What the hell?

"Hello?" he repeats.

I don't know what to say for a second. "Yeah, I'm here. I don't recall giving you my number," I say, now checking my hair. I run my fingers through the soft curls hanging over my shoulders, inhaling the fresh cucumber-melon scent. I whipped up a new batch of my personal beauty products and have been sampling them out on myself before using them on my clients. So far I like what I see, and so would Keenan if he were here.

"Nigel gave it to me when I asked him who hooked up his braids," Keenan says, the nervousness returning to his voice. "I was wondering if you could hook a brotha up when your calendar allows."

Satisfied customers are definitely the best advertisement. Maybe I don't need to waste my money on business cards when word of mouth does the job for free.

"Were you now?" I ask, smiling at his obvious attempt to flirt without flirting. I'm always about my money, first and foremost. Having a smart, funny, and fine new client is a nice bonus, too.

"Yeah, and I was glad to know it was you," he says, now being the confident brotha I met. My heart stops and I am again speechless. "You still there?" Barely. My mind has wandered to Jeremy and what he would think if he overheard this conversation. It's innocent enough for now, but I can see the energy between Keenan and I getting out of hand real fast.

"I'm sorry, Keenan, but I'm on my way out," I say, unlocking the front door. With all of the chains and other multiple security devices my mom's got in place, it's a wonder I can get out at all. "I'll call you back when I know my work schedule." I try to rush off the phone, but he's not letting me go so easy.

"Okay. But let me know soon if you can. I'd like my hair fresh for next week, and your boy says you're just the girl to get the job done."

Damn, why does he have to sound so sexy when I'm trying to save my guilty conscience? "I'll text you later, Keenan. I've really got to go," I say, ending the conversation. I don't mean to be rude, but if I stay on the phone any longer, I'm liable to go straight to hell for all the thoughts running through my mind.

I lock the door behind me and make my way down the

flight of stairs to the carport. I'll call my daddy while the car's warming up. I have to make this conversation short and sweet. My dad and I can stand each other for only about five minutes. After that, all bets are off.

"Hey, Daddy," I say, gently pressing the gas pedal to rev the engine. "Happy Father's Day."

"Well, if it isn't my baby girl," he says. "I thought you forgot about your old man."

He always tries to lay a guilt trip on me, but it never works.

"How could I?" I ask, closing the car door and getting comfy. I pull my portable sounds out, ready to get going. One day I'll invest in a new radio, but my ends have to be stacked high for that kind of purchase.

"Did you get your card?" I ask, knowing he did. My father's house is only five minutes from Mama's, and I mailed it from Compton Friday afternoon.

"Yes, I did. Thank you, youngin'. It was very thoughtful of you, Jayd. Although with all the money you're making over there, I was half expecting something else to fall out when I opened the envelope."

And just like that, he's gone too far. It's time to end the call before my head gets too hot to drive straight and keep from arguing with him at the same time.

"Well, I've got a lot of school activities and food to pay for," I say, pushing my own envelope. "But I'll keep that in mind next year." There's an uncomfortable silence between us. I know my dad wants to say something, but what can he say? I don't care if it's Daddy's Day or not: Right is right, and he knows he's wrong for that shit. I rev the engine again, ready to put the car in gear.

"Are you driving while on the phone, Jayd?" He sounds concerned. "You know you can get a ticket for that," he says, giving me the perfect out.

"You're right, Daddy. I guess I should go." Too bad my dad and I can't talk peacefully for long. Maybe when we both grow up a bit more we can have that warm and fuzzy father-daughter relationship I see in the movies.

"All right, youngin'," he says, clearing his throat. "Thank you for calling and drive safely."

"You're welcome, Daddy. Enjoy your day." I know my step-mother, Faye, is in the kitchen throwing down. I wish I felt comfortable enough to drop by and get a plate since I'll be in Compton anyway. But I'll stay on my mission of dropping off my grandfather's card, checking on the spirit room, and making sure everything's in order at Netta's shop. Then, on to Rah's house for the session this afternoon. Hopefully, the rest of the day will be all about relaxing.

With all of the new daddies in my life, this year was the most expensive Father's Day yet. I wasn't sure what to do for Nigel, so I got him one of those general Father's Day cards. I also bought cards for Rah and for Jeremy, too, even if he's not here to receive it. I'm mad as hell at Rah for allowing Sandy back into his home, especially after all of the drama I had to endure to get rid of her ass in the first place, but it's not my place to judge, even if I want to hit him over the head with a gavel. Maybe that'll knock some sense into his ass.

I already know Rah's going to give me grief about Keenan trying to holla at me last night, but he has nothing to say about what I do or who I do it with. And I intend on reminding him of that should Rah fix his lips to throw smack my way. Hopefully I can enjoy my friends and godbabies for the rest of the afternoon, because come tomorrow summer school and cheer camp will be in full effect.

I pull into Rah's driveway and see I'm the first of our friends to arrive. I can also hear him and his baby mama at it again and on Father's Day, too. That's what he gets for knocking up the wrong chick—not that I'm sorry Rahima was born, but Rah could've picked a nicer chick to lie down with. I exit my vehicle and brace myself for the inevitable disaster that is Sandy.

"It's yours, Rah, so get over it. We're having another baby, and there's nothing you can do about it," Sandy says as I approach the open front door.

I stop in my tracks, hoping I'm at the wrong residence. Did I just hear what I think I heard?

"What did you say?" I ask, stepping into the foyer and taking in the entire scene. It looks like a circus in here. Rahima's in front of the television watching cartoons like nothing's going on around her she's so used to her parents arguing. As usual, Sandy's scantily dressed with her green bra strap hanging off her shoulders and pink foam rollers dangling from the ends of her gold and black weave. What a hot mess.

"You heard me, trick," Sandy says, placing both hands on her hips as she fixes her lips into a snarl, satisfied with the blanched look on my face. "We having another baby."

Rahima turns around, noticing me at the front door. She attempts to run to me, but her mother stops her in her tracks, upsetting her.

"Another baby? How could this have happened?" I ask aloud, even if I'm really posing my inquiry to the ancestors who don't need a verbal summon to respond. Nothing in all of my intuition sensed that Rah and Sandy were back at it, but stranger things have happened.

"Do you really need me to break it down for you?" Sandy asks, snatching her crying daughter's tiny hand in her acrylic claws and leading her to the back of the messy house. Rah's too meticulous to be okay with his home looking like this. "Oh, yeah, I forgot you're still pretending to be a virgin.

Maybe you do need me to explain how the shit works so your slow ass can get a black man of your own."

"Sandy, watch your mouth in front of my daughter," Rah says, apparently just as traumatized by the whole scene as I am. He's acting like he's in a daze.

"And don't forget our new baby, too," Sandy says, rubbing her flabby stomach. No one said you had to be fit to strip. "I have a feeling it's going to be a boy, maybe a junior. What you think, Jayd? Rahima and Raheem, Junior: cute, huh?"

Is it legal to slap a pregnant woman if she's a total bitch?

I watch Sandy and Rahima go into the hallway toward the bedrooms. With the Father's Day card in my hand, I turn around and step onto the front porch ready to leave without wishing him a happy day. This shit is totally out of order and unexpected. I feel like Alice in Wonderland: dizzy and desperately in need of a way out.

"Jayd, wait. Please," Rah says, taking me by my right arm and turning me toward him.

"Rah, I need to get out of here. This is none of my business, and I don't want to get involved," I say, snatching my arm back as tears well up in my eyes. How could he lie to me—again? We're just getting back to a place of trust and now this.

"Jayd, I swear to God this isn't my baby," Rah says, looking panicked.

Against my better judgment, I'm actually inclined to believe him, but my head's too hot to make any decisions in the moment.

"How do you know it's not yours? Are they giving paternity tests in the first trimester now?" I ask. Tears fall down my warm cheeks, pissing me off even more. Now I have to blow my nose, and it's too hot out here for this shit.

"I know it's not mine because I haven't touched Sandy in years, Jayd. I swear to you, this is all news to me."

I look at Rah, focusing on the brown flecks in the whites of his eyes, cooling his mind even if mine is hotter than it needs to be. I see his sincerity and confusion, calming us both down. I know he's telling the truth, but so is Sandy. I didn't need to invade her thoughts to feel the life growing inside her.

"Then why does she think she can convince you that the baby's yours if you haven't had sex recently?"

"She says I slept with her one night a couple of weeks ago after Nigel and Mickey left a late-night session," Rah says, rubbing his temples like he has a migraine. "We were hella faded, but I know I wasn't that far gone. All I remember is passing out in the studio and waking up the next morning with the worst hangover ever."

That's why his ass needs to stop smoking and drinking, especially when in questionable company. This is the type of insane shit that can happen when you let your guard down around the wrong person.

"I assume you told Sandy the same thing," I say, lowering my voice. The last thing I want is another altercation with his baby mama. "How does she think she's going to get away with it?"

"Sandy never thinks shit through, Jayd. Can't you tell she's desperate? I don't know what happened, but I know I didn't sleep with that girl, at least not willingly. There has to be some sort of law against that shit or something."

I doubt anyone's going to believe Sandy raped Rah, no matter how true it might be.

"Okay, Rah. If what you're saying is true, there has to be a way to prove it," I say, looking down at the white envelope in my hand. I hand the card to him, realizing how awkwardly inappropriate it is to wish him a happy Father's Day when he's being accused of fathering another child with the mother from hell. "I'll see what I can do." I sympathize with Rah, but this shit is his fault.

"Thank you, Jayd, for everything." We look at each other, and for a moment it feels like we're back in junior high school. Everything was so much simpler back then, but those days are long gone.

"Hey, Romeo. We hungry," Sandy says, coming outside with an exhausted-looking Rahima on her hip. If I could take baby girl from her crazy mama and raise her myself, I'd do it in a heartbeat.

While Rah thinks of an appropriate response, short of telling Sandy to go to hell like I would say, Nigel and Mickey roll up with their daughter in the back. I guess Nellie's sitting this session out since Chance left town early this morning. She's a true daddy's girl anyway. I wouldn't be surprised if Nellie and her pops have plans of their own.

"What up, my nigga?" Nigel says, exiting his clean vehicle.

He needs to let me get the keys to the classic green Impala and take it around the block. Come to think of it, Chance could've let me babysit his Nova while he's in the A. I'll have to run that plan by him next time.

"Jayd, here," Mickey says, passing Nickey's car seat to me with the screaming baby inside. "She's working my last nerve."

"Hello to you, too," I say, taking my youngest goddaughter from her stressed-out mama and reaching for her pacifier in the seat. If I could free the other one from her mother, the three of us could go inside and chill. It's too hot out here for all of this madness.

"Mickey, I told you to stop saying the baby's getting on your nerves," Nigel says, glaring at his girlfriend with a similar look of hatred Rah's giving Sandy.

"And I told you that you ain't my daddy," Mickey says, slamming the car door shut.

What my girl needs to remember is that Nigel isn't Nickey's real daddy, either. And if she continues antagonizing him, she won't have a father for her child.

"Fool, did you hear me?" Sandy asks, stepping off the porch and walking toward us in the driveway. I focus on calming Nickey down by rocking her seat. She's refusing to take the pacifier, and her screaming's growing more intense every minute.

"What the hell is she doing here?" Mickey asks, gesturing toward Sandy's raunchy ass.

"What would Father's Day be without the baby mama to both his kids?" Sandy responds. No one was talking to her.

"Both?" Nigel asks, staring at Rah, who's still in shock.

I need to work on finding out the truth before Rah snaps and ends up in jail for committing bitchicide.

"Damn, nigga. You hit that skanky tramp again?" Mickey asks, again pointing her airbrushed blue acrylic nail at Sandy, apparently as horrified by the thought as I am. "Why?"

"I know you ain't talking shit," Sandy says, finally releasing Rahima, who runs straight to me, equally upset by all the commotion.

"Bitch, please," Mickey says. "I'm grade-A ass. You're nothing but a corner ho and we all know it."

Nigel and Rah look at their women go back and forth, powerless to stop them.

"The babies, y'all. Please," I say, but they can't hear me over the rude slurs Mickey and Sandy take turns slinging. Some session this turned out to be. "I'm out and I'm taking the girls with me. Rah, put Rahima's car seat in the back. Y'all can pick them up from my house when you're through acting stupid."

The mamas are too busy going at each other's throats to pay me any mind, and the fathers don't protest. Poor babies. I hope they grow up to be saner than their parents. Until then, I'll have to be their buffer from the crazy situations they were born into. If I learned one thing from my dream last night, it's that getting too close to fire will definitely get you burned.

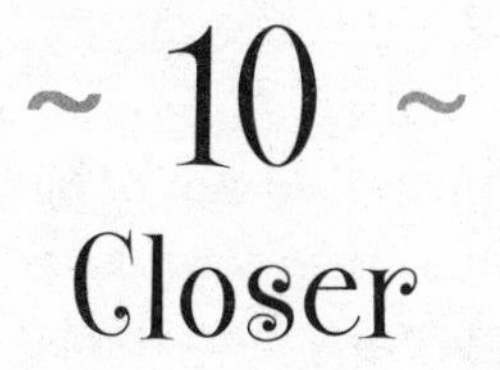

~ 10 ~ Closer

I don't mind us to build tension /
But we've got to move in the same direction.

—CORINNE BAILEY RAE

The smell of fresh paint seeps into my nose, burning its fragile skin. Without any knowledge of where I'm headed, however, I feel confident I'm getting closer to my destination. The four gray walls around me resemble a prison hallway. When I get to the end of the long, brightly lit hall, there are two large doors to choose from: one to my right and one straight ahead.

"Trust your instincts, Jayd. You know which way to go," a computerized voice says through the speakers in the corners. "The doors are identical, but only one way is correct."

"What am I looking for?" I ask to whom or what, I don't know. I look at the white speakers against the gray walls, following the white wire against the side of the massive door in front of me. Whatever type of institution this is, it doesn't look like people come here of their own free will.

I've always been taught to take the road less traveled, so I'm going to go with the less obvious choice.

"You're getting warmer," the voice says as I open the door to my right, entering the barely lit room. At first glance there appears to be nothing inside. But as I get closer to the back wall, I can see it's a mirage hiding an interrogation room with a prisoner inside.

It's Rah. He's been blindfolded and gagged with his hands tied behind his back. Rah looks unconscious, but his interrogator is completely aware of her actions.

The woman is Sandy, who wraps her massive legs around Rah's limp body, straddling him in the metal chair.

"Rah, get up!" I scream through the well-disguised window, but it's no use. He's out cold. "Rah, please wake up!" I try to break the glass with my hands, but it's too thick. Banging on the glass, I scream at Sandy, begging her to stop, but she ignores my pleading and continues on her mission.

I look around the room and notice a chair in the opposite corner I didn't see before. I run over, grab the chair, and throw it at the glass, shattering part of it. Sandy looks undeterred by my advance. I reclaim the chair from the floor and repeat the action twice more, finally breaking completely through.

"Get off of him, Sandy. He doesn't want you," I yell as I charge at Sandy and push her aside. When she falls to the ground, I free her victim, but it's no longer Rah. Who the hell is this brotha, and where's my friend?

"Do you mind? I'm working here," Sandy says, walking back over to her victim. "This ain't none of your business." Sandy climbs back on top of the brotha who is now smiling at her advance.

"It's not what it looks like," he mumbles, happy Sandy's back in position. Backing away from the X-rated scene, I accidentally step on a piece of broken glass with my bare feet.

"Ouch!" I scream, waking out of my dream to find myself bleeding all over the kitchen floor from a broken cup. Shit, not again. I haven't had a sleepwalking incident since the holidays, and I prayed that would be my last time. Apparently my days of insane behavior are not all behind me. I'd better get this cleaned up before I make an even bigger mess. Luckily we keep a first-aid kit under the sink, and I can patch this up without risking blood on the carpet. After making sure I was okay, my mom would have a hissy fit if I stained any part of her apartment.

I knew Sandy was lying, but now I have spiritual confirmation. The trick is finding out who the real baby daddy is, and for that I'm going to have to get inside of Sandy's head again. Just the thought of braving that crazy wilderness makes me sick. I never want to get that close to her again, but short of a confession, it looks like that's exactly what I'm going to have to do.

Obviously I'm not going back to sleep after a nightmare like that no matter how early in the night it is. Once Nigel and Rah came to get their little girls a couple of hours ago, I went straight to bed. Rahima's a handful at two years old, and taking care of an infant is no joke. I love my babies, but I don't envy my friends: Their daughters wore me out.

I could go to the coffeehouse and get some work done. No one's stopping me, even if I do feel like I'm cheating on Jeremy by doing one of our favorite pastimes by myself. Maybe it'll help put my mind at ease because I'm really tripping if I'm sleepwalking. And with Mama gone, I'm not confident enough to fall back into my sleep without fearing what will happen next.

Luckily the cut on my toe isn't too bad. It only hurts when I put too much pressure on it. I pick up the remaining glass from the kitchen floor before sweeping up the unseen shards with the broom. How it got here is a mystery to me, especially since it's from a cup I don't recognize. There's no evidence I knocked over anything else on my unsolicited vision trek, and I know I didn't break anything earlier. There are no signs that my mom's been home, either. I'll have to play detective later. If I want to get some work done tonight, I'd better get a move on. It's already after eleven, and I have to be at school by nine in the morning. Even if the reading group starts a little early in the morning for summer, it beats the usual seven o'clock call any day.

It amazes me that if you stay on almost any major street long enough in Los Angeles County, you'll travel through about ten different neighborhoods. It's close to midnight, and the parking on Fairfax Avenue is pretty tight as usual. A spot opens up close to the front of the quaint Ethiopian establishment, and I take it. I can see there's a crowd inside but still a few available seats to work with. Limping my way from the curb and through the front door, I recognize a familiar face at the end of my path.

"Jayd," Keenan says.

His smile melts my heart every time. "Hey, Keenan," I say, passing him by and claiming my seat before one of these sistahs in high heels needs to take a load off. I had no idea how busy this place would be on a Saturday night. Apparently Keenan's again my coffee neighbor.

"Cute Band-Aid," Keenan says, pointing at the Winnie the Pooh print covering my freshly painted toes. While Nickey slept, Rahima and I did our nails.

"Thanks," I say, making myself as comfortable as I can in the hard wooden chair. All the plush seats are taken.

"What brings you out this way?" Keenan asks, sitting across from me at the circular table and reclaiming his cup. His backpack hangs loosely over the side of his chair.

"I needed to get some studying done. You?" Maybe talking to Keenan will provide me with the distraction I need to get the nightmare I just experienced off my mind.

"Actually, I just got off work and figured I might as well hang out. As you can see, the vibe is pretty thick in here once the sun sets." He leans back in his seat and crosses his left foot over his knee, revealing his work apron with the coffee shop's logo across the chest.

"You work here?" I ask, surprised. I didn't get the vibe that UCLA athletes needed employment.

"Not all football players are spoiled, Jayd," he says, taking the thought out of my head. "Scholarships don't cover everything."

True that. Life's expensive in California.

"Touché, my brotha. Touché."

Keenan laughs at my sass, which makes me like him even more. This boy's going to distract me from the real reason I'm here. So far I don't mind the intrusion.

"How can a high school student have so much work to do all of the time?"

I take a deep breath and let out a sigh that seems to puzzle Keenan. If he only knew the half of it. "Because some of us work harder than others no matter what grade we're in." I smile at Keenan, and he smiles right back, loving the challenge.

"Touché, my sister. Touché." Taking another sip of his drink, he looks across the table realizing I don't have a cup of my own. "I'm sorry. I didn't even offer to get you anything," he says, rising from his seat, awaiting my order. He's such a gentleman, just like Jeremy and Rah when he's in the mood.

"You're off the clock, but thank you for the offer," I say. "I can get it myself."

"Please, let me. What are you having?" Keenan asks, putting his hand up for me to remain seated. He doesn't have to ask me twice.

"A green tea," I say, ordering my customary beverage.

"Excellent choice. I'll refill mine, too."

Good. That'll give me a chance to review a few of my spirit notes. I took the liberty of jotting down a few more things about my mom's younger days while I was at Mama's house earlier and need to review them.

After a few minutes of reading, I try to put my notes away before Keenan makes it back to the table but not before he notices my sloppy handwriting.

"Looks interesting," he comments, placing the two steaming cups on the table and taking his seat.

Keenan kind of reminds me of this guy I dated for two weeks in the eighth grade, except dude was a nerd who really thought he was one of the characters in *Dungeons & Dragons.*

"It is," I say, returning the notebook to my backpack before slowly sipping my tea. He looks like he wants to know more but doesn't press any further.

"So, Jayd Jackson, where are you originally from?" Keenan asks.

He has a laid-back vibe about him that I'm finding hard to resist. "Compton. You?" I reach for the honey packets he brought to the table.

"Oakland," Keenan says. "Ever heard of Too Short?" He leans back farther, taking in the buzzing atmosphere.

"Oh, I know you're kidding, right?" I ask, but it doesn't look like he's joking. "Yes, I have. Ever heard of Eazy-E?"

"Touché, Jayd Jackson. Touché," Keenan again says, laughing at his own ego.

I don't know what kind of girls he's used to dealing with, but I'm not the average chick, as he's quickly finding out. "How is it that a high school girl's hanging out at a coffeehouse on a Sunday night in West LA? Don't you have a rave or something to go to?"

"Oh, I see you've got jokes, huh?" I know Keenan thinks he's cute, but I'm cuter. He just doesn't know it yet.

"Who, me? Never," Keenan says.

The melodic tempo of the background music makes me

feel as if I'm time traveling through one of my dreams. Something about the Etta James classic tells me Maman liked the song when it was new back in her day, too.

"What do you know about 'A Sunday Kind of Love'?" Keenan asks jokingly.

Ignoring his smart comment, I close my eyes and sway my head to the smooth ballad. When I peek at my companion, Keenan's simply watching me enjoy the music. Sensing the change in vibe, he surrenders to the moment. I wonder how he'd take it if I told him he was in my dream a few nights ago—a dream that was more like a premonition than some random subconscious occurrence.

We continue sipping and vibing, enjoying each other's company without interrupting the song. I focus on the brown flecks in the whites of Keenan's eyes, easing my way into his mind. His thoughts are already cool and calm, allowing me easy access.

The dream of him and me as my ancestors comes to the front of my mind's eye, and I unintentionally share the vision with Keenan. He probably thinks it's his own daydream; he has no idea who Jean Paul and Maman are in relation to me. I glance around the coffeehouse and see the atmosphere has changed from a buzzing social spot to the quaint kitchen in Maman's house. When the song finally ends, so does our visual link. I didn't know I could do that without my grandmother. Mama and I have shared visions before, but neither of us has any control over that part of our powers.

"I think there was something in that tea," Keenan says, blinking his eyes as if that'll erase what happened. I feel like I momentarily fell asleep. I'll take that as my cue to roll.

"Yeah, I feel you," I say, shaking my head and rising from the table, careful not to step directly onto my wound. "I have to get going. I've got class in the morning," I say, hurriedly gathering my things.

"Wait a minute," Keenan says, following me to the door. "You just got here."

"I have an early day tomorrow," I say, pushing my way through the crowd. People are outside enjoying the warm night air. I wish my life were that carefree.

"Jayd, are you okay?" he asks, opening the car door. "Everything was going so well until that song came on."

With the memory of the soft voice singing about the kind of love she desires, I snap back into the vision, unable to still myself in this time period. Keenan's appearance is changing right along with my sight, causing me to feel woozy. I balance myself against the car and catch my breath.

"I'm fine. I just need to get some sleep." I place my things inside the car and get in.

"Drive safely and get plenty of rest. I'm looking forward to our next meeting," Keenan says, closing my door. Me, too, but I hope we can stay in the present the next time we meet.

I start the car and decide to stay parked for a few more minutes while I gather my thoughts but not before my eyes can play one more trick on me. If I wasn't sure of Jeremy's whereabouts, I could swear he and Cameron are in front of the restaurant across the street kissing. What the hell? I'd better get home before I bug out so bad I won't be able to make the fifteen-minute drive back to Inglewood. Regardless of my mental breakdown, I need to get some solid rest if I'm going to make it through tomorrow. Hopefully some of Mama's lavender and vanilla ointment will soothe my nerves once I get home.

"And go straight home, Jayd. No detours, you hear?" my mom says, interrupting my private time. I can't recoup with her in my ear.

"Mom, where would I go this time of night?" I ask aloud. My brain's too tired for any more telepathic ventures.

"I don't know. Over to one of your little friends' house or somewhere."

I would tell her she sounds like Mama, but I don't know how she'll take it.

"All I know is that if you're seeing things that aren't there, you don't need to be out."

"It was the strangest thing," I say, the kissing couple popping back into my head. "I could've sworn that dude was Jeremy." The crowd outside the coffeehouse is dying down a bit the later it gets. It's well after midnight on a Sunday, and these folks act like they don't have to work in the morning. I know some of them have jobs to go to.

"What about this Keenan guy. Who's he?" my mom asks.

She knows more about my new friend than she's saying, but she wants to give me the chance to explain, offering me some delusion of privacy.

"I had a dream he was Jean Paul and I was Maman. I was on fire, and he put it out. It sounds worse than it actually was," I say, trying to explain the vision, but it's no consolation. She was a young mother herself, so I know what's going through her mind.

"I see," my mom says. *"Jayd, all I can say is that you're young and single. Jeremy's good, but if you're having dreams like this about another man, then he's not all you need and that's okay. You don't have to compromise, Jayd. If you don't get everything you want the first time around, the next time you ask the Creator for what you want, be more specific. You deserve everything you can imagine having and more. Remember that."*

"It wasn't just about another man." I think back, remembering the vivid details. *"Jeremy and that girl were kissing in public, unashamed of their infidelious behavior."*

"Infidelious? Who talks like that, Jayd? Really?" my mom

says, totally off subject. The SAT prep words I've been studying are sinking in. *"Okay, but seriously, if you're having visions about someone cheating after you just left a date with someone other than your boyfriend, it could be your own guilt you're sensing and not the little white boy's. Just a thought. Bye, little girl,"* my mom says, finally leaving my head so I can drive home.

She might be right about me projecting my feelings onto Jeremy. Ever since meeting Keenan, I can't get the brotha off my mind. Just thinking about his slightly crooked smile makes me sweat. I hope he stays out of my dreams and my reality for the rest of the night so I can recoup from my recent experiences. Otherwise, I'm going to be no good to anyone come tomorrow.

As predicted, my lack of sane sleep has created a deficit in my brain function. Our first reading group started with a bang as Charlotte and Alia went back and forth about the white girl and black boy in our first novel falling in love. It was a heated conversation with Alia finally shutting Charlotte's know-it-all ass down. Because Alia's feeling Chance and it's no secret that he's proud of his black blood, I think she was extra sensitive about the topic. Alia's raw emotion was written all over her well-tanned face, which gave her an advantage over Charlotte that I usually possess. I was proud of my girl, although I have to admit Charlotte had a few relevant points. All in all, I think Alia's taking on a new swag, and it's about time. The girl's got gumption, beauty, and brains: three powerful weapons in her arsenal if yielded properly. I think she should use them more often.

Before heading to cheer practice, I rewrapped my injured toe in the girls' bathroom just to make sure it was okay. With all the new crazy stunts we've been doing lately, I need all the protection I can get.

"Jayd, get in the lineup," Ms. Carter says, snapping me out of my thoughts and back to the dangerous reality ahead. How the hell am I supposed to step on top of another girl's thighs to reach the second tier of the human pyramid when I can barely walk straight because of my injury? And an even better question is why the hell are we doing this shit? Since when do all of the cheerleaders have to participate in this physical abomination? Do I look like Dominique Dawes to these broads?

"But, Ms. Carter, Jayd's legs are too fat to hold me up properly," Ellen says. "No offense, but muscle's more supportive than jiggle."

If I weren't afraid for my life right now, I'd check this skinny bitch. But I have to agree with Ellen. Her ninety-pound frame is no match for my natural thickness. I may not be the biggest girl on the block, but I'm short and packing what I've got.

"I see what you're saying, but Jayd's got good upper-body strength. She can hold herself up with the bottom half," Ms. Carter says, pointing to my behind.

Why do I feel like a slave on the auction block? They're talking about my body as if I'm not here, and that's pissing me off. I'm too tired for this crap. "Don't I get a say in what I can and can't do?" I ask. Both of them look at me like I'm completely out of order. The rest of the squad is busy prepping, oblivious to the debate.

"This is serious business, Jayd," Ellen says, flipping her blond ponytail over her left shoulder. Someone should really tell her about her scrunchy fetish before she gets clowned. "This is your first year as a cheerleader, and you have to learn the game."

"The game?" I ask, feeling as insulted as I did a moment ago when she sized up my body. I didn't sign up for this.

"Yes. And there are rules to every game," Ms. Carter says

like she's giving me a private tutorial. "Rule number one: no talking while the captain is speaking with the coach."

Is this chick serious? I'll be damned if I follow any more rules. I already had to run a mile—sore toe and all—for being five minutes late. Now I can't even speak unless spoken to. And with the other two black varsity cheerleaders, Shauna and Alicia, officially graduated, the thrill is gone. Some summer this is turning out to be. With the writing workshop in the mornings and this shit right after, I feel like I'm back in school part-time with full-time heffas.

"I don't know what you've heard, but even mere cheer novices have rights, and I'm telling you both right now that I don't feel well enough to climb anybody today. I cut my foot this morning on a piece of glass; that's why I was late, if you'd listen," I say, officially pissing the little white girl off.

"You know what my daddy says about excuses?" Ellen asks, sounding like the authentic Southern girl she is. "They're like buttholes. Everyone's got one and they all stink."

Well I guess she put me in my place, or so she thinks.

"I've got one you can kiss," I say, not letting her get away with slamming me like that—damn the cheer hierarchy.

"You can't speak to me like that," Ellen says, now completely enraged.

I guess she's used to people bowing at her nimble, blond feet, but I couldn't give a damn about this fake-ass world.

"Why not? You're barely my equal, and I couldn't care less about who you think you are in Cheer Land," I say, rolling my neck like only a sistah can. It's bad enough I have to hold my tongue at debutante functions. All of this humbling myself to the wrong people is messing with my emotions.

Fully aware of the drama unfolding center court. The rest of the varsity squad shift their focus from the routine and hone in on our loud conversation.

"Okay, ladies. Let's all calm down," Ms. Carter says, attempting to regain control of the situation. "We only have an hour left to get this down."

Ellen doesn't budge and neither do I.

"Ms. Carter, I agree," Ellen says. "We don't have time for any losers on our team."

"Exactly," I say, stepping closer to her midget ass. She could double for one of the seven dwarfs if she was a dude. "This team was just fine before you arrived, so why don't you go back home where your country ass belongs. And take that funky red scrunchy with you."

The other girls snicker because they know I'm right about her choice in hair accessories. I've never done a white girl's hair before, but maybe I should start. Some of these girls could use the help.

"She can't talk to me like that," Ellen says, looking as pissed as I feel.

This is such a waste of valuable time. In all honesty, I could be making money right now. There's always someone in my mom's hood to braid up.

"I'm the captain."

There she goes with that title again.

"Okay, girls. Why don't you both take a deep breath and count to ten," Ms. Carter says. "The rest of you, get back to work. Jayd and Ellen will join in a minute."

I don't know about Ellen, but counting to ten isn't going to do much to calm me down. Whatever joy cheer gave me during tryouts officially left with the two senior sistahs. The last thing I need is to voluntarily deal with perky white bitches on a daily basis. College program or not, quitting the squad sounds damn good to me.

"We're not quitters, Jayd Jackson," my mom says, butting in as usual. *"Get your head straight and handle your business, girl."*

"Ready, set," Ms. Carter says, clapping her hands and calling us back into line.

I look at the squad and weigh my options. Ellen smiles, thinking she knows I'm out of here. But my mom's right: Williams women don't quit.

"Okay," we respond, clapping in unison and getting back into formation. I take my place at the far right end of the line. Once the second row of the pyramid is firmly secured, Ellen begins her climb to the top. She's too close for my comfort and she knows it.

As Ellen mounts my right thigh, she purposely presses her heel into my knee and that's her final bad. With the added pressure, my injured toe can't take the pain. Attempting to focus on something else, my mind falls back to Jeremy and Cameron kissing, breaking my concentration and stability. With the pain coursing through my foot, I can't hold on much longer.

"She's going to fall!" Another teammate screams from the second tier, trying to hold herself and Ellen up, but it's too late. My legs buckle, and like Humpty Dumpty, we all fall down.

"Shit!" Ellen shouts.

For a little proper miss, she sure does have a dirty mouth. I guess that comes with the assumed power of her position. We're all okay, but Ms. Carter is not pleased.

"Let's call it a day," Ms. Carter says, totally exasperated with her girls. The two boy cheerleaders don't come on until the fall. "Get some good rest tonight and come back with a different attitude tomorrow. Otherwise we're not going to survive as a team."

That's the best idea I've heard all day long.

After a couple of hours of resting my toe, I'm ready to get some studying done. Unfortunately, I can't get the image of

Jeremy cheating on me out of my mind. I know the vision wasn't real, and because it wasn't a dream, I don't know if I can trust it as a premonition. However, something in my bones tells me I'm right. I don't want to believe that Jeremy would do that to me after the rap he gave me about not being Rah, but he's still human, and we all screw up.

Between this weekend's dramatic events and this afternoon's practice, I wish this week were over, but it's only Monday. As if my life weren't uncomfortable enough, my skin's breaking out—another side effect of not sleeping well. I need one of Mama's honey-molasses masks to clear my skin, but I'll have to settle for making my own. My imperfect mixture will have to do until Mama returns.

Speaking of missing loved ones, my phone rings and I know it's Jeremy. If he doesn't get back soon, I'm going to change his ringtone from Usher's "There Goes My Baby" to something not so sweet.

"There's my girl," Jeremy says, sounding like he's in a much better mood than I am. Maybe there's a good reason—or person—for that.

"Are you referring to me? Because this girl is feeling deserted." I walk into the bathroom and look at my face in the mirror. My brown skin is smooth until my fingers get to my chin, my problem area. Unlike my cousin Jay, who has acne, I don't usually break out unless I'm stressed out about something.

"Jayd, don't be like that. I miss you, too, baby."

Any other day, Jeremy's deep voice would calm my nerves, but not today. I'm over it.

"Are you sleeping with Cameron?" I ask him point-blank. It might be because of my guilty conscience about feeling Keenan, but he doesn't need to know all that. He doesn't sound so innocent himself.

"What? No. Hell, no," Jeremy says, thrown off by my accusation.

He sounds pretty convincing, but I'm still not sure he's telling the truth. Something's going on, and I'm going to get to the bottom of it. My visions don't lie, but dudes do.

"Jeremy, I know you're cheating. Just admit it," I say into the phone while pinching my chin. These blackheads are driving me crazy. If I keep picking at my face like this, I'm not going to have any skin left.

"Jayd, I'm not cheating on you. What's up with you lately? Are you feeling okay?"

"Yes. I'm feeling fine," I say, squeezing my skin with my fingernails until I bleed, but I don't care. I can't take these bumps on my face any longer. They have to go. "How you doin'?" I ask in my best Wendy Williams impersonation, not that Jeremy would catch that. I doubt he keeps up with the talk show diva.

"Jayd, seriously. Every time we talk, you sound different. I don't know what it is, but something's off."

Jeremy's right, but since he's not here to see for himself, he doesn't have much to say. "Now you're calling me off?" I ask, officially scratching the shit out of my face. I can't stop until it's smooth. "You really sound guilty, Jeremy. Why don't you just confess, because I'm not going to stop until I get the truth."

"That is the truth," Jeremy says, upset himself. "Damn, girl, you're acting a bit insane. Have you been sleeping?"

He sounds too much like Rah for my taste. "Actually I haven't, because I keep having visions of my boyfriend kissing another girl. He's supposed to be vacationing with his family when all he really wants is a vacation from me. And you know what? You've got it. You're free to frolic with whomever you please." I take a tissue from the box on top of the toilet, soaking up the fresh wounds I dug into my brown complexion. If Mama were here, she'd have my ass for damaging my skin.

"Jayd, what the hell is wrong with you? I'm calling Chance to come check on you."

He can call Dr. Phil for all I care. I know I'm right, and I don't need any help. What I need is an admission, and he knows I'm getting closer to the truth. Otherwise Jeremy wouldn't sound so nervous.

"You mean Chase? He's in Atlanta, or haven't you heard he's going black nowadays?"

"Okay, then, where's Nigel?"

"Busy playing baby stepdaddy somewhere," I say. I leave the bathroom and go into my mother's room. I know she's got some scar cream in here somewhere.

"Jayd, for real. I'm worried about you. You don't sound right, and it's scaring me. Please take care of yourself."

Jeremy sounds so concerned about my well-being I almost feel bad for tripping on him, but I know I'm right. Why won't he just tell me the truth so we can work it out? Dudes will lie to the very end. I've had it with his denial for today.

"And you do the same. I've got to go." I hang up the phone and look at my reflection in my mom's closet mirror. With the white tissues stuck to my bleeding face and my hair buck wild from lying down, I look as crazy as I feel. If I take care of myself this evening, I won't be so easily disturbed by others tomorrow.

It's hot as hell in my mom's apartment, and I've got two floor fans blasting. I'll start with a shower, then do a much-needed facial to heal my self-inflicted damage. By the weekend I should feel myself again. Maybe I'll be better prepared to deal with my man next time he checks in. The last thing I want to do is destroy the best relationship I've ever had.

~ 11 ~

Crazy, Sexy, Cool

My love is warmer than a chocolate fudge / That's why I don't want no ice cream love; it's too cold for me.

—JOHNNY OSBOURNE

The first week of summer school wasn't bad, other than Monday's events. After falling, Ellen was quiet for the rest of the week. And once I got myself straight, my head was cool and my thoughts positive. It helped that I spent time in the spirit room every day after school since my services weren't needed at Netta's shop. I also learned that the annual Fourth of July block party is on this weekend. Everyone on Gunlock Avenue will be out enjoying the holiday. I might come through for a little while if for no other reason than to get a plate. Free barbeque is the best kind there is.

Mickey and I are supposed to check out day cares in the neighborhood today, since her grant from the county came through. She's already on public assistance, and now she needs a part-time job to save up for an apartment. I guess she's finally coming to the reality that in order to take care of her little family, she's going to have to pitch in.

Mickey's hood is only two miles from Mama's house, but the loyalties are different. I don't like coming into Blood territory—not that the Crips on our block are any better, but at least the gangs in my hood know my family. Over here I don't feel as safe. When KJ and I dated last summer, I had to come over this way to visit him. Even if he considers himself living in Rosewood—a small community within Compton's perimeters—he's still in the heart of Piru gang territory, the same gang Mickey's ex-man and Tre, her baby daddy who saved Nigel's life, belonged to. I'll never forget that day as long as I live.

"What are you doing on this side of town?" Misty says, catching me off guard. I stopped at CVS to get something to drink and of course Misty would be shopping here, too. Cheer practice always leaves my mouth dry.

"Minding my business. You?" I would ignore Misty but that never works with her kind.

"Minding my man's business," she says, looking back at KJ, who's at the other end of the aisle talking on his cell. She's so stupid to believe that he'll ever be faithful to one girl, but neither one of them are my problems anymore. It's hard to believe that a year ago Misty and I were as thick as thieves. Now we can't stand each other. But like all relationships, it's heavy when it's hot and cold when it's not.

"Whatever," I say, grabbing a bottled water out of the cooler and walking toward one of five cashiers. Before I can check out, Misty follows me to the front of the pharmacy. She must be bored, because she knows I want nothing to do with her ass.

"How's your white boy?" Misty asks. She bats her thickly coated lashes and smiles like she knows something I don't.

She's no friend of mine, and I'm done with the polite act she's giving. "Don't worry about me or mine, you hear, Misty?" I say, tired of her games. She's like an evil leprechaun that won't leave me the hell alone. "And by the way, tell your wicked godmother to get off my jock, too. You both need to learn when your concern is not wanted."

"Damn, Jayd. You've got a lot of pent-up frustration," Misty says, sucking on her Blow Pop like a professional. "You still not giving up the cookies, huh? Not even for the rich boy.

What will it take to get you to drop those rigid panties, girl? A pro-ball player? Oh, I forgot. You had KJ but didn't know what to do with him, and you know my boo's a star."

This girl's so delusional I almost feel sorry for her—almost.

"It'll take a whole lot more than that trifling, cheating fool to get at this. And as you know, he tried his best, but some of us have high standards," I say, pointing at KJ, who's still absorbed in his phone conversation. Misty slits her false blue eyes at me, sensing I'm telling the truth, but she doesn't want to hear that. She likes living in her fantasy world where KJ is faithful. That'll never happen and we both know it.

"What are you trying to say?" Misty asks, getting indignant.

I don't have time to engage this heffa. It's after four and the childcare centers close at six. I want to be there for my goddaughter, because her mama's too anxious to turn her over to just about anyone who'll take the county's voucher.

"When have you ever known me to try and say anything?" I ask, getting in the shortest line, but they're all moving too slow for me.

"Jayd, you're too conceited for any nigga to deal with for too long, including that surfer you call your boyfriend," Misty says louder than necessary. If I could slap her without the risk of her slapping me back, I would. But I'm in no mood to fight with this broad today. "You wait and see. You're going to be the only virgin left in the LA area—and a lonely one at that."

"So be it, then," I say, advancing in the line. The people around us look at our drama, uninterested. I'm sure this kind of thing happens in here on a daily basis. "I'd rather be a lonely virgin than a busy ho."

"Who are you calling a ho, trick?" Misty says, now completely beside herself.

Finally finished with his call, KJ joins us at the register, smiling big at the sight of a chick fight in his honor. I can't believe I ever fell for his bull.

"Jayd, what brings you across the train tracks?" KJ asks, putting his hands around Misty's waist. Misty smiles victoriously as if KJ claiming her wide ass is all the proof she needs that she's right and I'm wrong. As if that'll ever happen.

"None of your business," I say. It's my turn in line, and I couldn't be more ready to get out of here.

"Damn, what's up with you?" KJ asks.

I roll my eyes at him, hand the cashier two dollar bills, and take my water without saying bye to my schoolmates. It's bad enough I have to see them during the year, but around the neighborhood is pure torture.

Following me out of the large drugstore, Misty and KJ can't help but make a spectacle of themselves by making out when they reach his car. Yuck. The two of them deserve each other and whatever communicable diseases they exchange. KJ already gave Misty gonorrhea, which Mickey made sure the entire school knew about after Misty spilled the beans about Mickey's pregnancy prematurely. Even after KJ publicly blamed Misty for his obvious infraction—even though she was a virgin before they got together—she still didn't learn her lesson.

"Bye, Jayd. And tell Mickey I said hi," Misty says as I drive off. Why would she say something like that? Mickey and Misty tolerate each other at best. But Mickey has been on Misty's jock for changing up her physical appearance. I don't know what that's all about, nor do I care. My only concern is Nickey and quenching my thirst.

When I arrive at Mickey's house around the corner from the store, I walk through the small home to my friend's bedroom, which is a complete mess. The small room has been inundated with baby gear. Mickey's eight-year-old sister has had to make room for the new arrival, poor child. It must be no fun sharing a room with a selfish sister and a new baby. Nigel's trying to find somewhere for them to live together, but it's not easy to find someone to rent an apartment to two teenaged parents: They don't exactly scream *responsibility.*

"Hey, Mickey," I say, stepping over the clothes and shoes covering the floor.

"What up, Jayd?" Mickey says, not taking her eyes off her own reflection in the mirror.

We're going to look at day cares and she's dressing like we're going out for the night. Nickey looks like she needs some attention, because I can tell her mama's paying her no mind.

I pick up my goddaughter, who's whining from discomfort, from the equally junky bed. Her diaper's heavy and reeks of pee that hasn't been changed in hours.

"Mickey, did you know Nickey's wet?" I ask, putting the baby back in her crib and taking a diaper from the near-empty bag on the bed.

"Then change her," Mickey says, now applying makeup. "I've been busy all day, and she's almost out of diapers. She'll be fine until Nigel gets here with her stash."

I remove the soaked diaper and let her air out. I look more closely at Nickey's bottom and cringe at the sight. How could her mother let it get this bad? After a few minutes, the baby calms down but I'm just getting started.

"Mickey, she's got a severe diaper rash," I say, looking at the millions of tiny red bumps covering Nickey's cocoa skin. I gently wipe her clean, causing her to scream in pain. Poor baby. Mickey's really slipping on her motherly duties. Someone needs to check her before she goes too far. If Mama were here, she'd slap my girl straight.

"Shut up all that crying, Nickey. Damn," Mickey says without even looking at her daughter.

What happens when I'm not here?

"Don't talk to her like that. It's not her fault she's in pain," I say, slathering a thick layer of the baby bottom cream I made for Nickey all over her before fastening her diaper shut and picking her up. I soothe my upset godchild and kiss her gently on her head, noticing her cradle cap isn't getting any better, either. If Mickey would've used the products Mama and I made before she left, all of this could have been prevented. But Mickey's top priority is herself, and that's not a good thing. I look on the dresser for the head cream and notice a small bottle of pills. The label looks very familiar, but I can't place it.

"What are these for?" I ask, seizing the dark blue bottle with a simple label of a bird on the front. Where have I seen that symbol before?

"They're vitamins to help new mamas shed the baby fat," Mickey says, snatching the bottle from my hand and placing them on a shelf where I notice two more just like it.

"Mickey, you can't be serious," I say, patting Nickey on the back. "Your daughter's health and well-being are more important than your waistline." I've noticed her weight dropping in the last week and thought it was natural, but now I know that's not the case.

"Speak for yourself. I'm over it," she says, smoothing her skin-tight jeans over her behind. "You didn't just push a big-ass baby out of your body. I've got to get back in shape before the end of summer, girl. I've got a reputation to uphold."

Mickey's back to being her normal, conceited self, and it seems to have gotten worse.

"I'm positive there are better ways to lose weight than popping pills, Mickey." I take out one of Nickey's cute outfits from her diaper bag—courtesy of godmother Nellie—and change her clothes for our outing. She's a cute baby, and we should garner plenty of attention on our mission.

"What up, chicas?" Nigel says, stopping at the bedroom door and tossing a bag of diapers on the bottom bunk. There's no more room in here for another person. Mickey's sister's playing outside with her youngest brother, probably more out of necessity than desire. Who wants to be cooped up in here with Mickey's narcissistic ass? "Are we ready to roll?" Nigel's taking his parental roll more seriously than Mickey, and he really doesn't have to. Lucky for Nickey one of her parents has some sense.

"Yeah, I guess so," Mickey says. "How do I look, baby?"

Nigel looks at his girl without responding. He's over her selfish ways, too, I see.

"Mickey, we're going to look at day cares, not going out for dinner," Nigel says, reaching for the baby.

I step over the messy floor and hand her off, anxious to reload her diaper bag. I have to keep a close eye on her rash to make sure it heals quickly. At first, Nickey's excited to see her daddy, but when I walk back over the pile of clothes, she starts to fuss.

"There she goes again," Mickey says, grabbing her purse off the top bunk and passing by her man and child in the hallway. "Mikey, we're leaving," she yells outside. Her little brother's anything but a sitter, but with both of her parents constantly working, they don't have much of a choice.

"Why don't I take Nickey and y'all can check out the centers," I say, reclaiming my godbaby from Nigel. Nickey quiets down in my arms and sucks her fingers, an indication that she needs to rest.

"Fine," Mickey says without protest. Nigel looks like he wants to intervene but doesn't. "We'll holla when we're through. Come on, Nigel."

"Thanks, Jayd," Nigel says, kissing Nickey on the forehead and giving me a quick hug. Mickey looks at the three of us, and I can feel her jealousy. If she were a better mother, my presence wouldn't be needed. She only has herself to blame if she doesn't like what she sees.

"Nigel, come on. They'll be fine," Mickey says, leading the way out.

"I forgot the diaper bag," I say, going back into her room. I take the bag from the bed and the open bottle of pills Mickey's so protective of, and I remember where I've seen the label before: Esmeralda. Which means they probably came by way of Misty. No wonder she told me to tell Mickey hi. If she misses the diabolical pills, their absence can be blamed on this disheveled room. The carpet can get lost in here. Since we have the evening free, I say we pay a visit to Dr. Whitmore and let the good doc investigate these so-called vitamins. My mom's been after me to go see him anyway. I can also show off my goddaughter on my side of Compton.

The five-minute drive from Mickey's hood to mine was enough to calm Nickey down, although she didn't fall asleep. She's too fascinated by the artifacts and bright colors in Dr. Whitmore's Chinese-inspired office to nap even if she needs to. After we leave here, I might take her to the South Bay Plaza and walk around. The stroll should make her fall asleep. Hopefully Mickey and Nigel will be done in a couple of hours.

Dr. Whitmore's been inspecting the tablets for the past fifteen minutes and looks distressed by his findings. Thank God he hasn't questioned me about how I'm feeling. The last thing I want is another one of his horse-pill prescriptions. I had a hard enough time taking them the last time I needed them for sleepwalking.

"They're labeled as simple postnatal vitamins, but they're a lot more than that," Dr. Whitmore says, inspecting the small pink pills under the microscope. His office is a cornucopia of traditional medical research. Some call him a witch doctor because of his association with Mama, but that's tantamount to calling a priestess a witch, and he doesn't like the term any more than we do. "These will drive someone crazy if they take them for too long. Where did you find them?"

"Mickey's house, my friend who just had the baby," I say, looking at Nickey's stroller next to me. Dr. Whitmore didn't even ask whose baby she is. As long as it's not mine, I guess he doesn't care. "I found them in her room and recognized the bottle from Esmeralda's collection."

Unfortunately, I have been in Esmeralda's house on more than one unpleasant occasion. She has her own containers and labels for her line of products. Esmeralda's never cultivated her skills like Mama and Netta but still does her own thing. Money rules Esmeralda's business, unlike Mama and Netta who are led by the spirit to heal. If the client is willing to pay, Esmeralda's willing to concoct her potions no matter how dangerous they may ultimately be.

"Esmeralda," Dr. Whitmore grunts. I don't know the entire history between him, Esmeralda, and my grandmother, but Esmeralda's name gets a rise out of him every time. "When will that woman ever learn her evil tricks are no good?"

"Never." I take a seat on the futon up against the wall and let him continue his scientific experiment. Mickey thinks I'm driving her crazy and that Nickey's also to blame. Wait until she finds out it's the magic diet pills Misty gave her that's irritating her. I'd hate to be my nemesis when Mickey learns the truth.

"Here," the doctor says, handing me a clear plastic bag full of pills very similar to the ones in the bottle. "Replace Esmeralda's pills with these and make sure your friend takes them daily, just like the others. She should start to feel normal again very soon. And please tell her to stay away from Esmeralda and her disciples at all cost. That woman's no good."

"Thank you, Dr. Whitmore," I say, claiming the medicine. I need to get some food in my growling stomach. Chinese from the food court at the mall sounds good. Nickey's probably hungry. I'll feed her when we get to Redondo Beach.

"And how are you faring without your grandmother, Jayd?" Dr. Whitmore asks, shining his tiny light in my eyes. He's looking for more than my emotions with the shiny tool. I don't need a mini flashlight to see that Dr. Whitmore misses Mama. They have lunch at least once a week and see each other regularly for spiritual business, working on remedies and ridding negative energy from their individual clients.

"I miss her and Netta, but I'm glad she's enjoying her trip. She deserves it," I say, looking at the wall where a picture of Mama in all white hangs with the other photos. He and Mama go way back. My instincts tell me that they were more than friends back in the day.

"How's your sleep?" he asks, tilting my chin up and taking a closer look.

No sense in lying about it when he might be able to help. "Not so good lately," I say. He directs me to stick out my tongue. Nickey looks at us more curious than ever. She doesn't have to talk to communicate with me. As caul babies, we have our own unique language.

"Did you finish the last round of herbs I prescribed for your sleepwalking incident back in February?"

Dr. Whitmore knows as well as anyone I hate taking the meds he prescribes for my issues. I didn't finish the round because I've been feeling better, but I know I should always follow his directions to the letter.

"No, sir," I say. He looks at me, disappointed. Without further inspection, he packs up a bag of goodies for me to take.

"Call me if you need anything else. And, Jayd, please be mindful of your sleep. You know as well as I do there are real enemies just waiting for the opportune moment to take over your dreams again," he says, bending down and softly pinching Nickey's right cheek. They look at each other as if they've met before: knowing both of them, they probably have. "It would be a shame if you lost your gift of sight before you had time to master it. Think of all the people you could help with your blessing."

Dr. Whitmore's warning scares me into submission. "I will finish this round, Doctor. I promise."

Dr. Whitmore smiles as he opens the door for us. "Don't promise me a damn thing, Jayd," he says, standing up as I gather the baby's things and my own. With the diaper bag, stroller, and car seat, carrying Nickey around must be heavier than toting three adults. "Promise yourself that you'll put your health first. You'll do none of us any good if you suffer another breakdown." Feeling crazy is worse than menstrual cramps, and they make me feel like I want to die. No matter what's in this paper bag, I'm going to tolerate it. The alternative is a line I don't want to ever cross again.

The thick aftertaste of the bitter herbs I swallowed three hours ago creeps up my throat, causing me to belch loudly. I turn my head into my elbow and narrowly avoid spreading my gaseous air over my client's hair. That would ruin the mango-scented finishing cream I just smoothed all over Miller's braids. He's a new client, who doesn't say much and pays in singles. I don't know what he does, but Shawntrese recommended him, so I know he's okay.

"Excuse me," I say, undraping the brown towel from around his shoulders.

He looks in the large hand mirror, pleased with the results. "You're excused."

Miller hands me exactly forty one-dollar bills. My guess is he's a busboy and lives off his under-the-table earnings, which is why he can't afford to tip me. But I'm not tripping. I understand being that tight on cash. I haven't been grocery shopping at all this week and can't wait for the block party that's already going on. I told my crew about it, and they're probably already enjoying the festivities. A sistah like me can't afford to pass up cash. Surprisingly, the holiday hasn't stopped me from having a very busy morning.

"Enjoy your day," I say, opening the front door for my last client of the day.

"I will. My mom and I are going to watch the fireworks at the Queen Mary," he says, slowly walking down the stairs.

That explains his quiet demeanor: Miller has *mama's boy* written all over his thin frame.

"Have fun," I say after him. I close the door and head to the bathroom to shower and get dressed as quickly as I can. I'm hungry and I know the food's ready. I can practically smell it from Compton I'm so excited. I just hope my uncles keep themselves in check. Every year, one of them seems to go too far, but we're not the only family on the block with embarrassing relatives. It's always a crapshoot to see who'll go off the deep end every holiday. Hopefully, this year we won't win that title.

The closer I get to Mama's block, the louder my stomach growls. Granted, I don't eat all of the dishes that'll be served at each house, but there are still a few neighbors who make the best potato salad, baked beans, and chicken hot links I've ever tasted. I used to be the girl cleaning chitlins—the most disturbing kitchen job I've ever been forced into. I'm so glad Mama gave up pork when I was ten years old. However, it is the smell of the boiled and fried pig intestines that welcomes me home.

"There goes my baby," my ringtone sings, indicating a call from my man. I park around the corner from my grandparents' block and answer his call.

"I didn't think I'd hear from you again so soon," I say, turning the engine off and opening the door. It's too hot to sit in the car without air.

"I was a little thrown off by our last conversation, Lady J, but I missed my baby," Jeremy says, melting my heart. He can be so sweet. "Have you seen her lately?"

"No, I haven't. But when you see her, please tell her to holla at me," I say, making us both laugh. It's been too long since we've shared a light moment. Our conversations are too strained and quick to establish a comfortable flow and this time's no different.

"You're a little crazy, but it's kind of sexy, so all is forgiven," Jeremy says.

I know he's only partially joking. I admit I'm a lot to handle, but I'm worth it. His life's not so easy, either.

"I love you, too." I imagine Jeremy bending his tall frame down to meet my lips, taking me in his strong, toned arms, forcing me on my tiptoes. Voluntarily, I surrender to his embrace. What I wouldn't give to see his deep blue eyes, to run my fingers though his sun-kissed curls that complement his olive complexion. Damn, I miss my man.

"I'm sorry I can't talk for long, but I'll be home soon, Jayd. We have a lot of time to make up for."

He's got that right. The summer will practically be over by the time he gets back from Europe.

"I hope so, baby. Bye and be good," I say.

"Tell everyone I said hi," Jeremy says before disconnecting the call.

I guess it's time to party whether I'm feeling festive or not.

I lock the car door and head down Caldwell Street. As I turn the corner, I notice Rah, Nigel, and Mickey kicking it with my uncle Bryan and cousin Jay. I should be able to slip these pills into Mickey's purse when she's not looking without having to travel to her side of town to do it. I'm tired and need to catch up on sleep after I throw down on some barbeque. Dr. Whitmore's herbs may taste like death, but they get the job done.

"Damn, girl. We thought you were working in the fields as long as it took you to get here," Bryan says, talking shit as usual.

"I get paid for my hustle, Mr. James," I say to my favorite uncle. I hug my friends and give my cousin dap before claiming the ready-made plate on the long foldout table with matching chairs.

"I got all you favorites," Rah says, making sure I know he's the one who made my plate. He knows me so well.

The neighbors are enjoying the vibe and every family's got a job to do. The Webbs up the block are the deejays. The Baxters across the street are holding down the drinks—alcoholic and non—and all of the yards have folding tables and chairs for plenty of cross-family socializing.

"Thank you," I say. I haven't talked to Rah about the dream I had with Sandy straddling a stranger, but I think I should let him know in private. I pull back the aluminum foil covering the paper plate and dig in with the plastic fork also provided.

"Hey, Jayd. Your boy's here," Bryan says, pointing at Mr. Adewale walking up the block.

I look up to see an unexpected guest coming our way, not that I'm disappointed. Since when did my uncle Bryan and Mr. Adewale become boys? I know they occasionally ball together, but them hanging out is a bit much.

Too bad Mama's not here for the festivities. She usually makes a slamming peach cobbler for the annual event. I miss her cooking and so does everyone else on Gunlock today. Nothing's the same without my grandmother's special touch.

"What's our teacher doing here?" Mickey asks, feeding Nickey a bottle and rocking her to sleep.

I'm glad to see she can be a good mother when she wants to be. Hopefully Dr. Whitmore's meds will help her demeanor improve permanently.

"He's only your teacher during school hours. Right now he's the fool who owes me twenty dollars for whipping his ass on the court last night," Bryan says, greeting Mr. Adewale. I suddenly have the urge to check my breath. This potato salad is scrumptious, but the onions are a bit much.

"Hey, everyone," Mr. A says. My friends and I say hi and continue eating. "And you can't have what you didn't earn, man."

It's weird seeing him interact with someone his own age for a change. Mr. Adewale's just a regular guy: fine, but still regular.

"Always talking but never walking," my uncle says, pointing to the backyard where the netless basketball rim is hanging above the garage door. My uncles wore that thing out years ago, and it's never been replaced. "First to twenty-one, double or nothing."

"Bet," Mr. A says, following my uncle to the back.

No matter how old they get, boys will be boys. Nigel and Rah would love to get in on the action, but food comes first and we're all digging in.

"This chicken is banging," Nigel says, licking barbeque sauce from his fingers. Rah nods his head in agreement and so do I. There's nothing like home cooking.

It's still early in the afternoon, and so far it looks like everyone's enjoying the party. This is one of those holidays where everyone comes back to the block to catch up on the latest news, visit old friends, and see the new babies, like Nickey.

"Mickey, why don't you take Nickey down to Tre's house?" I say, looking at his sister Brandy's growing baby bump as she and her friends play dominoes on their front lawn. They've seen a lot of tragedy in their small family: First their mother died and then their little brother, Tre. Hopefully her baby will bring some joy to their household and maybe Tre's daughter will, too. "His sisters know the baby's his by now, I'm sure." We don't need our own news channel in Compton if we need to get the word out. Our CNN is via hair salons, barbershops, and the corner store.

"Because I don't want to," Mickey says, sucking her teeth at the idea. Nigel and Rah keep silent even if I know they feel the same way I do. "And besides, me and Brandy got into it a couple of years ago in junior high, and I still can't stand the bitch."

"Mickey, that's so juvenile I can't even comment," I say, placing my empty plate in the large trash bag next to the table and wiping my hands on a wet nap. There's no being cute while throwing down around here. "I'll take her, then," I say, rolling my eyes at my girl, who returns the favor. She has to know she's wrong for keeping Tre's sisters from his only child that we know of. After he died saving Nigel's life from getting shot by Mickey's ex-man, the least she could do is be apologetic about the shit, but not Mickey. She's a gangsta girl until the very end.

"Good looking, Jayd," Nigel says. "Tre was a good brotha."

Rah nods his head in agreement, and Mickey feels out of the loop. I'm glad I'm not the only one who thinks her behavior's immature.

I take Nickey's stroller by the curved handles and make my way down the packed block, waving to our neighbors along the way. Nickey is a cute baby and garners me lots of attention when we're together, just like Rahima. I'm going to have to take both my goddaughters to the mall and get some serious love. When Nickey and I hung out yesterday, so many people stopped to comment on her beauty.

"Hey, Jayd. Who's the baby?" Brandy asks, rubbing her swollen belly like she's ready to pop. She's due any day now. It'll be nice for Nickey to have a cousin to grow up with like Jay and I. We were very close.

"She's your niece," I say, positioning the baby for Brandy to see. Maybe she can recognize family features Mickey and I can't. Nickey looks just like her mama to me. "Nickey Shantae. Say hi to your auntie."

"Oh," Brandy says, looking at Nickey. I can see her older sister inside the house talking on her cell. "Who's the mama?" she asks, knowing it's not me. Everyone knows Mama would kill me before she allowed me to get pregnant at such a young age.

"Mickey," I say, surprised she hasn't heard the latest news. Or maybe she has and she's feigning ignorance to be mean.

"Well, we can't help take care of no more babies. We got enough of our own." Damn, I didn't even say anything about all that. "Besides, Tre ain't here to vouch for her, so she ain't no kin of mine."

I look at her three friends, each focused on the dominoes in their hands. This heffa's really going to sit here and pretend like Nickey's not a part of her family. Trifling people get on my damned nerves.

"I thought you'd want to meet her, especially since Tre's gone," I say, giving Brandy a chance to redeem herself, but she's unrelenting in her cold attitude.

"Whatever, Jayd," Brandy says, taking a drag from her cigarette. This broad should be arrested for smoking while pregnant. "As many niggas as Mickey runs through, it's no telling who the baby daddy is."

Without another word, I turn the stroller around and head back down the street. I don't know what to say. Unfortunately, Brandy's telling the truth about Mickey's promiscuity, but her way of going about it is all wrong. Visiting Tre's house was definitely a mistake. Brandy and I have never been cool, but we've never had beef, either, until now. I wish Mickey would beat her ass again for that ignorant shit.

"Let's get some lemon pound cake from Mrs. Pritchard's house," I say, but Nickey's knocked out. I wish I could fall asleep that easily. Bryan and Mr. A must be done with their game, and from the looks of the money exchanging hands, I'd have to say Bryan won even if Mr. A's smiling like he's the victor.

"Where'd my folks go?" I ask, noticing Rah, Nigel, and Mickey have disappeared from our front lawn.

"They went to smell the trees, and I'm going with them," Bryan says, speaking in code for smoking weed. "You coming, man?" Bryan says to Mr. A, who respectfully declines the invite. I guess it's just my favorite teacher and me.

"Bryan told me you're going to be in a cotillion?" Mr. Adewale says, like it's not the interrogation it obviously is. He tries to be so coy about his shit, but he's not.

"That's right," I say, parking Nickey's stroller in the shade and putting the cover up so she can get a good nap in. "But it's not really by choice as much as for the benefit of my college applications."

"I think it's a good move, Miss Jackson," he says, taking a swig of his water on the table. "My fraternity will be there to support our sister sorority. You'll enjoy yourself, I promise," he says, smiling big and displaying his perfectly straight teeth. His dreadlocks are pulled back, showing off his well-defined cheekbones.

"You're going to be there?" I ask. Now I'm more nervous than ever about the ball next weekend. Before I wasn't really tripping, but now I want to be on my best behavior: Mr. Adewale always brings that out in me.

"I sure am and I can't wait to see you in all white." Mr. Adewale's bright hazel eyes glimmer in the afternoon sun, reminding me of several dreams I've had of me and him married. Something tells me that he's not talking about my white evening gown Mrs. Esop purchased.

Before we can get too deep in conversation, our friends rejoin us, much more mellow than they were a few minutes ago.

"Cake," Mickey says, going for my plate, but she's got another think coming if she thinks I'm sharing my dessert plate. There's enough food up and down Gunlock to satisfy her munchies without picking off mine.

"Is that roasted corn?" my uncle asks, spying the sweet cob on Mr. Adewale's plate.

Mr. A looks as serious about his food as I do about mine. "Yeah, and there's some more two doors down," he says, pointing toward Alondra Boulevard where we see an unwelcome visitor.

"What's Sandy doing here?" I ask Rah, pointing down the block. Sandy switches her way toward us with Rahima in a stroller, knowing the girl's too big for that tiny thing. Rahima will be three in a couple of months and is tall for her age, which is no surprise. Her father clears six feet and her mother's not far behind.

"Oh, shit," Rah says, shaking his head. "I told her where I'd be if there was an emergency or something." Emergency my ass. The only crisis is the one Sandy's about to create.

"Why do you do shit like that when you know the girl can't be trusted?" I ask, watching our semi-pleasant afternoon come to a crashing halt the closer Sandy gets to my grandparents' house.

"She said she was having some stomach pains or something when I left. I just wanted to make sure she knew where I was, just in case."

"It was probably menstrual cramps," I say, wishing Sandy were lying about the whole damned thing, not just about the baby daddy, who I know for a fact isn't Rah. Now, I've just got to prove it.

"Jayd, she's really pregnant. I saw the test with my own eyes," Rah says, looking at me cross when he should be throwing the evil eye to his baby mama. I know better than anyone that eyes can play tricks.

"Okay, then, fine. Why didn't you bring Rahima with you if she wasn't feeling well? That would have made more sense."

Nigel and Mickey stay out of this one.

"Because Sandy said she missed our daughter."

Yeah, right. He and I both know Sandy drops off the baby to whomever she can, whenever she can. If he fell for that shit, he's tripping harder than I thought. My uncle and teacher are engrossed in a conversation with our neighbor and eating the sweets I'm craving. Even Sandy can't ruin my appetite today.

"Rah, you need to take her. I've got to be somewhere," Sandy says, pushing the stroller toward us without any type of greeting. Where was Sandy raised, in a barn? This girl could use an etiquette class or two her damned self.

"I thought you were sick?" Rah asks, taking the stroller by the handles and turning it around so that Rahima's sleeping face is out of the sun.

"I was, but I feel better now," Sandy says, straightening out her short shorts. She looks at Nigel and me, then back at Rah, completely ignoring Mickey. I'd hate to see the two of them really go at it. "Bye."

"Damn, Sandy. You need to get your priorities straight," Rah says. "That's how you got yourself pregnant again." He parks his daughter next to Nickey so she can finish napping in peace.

"I didn't get myself pregnant," Sandy says, putting her left hand on her hip, displaying her bulging breasts for all to see. The strained pink shirt looks like it's about to burst. "Or did you forget how it works already? If so, I'll show you later when we get home."

No, she didn't just go there with me standing right here. I could choke on my cake I'm so pissed. "Sandy, your home is in a state penitentiary somewhere, not at Rah's house," I say. I've had it with this broad and her wannabe propositions. I know he's not my man, but damn. She should show a little respect that other people are present before throwing her cookies around. I don't want to hear that shit.

"Whatever, Jayd. You're just jealous because I've got everything you want and then some," she says, readjusting her breasts in her revealing top. Now this heffa's really gone too far.

"What exactly do you have, Sandy? An ankle monitor that fits like the rest of your too-tight clothing?" I point at the blinking tracking device on her right leg. "You have no car, no high school diploma, and no one claiming your mystery baby. I'm sorry, what am I supposed to be jealous of again?" Sandy's hotter than the link I ate a while ago, but I'm speaking the truth. Mickey looks satisfied with the drama in front of her.

"Sandy, you can go now. I've got baby girl," Rah says to a shell-shocked Sandy. When will my former friends learn not to mess with me?

Defeated, Sandy struts back from where she came from, causing heads to turn with each clack of her sandals. She needs to pick up her feet, as Mama would say. A cool breeze drifts up my shirt and to my cheeks, calming me back down. That trick always gets a rise out of me. Speaking of heffas, Misty appears on her godmother's porch, reminding me to slip the pills into Mickey's purse while she's distracted.

"Hey, y'all," Misty says from the safety of the gated entrance. "Mickey, you good?" She sounds like the dope man checking for customers. Mickey looks embarrassed by Misty's unsolicited greeting.

"I'll be right back," Mickey says, walking across the yard. If she's going to Esmeralda's house, I can't let her go alone. Against my better judgment, I follow my friend.

"I'll come with you," I say, but Mickey looks mortified at the thought.

"No," she says, stopping me from going any farther. "I got this, Jayd."

I look at Mickey and realize she's not sure she can trust me after I told her about helping her through her labor. One day she'll see that was for her own good.

"Fine," I say, walking up the front porch and through the door. I can hear and see everything on Esmeralda's porch through Mama's living room window.

"What's in these pills, Misty?" Mickey asks, shaking them in Misty's face. "I've been losing weight, but I also don't feel right," Mickey says.

We're not at school now. If Mickey wants to whip Misty's ass, there's no one here to stop her. I hope she doesn't, for her own good. The last thing she needs is to catch an assault wrap with a two-month-old baby at home.

"Nothing, Mickey. Damn, you're acting crazy." Misty looks at me, the last word dangling in the air.

Crazy. Misty gave Mickey the diet pills, causing my girl to slowly lose her mind. I should've known sooner her evil ass was up to something else: Misty's been too quiet for anyone's good.

"All I know is that if there's anything foul in these vitamins, you won't be smiling like that for long." Mickey walks off the porch and back to where our friends are chilling. Good thing I changed the tablets. Now I have to pull the rest off her shelf and fix Misty for this shit. Good friends do what needs to be done whether they get credit for it or not.

"What up, Jayd?" my uncle Kurtis says, coming into the living room from the hallway. Unless he was in the bathroom, he has no business back there. Actually he has no business in the house at all.

"What are you doing here?" I ask. He moved out weeks ago, and in my opinion that means no visiting when Mama's not here. Daddy and the rest of the boys are making their rounds around the block: It's just us in the house.

"Damn, I can't take a leak?" he says, smiling sinisterly.

I head to Mama's room, feeling like something's wrong. "Move out of my way," I say, pushing past him in the hallway. I look at Mama's closed door, seeing the locks have been tampered with. This jackass tried to pick Mama's locks.

"You punk! Get out of Mama's house now," I say, punching my big-ass uncle as hard as I can in his left bicep, which only amuses him more. Kurtis trying to hurt Mama is way beyond any line of respect that can be drawn.

"You better watch yourself, Jayd. Mama can't protect you now." Kurtis doesn't budge, pushing me to my limit.

I don't give a damn if he outweighs me by more than a hundred pounds. This fool's going down this afternoon, and I'm going to be the one to take him there. Mama left me in charge of her things and that includes her bedroom.

"You'd better watch yourself, Kurtis. You have no idea what I'm capable of."

He grabs my arm hard, squeezing as tight as he can. It hurts but not more than my nails digging into his neck. "You little bitch!" Kurtis yells, letting me go to focus on his bleeding skin. I try to escape, but not before he grabs me again, this time picking me up.

"Let me go, fool!" I scream, thrusting my feet up, trying to get in a solid kick to his most sensitive area. He spins me around in the air like he used to do when I was a little girl, but I'm not a child anymore. I close my eyes and bite down hard on his shoulder, causing him to let go. As I fall to the floor, Kurtis snatches my feet, pulling me back into the hallway. I turn over on my back and kick him as hard as I can in his fat gut.

"Shit!" Kurtis screams. His eyes have gone blank like an insane person: I know I'm in for it now.

"What the hell is going on here?" Bryan asks, busting through the front door with Mr. A and my crew also witnessing the fight. "Let her go, man."

The neighbors within earshot also get a good look at the scene. I guess we know which family won for most embarrassing block party moment, even if it is taking place indoors.

"Hell, no. This little bitch bit me and she's going to pay."

My uncle Bryan intervenes and Kurtis backs down, knowing his younger brother has a black belt in Tae Kwon Do. I may not be able to kick his ass, but Bryan can in one quick move.

"This is your niece, Kurtis. Don't call her out of her name again." My friends look stunned, but this kind of thing happens around here on the regular. "Are you okay, Jayd?"

"I'm fine," I say, picking myself up and straightening my clothes. "He tried to break into Mama's room," I say, pointing toward the scene of the crime. "I told him to get out, but he wouldn't listen." My adrenaline's pumping, and my head doesn't feel so good. That fall really hurt.

"She's crazy, man," Kurtis says. "She doesn't know what the hell she's talking about."

"I may be crazy, but I'm no liar."

Bryan points at the front door, and Kurtis leaves. I think it's time for me to go, too. My medicine is at home, and something tells me I need to take an extra dose when I get back to my mom's house. I don't need to stay for the fireworks. That was enough excitement for me.

~ 12 ~
All Hail the Queen

I remember I remember when I lost my mind /
There was something so pleasant about that place.

—GNARLS BARKLEY

After last week's block party, it's been pretty quiet around Mama's house. I guess going buck wild on my uncle Kurtis was the right thing to do. Mama told him to be out weeks ago, and because she's not here, he thinks he can take advantage of the situation. Daddy might not want to check his ass, but I don't care. I've had enough of people taking my kindness for weakness and that goes for Mama's, too.

With the cotillion tomorrow evening, I have a lot of work to do between now and then. Not only do I have to get my nails done and pick up other last-minute necessities, but I also have to fill a few clients' orders and drop them off at Netta's shop before heading over to Nigel's house for my final fitting. Mrs. Esop wants to make sure the shoes, dress, and jewelry are all in accord before the big night. I feel like I'm getting married, the way she's fussing around like the mother of the bride. The amount of money Mrs. Esop's already spent is really ridiculous. I'm just glad I didn't have to come out of pocket for a damned thing, because I don't have it like that even if I am making a killing off braiding hair this summer.

I've been averaging three heads a day, and depending on the style, I usually end up with at least a hundred dollars in my pocket. That might be considered small cheddar to Nigel and Rah, who can make that in one sale if the herb is superb, but I'm proud of my hard-earned money. Mama would be pleased with how I'm handling my earnings. I've saved almost every dime for the last month, and my bank account is stacking high. I do miss working at Netta's, though. I can't wait until Mama and Netta both return from their vacation and we can get back to normal. Without them my days don't have the same flavor or balance. I need the elder wisdom only they can give. The shop doesn't even feel the same.

"Well, well, well. Look what the cat dragged in," Rita says, clamping the flat iron loudly before running it through the client's hair. The smell of freshly pressed hair and honey shampoo fills the warm air in the quaint shop.

"Good afternoon, Miss Rita," I say as she buzzes me in. I set the large bag full of creams, sprays, and other beauty products Mama had me fill for the shop down on the table next to the front door. Our clients come here to pick up their regular regimens, and I'm responsible for maintaining the clients' boxes and other supplies for the shop. I don't get to help with the clients' heads anymore until Mama and Netta return. I'm under strict supervision by my godmother and grandmother all of the time.

"Is that little Jayd?" Miss Celia asks from the washbowl area. I greet the three customers sitting under the driers, recognizing two of them. The other lady is new to me. "If so, please tell her to wash these towels and stack us some new ones in here." Work, work, work. It's a wonder I have a social life at all, although with my boyfriend having big fun in London, I have more time on my hands than usual.

"Yes, ma'am," I say, heading to the back with my loot. It's already after four. By the time I finish my work here, it'll be the early evening. I should've eaten something before getting here, but I didn't think about it until now. Hopefully my friends will have food at the session when I get there. We're having it at Nigel's house tonight, which is convenient for me. I have to try on my dress per Mrs. Esop's insistence. It's all good as long as we can kick it after.

I want to talk to Rita and Celia so bad about their beef with Mama, but we've kept a safe distance for the past few weeks. I don't know if Mama gave them the same directions she gave me. Other than shop business, we don't chat. I know Netta will give me the lowdown when she returns. Mama can't keep my godmother from talking to me. Until then, I'll do my work and enjoy the extra time to chill with my crew.

Most of my crew's already at Nigel's pad, ready to get this party started. Mickey and Nellie arrived a few moments before me, and Rah had to run an errand but will be here shortly. Tomorrow's the ball, and Nigel and I will be tied up all evening at some fancy hotel in Sherman Oaks. I've never been to the valley before, and from what I've heard, I'm not missing much.

"What's Nickey doing here? I thought the shorties were staying at home tonight?" Nigel asks, holding the front door open for us.

"I can't get anybody to watch this baby at night with my mama and daddy both working double shifts," Mickey says, throwing down her diaper bag and purse onto the couch. She looks worn out and so does Nickey.

"This baby?" I repeat, putting my purse down next to hers. Mickey's language toward her daughter has been growing more distant lately. I replaced all of the pills with the identical but healthy tablets Dr. Whitmore prescribed last week. I hope she didn't stop taking them after her tense conversation with Misty last weekend. Mickey needs to take them to reverse the damage that's already been done.

"How are we supposed to smoke with a baby in the room?" Nigel asks, concerned about his freedom once his parents leave for the night. They always have some gathering to attend. I've never known two more socially busy people than the Esops. After spending time with Mrs. Esop on a social level, I can see why Nigel needs a break: His mom's one intense sistah.

"When has a baby ever stopped people from kicking it how they want?" Mickey says, handing me the baby.

I'm glad to hold her. She's the plumpest two-month-old I've ever seen. I hate to say it, but I know it's the formula her mama's giving her. I wish Mickey would've breast-fed for a little longer. Mama said some milk is better than nothing. Thank God Nickey's a strong little girl. She has to be to have a mother like Mickey.

"I'm just tired of changing her and carrying her and feeding her," Mickey says, straightening her tube top and smoothing down her short jean skirt.

"Mickey, why don't you ask Nickey's aunts to watch her? I'm sure they would love to get to know their niece," I say, reminding her that Tre's family is grieving the loss of their brother. Nickey's presence might be just what they need to heal from the tragic shooting. No mater how unwelcoming Brandy was at the block party, once she realizes Mickey's not asking for a dime and that Nickey's indeed Tre's daughter, hopefully she'll open up a bit. Besides, I think once Brandy's own baby is born, her attitude toward Nickey will change.

"And why don't you mind your own business?"

Mickey's got one more time to snap at me before my forgiveness runs out.

"Damn, Mickey. Jayd's just trying to help," Nigel says, having my back as always, officially pissing Mickey off.

"Y'all are enjoying rehearsing for the ball, huh?" Mickey says, taking a stance too familiar to Sandy's for my taste. "Pretending you're a couple and shit."

Nigel and I both choose to ignore our girl's jealous comment for the sake of the baby in the room. Otherwise, I'd tear into her like a pit bull after a Chihuahua.

"I can't speak for Jayd, but I can think of a million places I'd rather be than the hot-ass valley on a Saturday night."

I'm with Nigel. This ball's taken up too much of my time as it is.

"Jayd, why don't you just ask Rah to be your escort? He's closer to being your man than Nigel is," Nellie asks, coming into the den from the kitchen with a glass of sparkling water.

She likes coming over here and pretending to be the lady of the house, unlike at Chance's crib. She can barely move from room to room without looking over her shoulder to see if Mrs. Carmichael's watching her. Chance's mom will never like Nellie for her son.

"I wish I could," I say, eyeing the white gown hanging on the back of the den door, afraid to touch it too much. The last thing I want to do is mess up this dress. "Mrs. Esop's got full rein over my wardrobe and my date. She's already made it very clear that Rah's a no-no. She wants me on her son's arm—no other dudes allowed." Mrs. Esop has even suggested hairstyles, like I need help in that department. I'm already going crazy enough as it is. The last thing I need is someone up in my head. Mama would kill me if I let anyone other than her, Netta, or my mom touch my crown.

"Oh, Jayd," Mrs. Esop says, walking in on our private conversation, but we can't say too much. This is her house even if we're beginning a session.

"I know, right? Isn't she going to make a lovely bride?" Nellie asks, obviously joking, but Mickey takes it to heart.

With Nigel's tux hanging on the back of the closet door next to my dress, it does look like somebody's getting married.

"It's a stupid ball, Nellie. Not a wedding." Mickey shoots our girl a look while Mrs. Esop ignores the jealous outburst.

I already know it's her secret wish for Nigel and I to be together, but that'll never happen. I've known Nigel since junior high, and we've always liked each other in a brother / sister kind of way—nothing more. Nellie's on the outs with Chance. Maybe Mrs. Esop can turn her sights toward Nellie and Nigel hooking up if he and Mickey don't make it. Nellie still has the hots for Nigel no matter what she says, and Mickey's bitchiness just might turn Nigel off for good. I really don't care either way. As long as they take care of Nickey, I'm good.

"Why don't you try it on, sweetie?" Mrs. Esop says, gesturing upstairs. "Let's make sure the tailor didn't miss anything."

Mickey glares at Mrs. Esop and then at me, feeling defeated. Nellie excitedly takes the gown down and cradles it across her arms in true bridesmaid fashion. She's more excited about the ball than I am. I have to admit, I am starting to get little butterflies in my stomach. I can't believe it's finally here. All of the training and rehearsals to come out to a society I'm not even a part of seemed ridiculous at first, but now I'm ready to show off all of my hard work.

"Yes, ma'am," I say, taking the dress into my arms and heading to the bathroom in the guest bedroom upstairs for more privacy.

"Here, Jayd. Take the shoes with you." Mrs. Esop directs Nellie to hand her the silver box on the den floor and hands it to me. "Let us know if you need any help."

"I think I can handle it." I walk into the immaculate bathroom and lock the door. Knowing Mrs. Esop, she'll want to make sure I'm wearing the right underwear, which she also provided. I didn't wear a strapless bra today, but what I'm working with will have to do.

"Everything all right in there?" Mrs. Esop asks a few minutes later, knocking on the door.

I've barely had time to slip out of my short jumpsuit. "Yes, I'm fine." I work my way into the form-fitting gown, admiring the finished product. It's stunning. I open the door, allowing everyone to take in the sight. They couldn't wait for me to come downstairs.

"Oh my, Jayd. You look gorgeous," Mrs. Esop says, near tears.

I walk across the hall into Nigel's room to look at my reflection, seeing what they all see: a true lady coming out of my teenaged self. I wish Mr. Adewale could see me now. I also wish Jeremy were here to celebrate this night with me. But I'll see him soon enough. He'll be home by the end of the month in time to celebrate his birthday.

"Damn, girl, you clean up nice," Nigel says, checking me out. That's the same look he had on his face the first time he saw me in my mom's cream suit at the first debutante tea. "That dress looks good on you."

"Doesn't my son have excellent taste most of the time?" Mrs. Esop says, hesitating slightly, watching Mickey's scowl deepen as she walks out of the room.

The last thing I want to do is make my girl feel any worse than she already does. It must be hard to watch Nigel's mom and I together, not to mention Nigel complimenting me on a dress his mother bought when she doesn't even respect Mickey enough to acknowledge her when she's in the room.

"Mom, be nice," Nigel says, feeling Mickey's heat. "She just had a baby, for God's sake."

I smile at my boy defending our girl against his mother. That's the way it's supposed to be. Mickey and Nigel's love has been passionate during their short, tumultuous relationship. Even now Mickey's trying to get back in tip-top shape because she thinks it'll make her man happy. But I think Nigel would like Mickey no matter how much she weighed. He just loves him some her and vice versa.

"Yes, and must I remind you that it's not your baby?" Mrs. Esop says, fidgeting with her couture investment. "Why is the baby even here?" Mrs. Esop looks disgusted by her son's choice in a companion and makes it known every chance she gets.

"Where else is she supposed to go? I told you, Mom. I'm the only daddy Nickey's got, and I intend on doing right by her and her mother."

Mrs. Esop eyes her son in the mirror's reflection with a look of complete bewilderment. Seeing that this argument is going nowhere productive, she smiles and changes the subject. "So, we need to make sure we have the walk down. Let me see you escort your date in her stunning gown, Nigel." Mrs. Esop ushers me to take Nigel's arm as we've practiced at least a hundred times. I never thought I'd be ballroom dancing with anyone, especially not Nigel.

"Oh, you two look lovely. Simply stunning," Mrs. Esop says, clasping her hands over her mouth in the most dramatic fashion ever.

"Here you go," Mickey says in the hallway, trying to soothe a crying Nickey. She steps into the doorway, taking in the sight of her man and me arm in arm. Mickey walks back into the room with a fresh bottle for Nickey's dinner, hoping the warm fake milk will put her to sleep for the night. The two-month-old is restless in her mother's arms, obviously overtired. I gave her a book on healthy sleep habits for children, but I doubt Mickey read it. If it's not a fashion, hair, or music magazine, she's not too interested in reading.

Nickey hungrily gulps down the concoction while Mickey eyes my outfit, taking in the bright, white sight.

"It is a pretty dress," Mickey says, walking over to get a better look at the exquisite detail. Mrs. Esop didn't spare any expense.

"Isn't it magnificent?" Nellie says, rubbing salt in Mickey's wounded ego. Nellie gets too enveloped in fashion for her own good. Can't she tell Mickey's hurting?

"Here, baby," Mickey says, attempting to feed Nickey the rest of her dinner, but the baby's still restless in her mother's arms. Mickey shakes the bottle vigorously, causing the nipple to fly off, spilling the thick baby formula all over my formerly immaculate gown. Nickey screams loudly and so does my benefactor.

"Damn it!" Mrs. Esop yells, coming to my aid. I've never heard her cuss before. If Mickey wasn't healing from Misty's influence, I'd whip her ass with that bottle. She looks sorry and completely shocked by the mishap. Maybe it was just an accident, but I'm sure she got some pleasure out of ruining my dress.

Nellie runs inside the bathroom to grab towels while Mrs. Esop guides me toward the door.

"Damn," Nigel exclaims, wiping the small amount of foul-smelling liquid from his Lakers jersey. "This is going to be hard to get out."

Mickey's frozen in place, holding an empty bottle and a screaming baby.

"You did that on purpose," Mrs. Esop snarls at Mickey. "Jayd, take the dress off. We have to get it to the cleaners, now. And you, out," she says to a now-sobbing Mickey. I feel bad for my girl.

"I'm sorry, Mrs. Esop. It was an accident, I swear," Mickey says, looking confused. She doesn't know whether to try and clean up the mess she's made, soothe her baby, or leave as instructed.

"Of course it was, dear. Just like that baby you're holding,"

Mrs. Esop says, causing more tears to fall from Mickey's eyes. Thank goodness for waterproof mascara. Otherwise, Mickey could give Erica Kane a run for her money.

"Okay, Mom, that was completely uncalled for," Nigel says, taking Nickey from her mother's arms, attempting to calm both his girls.

"The hell it is, Nigel. This girl is a walking disaster, and I'll be so glad when you finally wake up and snap out of it," Mrs. Esop says, frantically dialing her cell and directing me back into the guest bathroom to change out of my wet dress. "Call the maid in here to clean this mess up and prepare Jayd's dress for the cleaners. I'm calling them now to see if they can come pick up this 'accident' before it's too late."

Completely unremorseful, Mrs. Esop storms out of the room as I exit the bathroom with my devastated dress in tow. I hope it can be cleaned by tomorrow. It would be a shame to let such a beautiful gown go to waste.

"Nigel, is your mother up there?" Mr. Esop yells from downstairs. "If she is, tell her we have to go."

"I'm coming, dear," she yells, recomposing herself.

"What's everyone doing up here?" Mr. Esop asks. When he reaches the top of the stairs and sees the mess, he understands.

"Jayd, we're meeting here promptly at ten o'clock tomorrow morning to prepare. Please be on time," Mrs. Esop says. She gives Mickey one final glare before following her husband out, both of them dressed to kill.

"Let's get this party started," Mickey says, stepping back into Nigel's room like nothing just happened. She takes the blunt out of the box under the bed and attempts to light it, forgetting her daughter's lying on the futon next to her almost asleep. She's really gone off the deep end, and it's not cute.

"Mickey, the baby," Nigel says, taking the filled cigar and

lighter from her. Nigel finally got her calmed down, but she probably needs more to eat before she's out for the night. I guess her pacifier will do for now.

"Why you tripping?" Mickey asks, snatching the items back and causing Nickey to stir in her sleep. No wonder the child doesn't sleep through the night. She's too nervous with all the drama constantly going on around her, courtesy of her selfish mother. "You never check Rah for smoking around his daughter."

"That's because I never do," Rah says, entering the room and adding his two cents.

Oh, shit, Mickey's about to really go off. I'd better rescue my goddaughter before she ends up falling off the futon.

"Whatever, nigga. I know you've smoked around that baby at some point." Mickey tries to reclaim the blunt, but Nigel's not having it.

"No, I haven't, mostly because my baby just came into my life nine months ago. And it's unhealthy for any kid to be around smoke, especially a baby."

Feeling outnumbered, Mickey looks around at her friends, pissed as hell. I pick up Nickey and cradle her in my arms, ready to transfer her to the blankets I've laid out for her on the plush carpet downstairs. She would sleep like an angel if her mama would chillax. I can remember arguments my parents had when I was a baby, and I know Nickey's feeling the same uneasiness even in her sleep.

"Maybe we should have a session where no one smokes," Nellie says, causing Rah, Nigel, and Mickey to eye her like she's lost her mind. If Chance were here, he'd give his estranged girlfriend the same blank stare.

"Or we can just smoke up here while y'all head downstairs where the pizzas and movies are waiting. Let's hit it, man," Rah says.

Nellie and I head out, leaving the smokers behind. I lay

Nickey facedown on the blanket. Mama says babies sleep better on their stomachs no matter what conventional wisdom says.

"What are we watching?" I ask Nellie, who sits on the couch. She and Mickey picked up the movies on their way here. I'm surprised she's here, but I guess without her man to drive her around, Mickey's back to being her main chauffeur. I know none of her white friends are driving to Compton to pick her bougie ass up.

"I'm not sure," Nellie says, retrieving a nail file from her Louis Vuitton bag. "I stayed in the car with the baby while Mickey went into Blockbuster."

"That's cool. I'm more concerned about the food anyway." Hopefully we'll all relax after we eat and get through the first flick. After all of that unexpected excitement, we need to vibe out.

The first movie was just what we needed to escape. There's nothing like watching Jason Bourne's fine self escape death multiple times. But if our girl doesn't slow down with the alcohol, she might not be so lucky.

"Mickey, haven't you had enough to drink?" I say, reaching for the bottle of liquor, but Mickey's determined to show her ass today—red G-string and all.

"Jayd, you ain't nobody's mama up in here, especially not mine," she says, taking the half bottle of expensive liquor straight to the head. I haven't seen my girl this far gone in a long, long time. The one good thing about her teenaged pregnancy was that it stopped her from drinking, which apparently she missed.

"Look, it's the Pussycat Dolls," Chance says, walking through the back door and scaring the shit out of us all. "What up, folks?"

"Damn, nigga. Announce yourself before you walk through

open doors," Mickey says, nearly spitting the brown liquor out on the white carpet. If she did, that would truly be her ass. Nellie and I look at our inebriated homegirl and shake our heads.

"Chance, I'm so glad you're back," I say, giving my boy a bear hug, damn his testy soon-to-be-ex-girlfriend. Nellie doesn't even look happy to see him. What a shame she doesn't know what she's got in Chance.

"What did I tell you about that, Jayd? It's Chase," Chance says, hugging me back. We used to hug like this all the time before he and Nellie started dating. Now, for jealousy sake, we stick to the simple quick hug you give acquaintances. Nellie's a trip. She acts like she doesn't want her man, but let another sister give him some attention and she's all over him like white on rice.

"Well, look who decided to show up," Nigel says, walking down the stairs by twos, smiling and reeking of herb smoke.

I guess Rah's still getting his fix.

"Ah, man, you know I couldn't miss a session. I just landed an hour ago," Chance says, giving his boy a one-armed hug.

"How'd you know about our session?" I ask. I'm all for surprises, but this was a big one.

"You know I had to holla at my boy and let him know I was on my way home," Chance says, playfully punching Nigel in the chest.

I guess guys have their secrets, too.

"How was your trip?" Nellie asks, the first thing she's said to her boyfriend since he walked in. Trust, if Jeremy walked through the door, I'd be all over my man. He doesn't get back for a couple of weeks, and like a clock on the wall, I'm counting the minutes until our reunion.

"It was great," Chance says, overly excited even if Nellie's curiosity is insincere. She looks like she wants to go off on him she's so angry. I can feel her heat from across the room. "Man, I've got about a hundred cousins, aunties and uncles, nieces and nephews. It's awesome and they all welcomed me with open arms," he says, getting out his new iPhone to show us the photos. I'm happy for our boy. There's nothing like family, even if they can work a nerve like no other.

"Nobody gives a damn about your newfound relatives, Orphan Annie," Nellie says, sounding as bitter as Mickey can get, who is still sipping on her syrup by the bar. When Nigel's parents get home, they're going to be pissed about their liquor cabinet being lighter than when they left a few hours ago. And they'll be even more pissed when they find out who did it.

"What did you just say to me?" Chance asks, looking like he's ready to slap some sense into Nellie, who looks ready to throw a couple of blows herself.

Oh, shit, it's about to be on and cracking in Lafayette Square this evening.

"You heard me," Nellie says, rising from her seat and walking over to Chance, finally greeting her man even if it's not as warm and fuzzy as it should be. "You act like we're supposed to really care about your Southern roots when you deserted us without any notice."

By "us" she means *her* because I don't feel that way, and I think it's safe to say that the rest of our crew doesn't feel that way, either. I know Alia missed him terribly. She's asked about him every day during summer school.

"Well hello to you, too, baby," Chance says, attempting to give his girl a hug and chill her out, but it's no use. Nellie's tripping and we're all here to witness her fall.

"Don't baby me," Nellie says, pushing his arms down. "You left me, Chance. And I'm over it."

"What's that supposed to mean?" Chance asks, putting his

phone back in his jean pocket and turning his full attention to his enraged girlfriend.

I guess the family photos will have to wait. I personally can't wait to see what his birth family looks like, but right now I think we're all more interested to see where this argument leads.

"It means that I've had enough of your soul searching. You found your blackness and I'm happy for you, but I can't do this anymore."

Rah comes down the stairs, lit as all outside and apparently confused by the drama unfolding in the living room. I can hear Nickey stirring in her sleep from her cozy spot. But like Mickey so eloquently stated, I'm nobody's mama. I might be the only one able to take care of the baby in a minute the way this evening's turning out, and I for one am tired of babysitting. I love my goddaughters, but I don't work for free.

"So, what, are you calling it?" Chance asks, all of us waiting for the answer.

Is this finally the end of Nellie and Chance? Mickey breaks the still air with a belch loud enough for the ancestors in heaven to hear.

"Excuse me," she says, hitting her chest to make sure it's all out. If Mrs. Esop could see her now.

"That was real ladylike, babe," Nigel says, smiling at his girl.

Aren't they a perfect pair? Chance hasn't moved an inch and neither has Nellie. She'd better seriously think about what she's doing letting him go. Chance treats her like a queen, and she's not the easiest chick to deal with, which says a lot about Chance's patience. I never understood why they were together in the first place, but they are and I've learned to deal with it.

"I'm out," Nellie says, going nowhere fast. She rode with Mickey, and unless Chance takes her back home, she's out of a ride. Mickey's in no state to drive anyone anywhere, and I'm not about to waste my precious gas taking her ass home, so she needs to get over herself and be happy for Chance. Is that really so impossible to do?

"Where are you going?" Chance asks, following the drama queen out of the living room and into the foyer. "We're in the middle of a conversation. You're just going to walk away?" Nellie keeps walking and Chance follows. "Real mature, Nellie. Real mature."

"Whatever," Nellie says, taking her purse and exiting the house without saying good-bye to any of us.

Why is she so upset, and where is Nellie going with no car and a serious aversion to public transportation?

"Damn, y'all are really tripping," Mickey slurs, barely able to stand up. She needs to sit her drunk ass down somewhere before she passes out. "It's not like Chance knows about David. Oops," Mickey says, covering her mouth for letting that secret slip out.

Chance looks at Mickey and back down to Nellie, who stops in her tracks. If her dark brown skin weren't so perfectly kissed by the summer sun, I'm sure we would all see just how red her cheeks are from being busted.

"David? Who the hell is David?" Chance asks, feeling out of the loop. He walks out of the door and down the steps to Nellie in the driveway. Damn, why did Mickey have to get drunk and open her big mouth? The last thing we need is our crew falling apart again. I don't know if I can fix this mess, mainly because I don't know anything about this mystery guy. Who knew Nellie had it in her to cheat?

"He's a friend from church," Nellie says, crossing her arms in quiet indignation like she has nothing to be sorry about.

Her phone buzzes in her hand, and Chance snatches it up and reads the text aloud.

" 'See you at Popeyes on Crenshaw in five. David,' " Chance says, tossing the phone back at Nellie. Well I guess she does have a ride after all. "For real, Nellie? You're cheating on me with some dude you met at church?"

"I'm not cheating on you," Nellie says, looking down at the phone. "And like I said, I've had it. I don't owe you an explanation, especially since you weren't here to take care of me like a good man would."

"A good man? Bitch, please," Chance says, calling Nellie out of her name for the first time ever. There was a time when he would have slapped anyone who dared disrespect his queen, but she's been officially dethroned and we're all present to witness it. "Let your new nigga know I said good luck and good riddance," Chance says, waving bye to Nellie and walking back inside the house, slamming the door. That was cold, even for this messed-up situation.

I walk back inside to grab my purse. Chance heads upstairs to blow off some steam, and our boys are right behind him. They've been where he is on more than one occasion, and I know they can't talk freely among us girls. I look back at Mickey, who's finally laid out on the couch. I turn around and head back outside to check on Nellie, who's halfway up the block by the time I catch up to her.

"Nellie, wait up," I say, running to my girl. Damn she walks fast. Nellie's crying and looks like she wants to be alone, but I can't leave my girl hanging even if this ordeal is her own damned fault.

"Jayd, we had sex. I'm deflowered and I gave it up to the wrong person. What am I supposed to do now? No one will want me all used," Nellie says, crying into her soaked tissue.

I wish I had a napkin or something to offer my girl, because she's crying the ugly cry, for real. I would ask her if she's on her period, but I don't think it would go over too well.

"Nellie, this isn't a sixties sitcom," I say. "People don't get 'deflowered' anymore. And it could have been much worse. Chance isn't a bad guy."

"He's not the same guy, Jayd. If I wanted to be with a confused black boy, I'd be with Mickey's man."

We continue walking down the block, turning on the main street at the corner.

"So David is your rebound guy?" I ask. The smell of chicken and biscuits permeates the air, drawing us closer to our destination.

"No. David's a good guy from the summer Bible institute at my church. And he's a good listener. David's always there for me, and he makes time for the important things."

"Look, Nellie," I say, attempting to reason with her. "I know it's been hard on you with cheer tryouts and Nickey being born, but breaking up with Chance isn't a good thing."

"He left me, Jayd. We slept together the night before, and he left me without a word. How could he do me like that?"

"Nellie, talk to him. Tell Chance how you feel," I plead as we enter the bustling lot. The drive-through line is packed and nearly every spot is taken.

"He doesn't want to hear it. All he cares about is his family reunion."

A guy I assume to be this David character pulls into the Popeyes parking lot looking like the sucker he is, preying on someone else's girl. Nellie's feeling vulnerable, making her easy to manipulate. I don't need to jump into David's mind to see his true intentions: They're written all over his smiling face.

"David. Thank God," Nellie says, quickly walking up to his

white Ford Focus. If there's such a thing as a virgin mobile, this must be it. "Let's get out of here. I'm starving."

So am I and as fate would have it, I'm in the parking lot of one of my favorite chicken spots. I'll treat the rest of my crew to a family meal, and we can catch up once the dudes are finished bonding.

When I make it back to Nigel's house, Nickey Shantae's wide awake and her mother's passed out on the couch. The menfolk are still upstairs. I guess it's just her and me. I could use a nap, too. I can't believe this time tomorrow I'll be stepping out in style for the cotillion. I'm not sure if I can stand being in the ball with all of the heffas I have to deal with, but I'm glad after tomorrow it'll all finally be over. My only commitment outside of work is cheer practice and the last month of summer school. Other than that, my time is mine and I can't wait for freedom to ring loud and clear. Then maybe I can enjoy the rest of my summer in peace.

~ 13 ~
A Midsummer's Nightmare

But at best a dream is just a fantasy /
When I touch his hand he'll disappear.

—Randy Crawford with Joe Sample

Motion. The fast pace of my bare feet takes me off guard. It's a hot night, but darkness is darkness and I'm not exactly comfortable walking on the ground with no protection. The green foliage is thick, and the jungle ahead looks even more dense than the bush hitting me in the face as I move along the path. Someone's clearing the way for me to only God knows where. I want to stop from exhaustion and fear, but something tells me to keep going.

"Watch your step," the voice says through the trees. I clear the brush, the smell of salt water tickling my nose. She's already at the shore draped in a white cloth: Only her green eyes are visible through the narrow slits in her veil.

"Maman?" I ask, uncertain of the woman's identity. Caution is necessary because I've been tricked many times before.

"Oui, ma petite," my great-grandmother answers in one of her native tongues. She reaches her hands toward me, and I move in her direction. I wish I spoke French fluently, but even in my dreams that's not the case.

"Where are we?" It looks like a deserted island somewhere in the Caribbean I've seen on the Travel Channel, but this ocean feels more familiar.

"Jayd, are you feeling okay?" Maman asks, feeling my forehead with the back of her hand. "It's the night of your wedding and now you want to have a meltdown. We're home, girl." My wedding? Oh, Lord, not again. The last time I dreamed about getting married, it was a shotgun wedding to Rah. "Let's get started. We don't have all night."

I carry the remaining bags to the blanket Maman's laid out on the white sand. I follow suit, emptying each of the bags' contents out and taking note. Our spirit tools haven't changed much since Maman's time.

"The spirit book," I say, holding the ancient text in my hands. This is the first time it's appeared in one of my dreams.

"We're going to need it tonight more than ever." Maman looks pleased with my affinity for the leather-bound book.

I flip through the pages, not expecting the last page to be up-to-date, but it is. This ritual is happening in the present day—highly unusual for a dream with Maman in it.

"You know it's your job as the youngest in the lineage to protect the book, Jayd," Maman says, taking the text and setting it down on the blanket beside my foot. She directs me to sit down, and I'm glad to rest. It feels like we've been walking all night.

"Yes, ma'am, I do. And I'll do my best to take care of it," I say, massaging my wounded toes. The cut is healing, but I still remember the pain.

"I know you will. It's a huge responsibility, taking on your dreams the way they were born to function." Maman takes several of the ingredients and places them in a cast-iron cauldron to cook over the bonfire burning nearby. "We are walking shrines to the ancestors and orishas, Jayd. We don't exist solely for our own purpose. Sometimes you're the only book people will read."

"Don't we have the right to choose our own paths?" I had

this same conversation with Mama, and I have a feeling Maman's in full agreement with her daughter on this subject.

"Of course you do, as long as you acknowledge that a part of your destiny is living for those who came before you," Maman says, reiterating Mama's lesson. "The only way to make sure you don't go crazy is to fully submit to your powers, and that starts with becoming a bride."

Maman pours extra-large containers of molasses, honey, and brown sugar into the heavy pot, the fire rising with each addition.

"Who do I have to marry?" I ask, watching Maman work.

"It's not as important who you marry as much as that he has all of the qualities you ask for."

My mom said something similar to me after my last meeting with Keenan. Being specific is very important when petitioning the universe.

"You know that I conjured up your great-grandfather. I wasn't clear enough about what I wanted and ended up with a damned fool," Maman says, sniffing the thick brew as she continues stirring. "Add more vinegar. We don't want him to be too sweet." Maman brings the large wooden spoon to her lips to taste the concoction.

"What do you mean conjured?" I ask, obediently tasting the steaming liquid. It's bitter all right: too bitter if you ask me.

"I mean I made my man just like I'm making yours. And this time we're going to get it right." Maman finishes stirring, satisfied with her work. She takes a dipping spoon from one of the bags, fills it with the potion, and hands it to me to drink. "Three spoonfuls and be very precise with your desires as you swallow each serving. This is your life mate we're summoning. The devil's literally in the details."

I take the first spoonful, wincing at the hot, bitter brew going down my throat and immediately feel different. I take two more as directed, feeling my head lighten as I surrender to the vision.

"Jayd, let go."

I lie down on the sheet and let the dream take over my mind, seeing my image of a perfect man come forth. This bright ball of light must be my soul mate, but it has no shape or form: I thought I was more specific than that.

"It's the spirit that matters most, not the actual physical appearance." Maman's eyes begin to glow as she kneels by my side, her focus on our creation. "He's yours," Maman says, blowing the spirit my way. I open my arms, welcoming the male energy within my reach. Before my man is able to fully manifest, a female form emerges from the ocean, interrupting our nuptials.

"You!" Maman cries. "You won't ruin another one of my girls. I won't let you."

Esmeralda flies out of the water, morphing into a crow as she touches down on the sand.

"Who's going to stop me?" Esmeralda squawks, her long, black wings fully spanned. "The little girl you're trying to pass off as a bride? I could have her for lunch if I wanted."

"She's not alone," Maman says, also shifting her form to a ball of light. "Jayd is all of us combined in one: your worst nightmare."

My spouse-to-be disappears into the dark sky, and Esmeralda looks pleased.

"Your potions are weak! You and your precious descendants are worthless, Marie," Esmeralda says, her feathers rustling in the sea breeze.

Maman's energy circles my head three times before landing on top. She enters my skull, cutting me as she takes over my consciousness.

* * *

"Ahhh!" I scream, holding on to the top of my head. I could've sworn there was some blood shed, but my fingers are dry. Luckily I didn't wake anyone up with my loud mouth. Nickey's sound asleep in the same spot on the futon I placed her last night, and the rest of my friends are passed out in various positions around Nigel's room. My dreams have grown in intensity. I should've brought Dr. Whitmore's herbs with me last night, but I didn't know I wouldn't return home to take my nightly dose.

The sun's up and I doubt if I can go back to sleep. I need something cold to drink to shake off that nightmare. I step over my sleeping friends and carefully open Nigel's bedroom door. I don't want to disturb anyone with my early morning thirst. When I make it downstairs, I see Mrs. Esop in the kitchen fully dressed. From her outfit, I can tell she's just getting in from playing tennis.

"Oh, Jayd, good. You're here early. I knew you'd eventually get excited about the ball this evening," Mrs. Esop says, not realizing I never left her house from yesterday afternoon. Do I always look this undone to her? "We need to get you fitted again for your gown. Sometimes the cleaners can unknowingly shrink a dress. If that's the case, you'll have to fast all day long from both solids and liquids." This chick is tripping if she thinks I'm going all day without eating to fit into a damn gown no matter how gorgeous it is. I'd rather wear something else than starve myself for anyone.

I step into the bathroom off the kitchen near the laundry room and change into the cleaned white silk dress, thankful it fits even if it is a bit tighter than it was yesterday. I think it was the fried chicken, red beans and rice, and biscuits I threw down for dinner last night, not to mention the pizza I had as an appetizer. I don't regret a single bite, but I can't say the same thing for Nigel's mom, who looks at the snug fit, unpleased.

"Make sure you eat nothing, Jayd. Not a thing. And I'll have the maid make you some tea that should help relieve some of that bloating around your stomach." Did she just insult me? If she wasn't my homeboy's mama, I might have to have some words with her no matter how old she is. "Now, get some rest. We're going to rehearse in an hour. By then the makeup artist and hairstylist should be here. Perhaps I should call the seamstress, too. Maybe she can let the gown out a bit."

"Oh, ma'am. I can't let anyone touch my head," I say, unconsciously feeling my wavy locks. After that crazy dream, I'm surprised I'm as cognizant as I am. I took my cornrows out yesterday and planned on doing my hair this morning, but that didn't happen. I can still get it done if I get home soon and shake this feeling.

"That's nonsense, Jayd," Mrs. Esop says, dismissing my very serious objection with the wave of her diamond-studded hand. Can a sistah get one of those rings? "I told you there would be none of that hoodoo mess in this house. This is the house of the Lord, and my hairdresser is an upstanding woman and a longtime friend." Still not feeling me, she takes the dress and begins to walk out of the room, but I can't let her win this one. I know my limits, and they begin and end with me not removing my bracelets or allowing anyone else to touch my hair.

"It's not hoodoo, it's voodoo," I say, following Mrs. Esop, who halts her trek to hear me out, mostly amazed that I'm further contesting the issue. Any other sistah would be thrilled with a free makeover, but I'm not just another girl. I'm a priestess in training, and I have to hold my ground on this issue. "And I do my own hair—no exceptions."

"Yes, Jayd. I'm aware of what you and the women in your family practice. And I'm also aware of your little hair business. Cute, but not proper for this event. Please trust me and let this go. We don't have time to argue about this today, young lady." Mrs. Esop's used to having her way, but not this time.

"You're right: There's no argument. I'm good at what I do, and I'm doing my own hair."

Mrs. Esop stops drinking her orange juice and looks at me like I've lost my mind.

"You ungrateful little girl!" Mrs. Esop yells. "You will get your hair and makeup done by the stylist I hired—end of discussion."

Damn, she can get live when she wants to. Nigel comes downstairs, rubbing the sleep out of his eyes. Mickey also emerges with Nickey on her hip, really setting Mrs. Esop off.

"What the hell is she doing here? I told you about them spending the night in my house, Nigel," Mrs. Esop says. She doesn't need any more reasons to go off, but she's got two more right in front of her. My head's still throbbing from the cut in my dream, and I need to calm down.

"Your house? Last time I checked, everything was in Dad's name," Nigel says, obviously still feeling high from the session last night to make that comment to his mother. He and Mickey look like they just crawled out of a hole filled with alcohol and ashtrays. Yuck. Chance and Rah are still upstairs knocked out. But if Mrs. Esop's yelling gets any louder, they'll be up like the rest of us in no time.

"This is an absolute nightmare!" Mrs. Esop shouts, tossing a kitchen towel at her son. "How dare you speak to me like that? This is what I'm talking about, little girl," she says, pointing at Mickey. "You are a horrible, manipulative influence on my son. Nigel, mark my words, this tramp will be your ruin."

"What have I told you about talking to Mickey like that, Mom?" Nigel says.

Rah and Chance, now awake, stop in the middle of the staircase, not wanting to get too close to the action in case something heavier gets tossed, and I don't blame them. I need to get out of this dress before we have a repeat of yesterday's tragic events.

"We don't have time for this, Nigel," Mrs. Esop says. "Jayd, go change. Nigel, take a shower and fix yourself up. We have to be at the hotel by noon for the final dress rehearsal."

"Forget the ball," Nigel says, taking Nickey from her mother and walking out of the kitchen. "I'm going over to Rah's. Come on, Mickey."

Mrs. Esop's jaw drops and I take a step back; she's about to blow.

"Nigel, if you walk out that door with that baby, don't you even think about coming back."

I know her threat is empty, but Nigel's weighing all of his options and chooses the one unexpected.

"Fine," Nigel says, his hot head unwavering.

Mama says we should never make decisions when our emotions are on high, and Nigel's definitely off the radar with his this morning.

"You can't do this to me!" Mrs. Esop screams after her only son, who's already upstairs. "Nigel!"

It's no use attempting to reason with him once he gets like this. I look around the nice home, thinking about how perfect the Esopses' life appears from the outside. But their entire house of cards has fallen with their baby boy stepping out on his own.

"Don't worry, Jayd. One of the fraternity brothers will escort you this evening," Mrs. Esop says, moving right along, even if her face has aged ten years in the past few minutes. First her daughter leaves, now Nigel. I guess this is how Mama felt when my mom, my aunt, and then I moved out prematurely. "Everything will be okay." I think she's talking more to herself than to me, but I feel her. Everything will be okay if we could just make it through the rest of the day.

Once I escaped Mrs. Esop's clutches this morning, I returned to my mom's apartment, where I showered and did my hair before heading back to Lafayette Square. It's been a day with Mrs. Esop's emotions raging out of control. At least she was too distracted by her son's exodus to care about my hair. I let her artist do my makeup, but there was no way I was letting her get up in my head. She actually could have used my skills, but I kept quiet and let the sister work.

So far the ball has been just as boring as predicted. The fancy dinner's just as bland, and it appears that I'm the only one not enjoying myself. Natalia, the head debutante, and the other seasoned debutantes are enjoying their nights as princesses, but I would much rather be with my crew. I don't know what Nigel's going to do about his living situation, but he can't stay with Rah forever. Nigel and Sandy don't get along, and as long as she's there, Nigel won't be able to handle it.

"Is there something wrong with your tea?" Mrs. Tyler, Natalia's mother and the vice president of Alpha Delta Rho, asks me, gesturing toward the cup on the dinner table in front of me. "And you haven't touched your food."

Mrs. Esop would be pleased with my loss of appetite. I think I've just had too much excitement in the past twenty-four hours to eat anything. Besides, the small potatoes, duck, and asparagus don't tempt me at all.

"I'm not that hungry," I say, eyeing the bread basket. Even the sourdough rolls look disgusting to me.

"Teresa, you've got this girl too scared to eat a thing," Mrs. Tyler says as Mrs. Esop walks up to our table.

She's plastered on a good front, but I know she's still reeling from her argument with Nigel this morning.

"She doesn't want to be too bloated before her first dance," Mrs. Esop says, touching my updo hairstyle and making me cringe.

"Please don't touch my hair," I say.

Mrs. Esop looks like she wants to push me out of my seat but restrains herself. I already warned her about people touching my hair and that includes her.

"She's such the perfectionist," Mrs. Esop says, again reaching for my head, and I move out of the way. "Have some chamomile tea, dear, and calm yourself. We'll be called to the dance floor momentarily."

I take a sip of the hot liquid, instantly recognizing the china pattern. It's from the sleepwalking incident where I cut my toe. I don't feel so good.

"I'm so sorry Nigel fell ill," Mrs. Tyler says, sipping her tea. "Did you find a suitable replacement?"

"Of course we did," Mrs. Esop says, pointing toward the door. "And here he is now." Mr. Adewale and several other brothers dressed in tuxedos walk through the door. He and his frat brothers definitely know how to make an entrance. "Ogunlabi is just in time to walk you across the stage, Jayd. And he knows the dance from last year, so everything should be fine."

Mr. Adewale's going to be my escort? How did this happen?

The deejay plays the same Etta James song Keenan and I enjoyed at the coffeehouse, causing me to fall back into my vision with Maman and I conjuring up my husband.

"I need some air," I say, rising from the table and running toward the back door. The night air is thick and humid, unlike the weather on the other side of the hill. No wonder people from the city rarely venture to the valley. It's too damn hot out here.

I hold on to the patio railing, attempting to steady my

spinning head, but it's no use. In my mind, Maman and I are on the beach battling Esmeralda for my man. I catch my reflection in the water and see Maman's green eyes staring back at me. I would scream, but I'm not in control of my voice or anything else.

"Jayd, I'm here. It feels so good to be real again," Maman says, her body moving in the lake's reflection. The line between Maman's time and mine are blurred beyond recognition: I am her and she is me.

"Maman, what's happening to me?" I ask, touching my head. It feels like my scalp is on fire. Maman smiles at me, her shape shifting with each ripple in the dark water.

"Jayd, it's time to start," Mr. Adewale says, coming onto the patio, but he doesn't sound like himself, either: It's only Jean Paul's voice I hear.

"Oui, mon amore," I respond in Maman's voice. I have to let my hair out of the hundreds of bobby pins holding up my evening do, damn the dance.

"Jayd, are you okay?" Mr. Adewale says, trying to help me back inside, but I don't want to go. I'd rather stay out here with Maman.

"Jean Paul," I say, running up to Mr. Adewale, whose shape is also shifting in and out of time. He's wearing a cream-colored suit as my grandfather and a black tux as himself. Either way he looks good to me. Like Maman said, it's not the physical appearance that matters: His soul attracts me the most.

"No, Jayd. It's me, Mr. Adewale," he says, pushing me back.

Still seeing through Maman's eyes, I kiss him on the lips. Without responding, Mr. Adewale again pushes me away and steps back, shocked at my actions. He knows something's wrong, and I'm in no position to stop it.

"We need to get you home now."

I can barely hear him, my mind's so convoluted with everyone's thoughts. Where's Mama when I need her?

"I'm right here," Maman says in my head. I look down at my dress, which looks yellow it's so faded and old. I look at the back of my hands, again recognizing them as my great-grandmother's instead of my own. I look up at my companion, who is not Mr. Adewale but instead is Maman's white lover and Jeremy's great-grandfather. This isn't good; I have no choice but to play it out.

"My love, is that you? You've come back for me. I knew you would," I say in Maman's time, reaching up for her lover's face. I guess this is when Maman lost it. I can't see Mr. Adewale; he appears more like the shimmering ball of light from my dream last night. What the hell?

"Jayd, can you hear me? Mama's home. Go home now," my mom says, shouting in my head. *"I'll meet you there. Leave now, Jayd, before you lose it completely."*

"No, Jayd. It's me, Mr. Adewale," he says, stepping away from my advance. He falls against the hard rail, unable to run.

"*Mi amore,* I knew you wouldn't leave me. I left my husband. We can finally be together now. I'm glad your wife understands it's in our destiny to be together." I reach for Maman's lover's face, attempting to kiss him again, but he's not having it. Mr. Adewale grabs my hands, forcing them down to my side.

"We need to get you home, Jayd. Now," Mr. Adewale says, making his way with a limp. I know I've hurt him in more ways than one. Did I really just kiss my teacher? Oh, this can't be happening, no matter how many times I've dreamed about this moment. "Your grandmother will know what to do." Even out of my mind, I'm glad Mama's home. I have a feeling she's the only one who can help me out of this mess.

* * *

When we reach Mama's house, all the lights are out except the one in her bedroom. She really is home. We walk up the front porch steps and into Mama's room, where our happy reunion is overshadowed by my breakdown.

"Alaafia, Iyalosha," Mr. Adewale says, properly greeting my grandmother. "I found her at the lake talking like Maman Marie." He passes me off to my grandmother, whom I haven't seen in weeks.

This wasn't the kind of homecoming I had prepared for her. I'm grateful he omitted the intimate details of my walk as Mama's mama. Me kissing my teacher isn't okay, no matter how it went down.

"Still waters run deep," Netta says, pushing aside the luggage on the bedroom floor to make room for us. We sit down on Mama's bed and let her work her magic.

"Running water is where your powers lie, Jayd. If you catch your reflection in still water while in a dream state, you will be stuck in that vision until your head is cleansed with moving water. Only then will your head cool."

"My powers?" I ask, unsure of what she means by that. "There's more to them than my dreaming?"

Mama and Netta share a loaded look between them. Mr. Adewale looks like he knows what's really going on with me but remains silent.

"Jayd, have you done any of your assignments?" Mama asks, impatient with my lack of progress.

"I was going to finish them when the ball was over. I've just been so overwhelmed with everything lately, and then the sleepwalking didn't make it any better."

"Childish ways must be left behind in order to become a woman, Jayd, and the queen you were born to be." Mama looks like she wants to put me over her knee and spank me like the child I'm reminding her of.

Silently, Mama leads the procession through the main

house to the backhouse. When we reach the spirit room, the door is wide open. The screen is torn and shit is everywhere. What the hell happened in here?

"Your uncle Kurtis happened, that's what," Mama says with tears in her eyes. I notice the spirit book on the table, and it's not in very good condition. It looks like it's been burned.

"How did the spirit book get like that?" I ask, equally upset. I knew I should've followed my first mind and taken the book home with me.

"He tried to barbeque it," Netta says. "It was a horrible sight, but luckily we were just in time to save it."

"Can you imagine if he succeeded?" Mama says, flipping through the untouched pages. "We have to protect our lineage, Jayd. Damn the rest."

I can hear Maman in my head agreeing with her daughter. I've let everyone down. "I'm sorry," I say, tears streaming down my face, but Mama's unsympathetic. I know she and Netta are tired from their long journey, and then she has to come and clean up my mess. "I'll do better from now on, I swear."

"This was a test, and you failed miserably, Jayd," Mama says, picking up the pieces of the spirit room. I have a feeling Mama's about to give me a whupping and a hug at the same time: her infamous way of loving the wrong out of her children. I used to be so confused as a child when Mama would spank me and then wrap me up in her soft, warm embrace. I didn't know which way to go, and apparently I still don't.

"Miserably," Netta says, chiming in. Netta sits me down on the bamboo mat near the shrines—the only thing still intact back here. Even my uncles know better than to mess with the shrines. "Who knew we'd get off the highway and go right back to work? Boy, I tell you," Netta says, rubbing her feet.

Again, I feel bad they had to come back from their vacation to the mess I've made.

"You melted under pressure like an ice cube in a pit of fire. I thought I taught you better than that." Mama's sorely disappointed, and I can't blame her. "Ogunlabi, have a seat, son." Mr. Adewale obeys and sits on my former bed.

"You did, Lynn Mae. She's just stubborn like her mama," Netta says, letting it all hang out. Usually she'd censor her criticism of my mother's youthful ways, especially in front of guests, but I guess she sees too much of me in her to let it go this time.

"I knew you weren't ready to handle this all by yourself, even with your mama in your ear."

So this really was all a test? They deliberately left me in charge to see if I would sink or swim, and I ended up drowning in my own pool of circumstances. I didn't see that one coming.

"Now, Lynn Marie did a good job. That girl's finally growing up," Mama says, directing Mr. Adewale to wash his hands. I guess he's going to help us. Adding a man to the mix is definitely an interesting change.

"Yes, she is. I also think that fiancé of hers has a little something to do with her maturity." Netta picks up a bag of efun and places the small balls of white chalk onto the kitchen table. She then claims the honey, oranges, cinnamon sticks, and molasses, ready to get it started up in here. When this evening started out with me in a beautiful white gown, I didn't think it would end like this.

"Jayd, I specifically told you to study. We even made it so that you had as few distractions as possible. All you had to do was maintain the spirit room and fill the client orders, which is all part of your training. But could you do that? Hell no. Instead, you had to go running around with your little friends, keeping secrets from me and shit. If your mother hadn't told me what was going on at the ball, I would have never gotten here in time to help your stupid little self," Mama says, now fully pissed off.

"You have to walk through your past to get to your future," she continues. "Your mama lost her powers right before you were born, and it had a profound effect on your birth story, my dear. You are getting the esteemed privilege of walking in your predecessors' shoes, so to speak. Instead of only reading about them from the spirit book or hearing their stories, you get to actually see their paths through your visions—the good and the bad. You get to see what went wrong and experience the pain of losing their powers and their lives. It's your warning, Jayd. Your lesson. Pay attention, child. Your destiny is here."

"But she's not ready, Lynn Mae. It's too dangerous for the girl to master her powers this early. She's not even initiated yet, for God's sake," Netta says. She sounds worried, but after all that I've been through lately, I'm ready to get on to the next experience on the list. Whatever's after this has to be better.

"No, she's not, but the gift has claimed her. You know that a severe meltdown is the beginning of her change, Netta," Mama says like she's talking about me starting my period. Mama says change is a part of life, especially a woman's. "She has to be initiated tonight. We can't wait any longer."

"Well, we have to make some sort of sacrifice if we're going to do this right," Netta says, thumbing through the spirit book. "I've never done an initiation on such short notice."

It takes months to gather all of the materials necessary for one. Because of the many ceremonies taking place this summer, the spirit room is stocked with everything we need. All they need is Mama's blessing.

"Yes, indeed we do. The child needs a bath. She has to be completely cool for it to work."

For what to work? And what kind of bath do I have to take now?

"The river should be warm this time of year," Netta says, still searching for guidance in our ancient family text. "Or rather a salt bath would do her well. It'll calm her hot head right down and scrub all that madness off of her at once." Netta stands up straight as an arrow and points at the page, apparently finding what she's looking for.

"What does it say?" Mama asks, gathering white towels, linens, and blankets from the tall pile in the corner of the room across from where I'm sitting. I hate when they act as if I'm not in the room. It makes me feel out of control.

"That's exactly how you should feel, because you are," Mama says, catching my whining in midthought. I also hate it when she does that. "And you need to surrender to the process, Jayd. Walk your path with as little resistance as possible and you will master your powers in a way you thought was possible only in your dreams," Mama says, her emerald eyes sparkling in the candlelight. I stare deep into Mama's eyes, seeing all that she sees in my lifetime, from before my birth to me as an old woman. Sharing the vision, I feel the power Mama's speaking of, realizing that for the first time, I control my dreams and, through them, the collective powers of my predecessors.

"See what I'm talking about, child?" Mama asks, directing the next scene in our vision quest. "You can borrow anyone's sight if you think about it and purposefully fall into a dream state." As I fall asleep, the power takes over my eyes and I wake up in my mother's vision. "You have to learn to fall into your dreams and come out with the power you intended to borrow. You also have to learn how to master sleepwalking with the other powers in our lineage. Why do you think I let you keep your mama's vision so long? I wanted to see what you would do with it and how you would handle so much power."

"You knew?" I ask as my mother walks into the room. "Mom, you told Mama about me keeping your powers?"

My mom looks at me sympathetically. "Jayd, when will you learn that you can't hide anything from Mama for long?" my mom asks, kissing me on the cheek. "I don't even try, but I did ask her to let me handle it since I'm the only one who knows my powers inside and out, or at least I was." My mom joins Mr. Adewale, smiling at Mama and Netta.

"Iya, what can I do to help?" Mr. Adewale asks.

I feel so bad for putting him in this predicament, but I know he understands.

"Do what you do best, Ogunlabi. Protect us. We're going in." Nodding in agreement, Mr. Adewale stands at the door. "Our enemies have waged war on our house, and we can't let them continue with this foolishness. With Jayd and I working together, we can squelch this madness once and for all."

"War?" I ask. I have no idea what's going on.

"Yes, Jayd. War. Emilio's godfather and Esmeralda have been working hard to get revenge, and we're caught up in their mess. That's the real reason we were gone. We had a lot of work to do and needed to be out of earshot to get it done." Mama looks at the spirit book, reading the information for herself and nods in approval.

"We also needed to be with our ancestors," Netta says. "We got a lot of work done in Nawlins. I sure do miss being home, even if it's not the same since Oya and Yemoja went buck wild with Katrina. There's nothing like the kind of havoc wind and water combined can wreak, is there, little Jayd?" Netta asks, her golden-brown eyes shining at the memory. None of her relatives were killed in the storm, but several of their friends weren't as fortunate.

"Let's get her to Mama's house," Mama says, referring to Yemoja's house, the ocean. Yemoja is known as the mother of Oshune, and is therefore also one of our mothers. Lifting me by my right arm and leading me out of the backhouse, she locks the spirit room door and directs Lexi to clear the way, checking for any obstructions in our path.

"A bembé," Mama says, acknowledging the commotion in Esmeralda's yard. "She's officially taken over as Hector's wife in their ile."

I look across the backyard and see Misty and Emilio kneeling side by side, dressed in all white.

"Is she initiating those kids tonight?" Netta asks, recognizing Misty and Emilio. "They're not ready."

Mr. Adewale looks sad at his male protégé playing for the other team, but what can he do? Ultimately, we all choose our paths, and Emilio and Misty have made theirs no matter how wrong they both are.

"And they're also not our concern," Mama says, continuing with her trek. I follow my elders, but the loud squawking of a crow circling above my head stops me from moving forward.

"I can't see!" I scream. The squawking is getting louder and louder as the bird lands on my hair, pecking at my forehead. "Ahh!" I scream, blood streaming down my face. I know this old crow is Esmeralda, just like in my dream last night.

"Jayd!" Mama screams, trying to hit the bird, but it's relentless in its attack. My mom, Netta, and Mr. Adewale gather around, trying to protect me, but the bird's too agile.

"You mustn't let her win," Maman says in my head. *"Open your eyes, child. Je suis ici."*

Fanning the bird above my head, I open my blind eyes and recognize the distorted vision from my time travels. Unafraid of the pain of the pecking bird, I reach up and grab it in my hands, stilling its fluttering. The black crow silences under my strong grasp, accepting that with one wrong move, I will snap its neck in half.

"Mama, look at her eyes," my mom says in shock. "They're green."

"Maman," my grandmother says, recognizing her mother's stare. "Maman's riding Jayd."

Netta and Mr. Adewale bow at my great-grandmother's feet, and Mom and Mama kneel at her powerful presence as well. I'm aware of my actions, but instead of controlling them, it's like I'm in the background watching it all go down.

"No!" Esmeralda screams from the other side of the fence separating her yard from ours. The drumming next door has ceased, and Misty and Emilio look at us. The rest of their guests can't help but wonder what's going on over here.

"It's over, Esmeralda," I say in Maman's voice. "You can't hurt us anymore." I walk over to the fence with the bird in hand, my eyes beaming as Maman's powers fully take over the scene. I toss the frightened crow at a shocked Esmeralda.

"Impossible," Esmeralda says, running toward the fence with a broomstick. Her tricks won't work on me now, and the frightened look in her cold, blue eyes reveals what her mind's not ready to accept. "But I fixed you good. I got you right where I want you, little Jayd. Your head's too hot to see straight, let alone beat me."

Esmeralda's followers begin to chant loudly to the returning drumbeat as she boldly stares into my eyes. Instead of avoiding her debilitating eyes, I look straight into them, Maman's powers coursing through my blood.

"Oui, Esmeralda. *Se mettre d'accord,"* I say, agreeing with Mama's archenemy. "My head's too hot. I need a cool mind

to finish you off." Focused on Esmeralda's vision, I slowly drain her mind of its cool advantage, transferring my heat to her head and vice versa. With every beat of Esmeralda's heart, Maman robs her of her sight, crippling her in her own house. Misty and Emilio watch in awe as my eyes beat their godmother at her own game: I bet her wicked ass didn't see that one coming.

"No!" Esmeralda screams. "I can't see!"

"Funny," I say as my enemy squirms from the pain she's used to wielding on her victims. "I can see just fine." Before I can get too cocky with my new swag, I feel faint and fall to the ground.

"Jayd!" Mama screams, coming to my aid. "We have to get her to the ocean. Her crown can't be put off any longer."

"I'll drive," Mr. Adewale says. He's proving himself to be quite handy in spiritual matters. I think they've done this before. We all leave the backyard and pack into Mr. Adewale's truck.

Mr. Adewale expertly maneuvers his Jeep over the rocks and sand off the main road leading to the pier. The ocean is calm tonight and the breeze warm. I miss spending evenings like this with Jeremy, but I can't think about that right now. I have to focus on getting my head straight.

We exit the vehicle and head toward the water. I still can't wrap my head around my maturing powers. If I can borrow anyone's sight through my dreams, we can bring back all of the powers mentioned in the spirit book. That's got to be the dopest shit ever.

"Jayd, sit down," Mama says.

My mom and Mr. Adewale serve as lookouts for any unwelcome visitors we might encounter, but this part of the beach is pretty deserted.

Netta takes my hand, leading me to the wet part of the

sand where the water turns to salty froth and kneels down beside me.

"All fresh water returns to the ocean. Daughters of Oshune always go back to their mother, Yemoja," Mama says, scrubbing my ankles with the sea salt and ocean water. The full moon fills the dark sky, blessing the ancient ceremony. This is the beginning of my journey to full initiation, my first step to becoming a priestess in my own right.

"It's about balance, Jayd. Yemoja is the cool, levelheaded mother while Oshune is the fiery, passionate one, but she can be cool as well," Netta says, washing my arms and hands in the same mixture. I can already feel my body cool down, but Maman's still in my head. "They both have their crazy moments, as evidenced by floods and tsunamis," Netta adds, checking the romantic side of both powerful female orishas.

"The point is that it takes all levels to become all the woman you were born to be. And you can't be afraid of your power. That's good for no one."

Mama's right about that. I've been no good to anyone lately.

Mama gently massages my scalp, parting my hair with her fingers. She then wraps a large white sheet around me, covering my white gown from this evening's ball. As she prays over me, Mama rips the delicate fabric away from my body, tugging me hard with every pull.

"Jayd, you're going to take off the dress and throw it into the ocean," Mama says, passing Netta one end of another sheet identical to the one I'm wearing.

Knowing Mrs. Esop's going to be extremely upset at both my disappearing act and the loss of the couture gown, I follow Mama's directions and let the dress go with the ebb of the receding tide. It comes back with the flow, and I again attempt to discard the new outfit, this time going with it.

Completely taken asunder by a wave, I'm unafraid because I can feel Maman's presence take over, eliminating any doubt that I'm doing the right thing. While underwater, I can see everything so clearly. It's all running together like a movie in front of my eyes. The heavy feeling I've been carrying on my head gently fades away with each ebb and flow of the strong tide. The blindness, the fall at cheer practice, the fight with Jeremy, Sandy's crazy-ass accusation of Rah being her new baby daddy, and last but not least, Mickey going to Misty for help losing weight, which in turn has made her lose her mind. In the quiet of the water, I can hear the answers to all of my inquiries. I now know what to do.

"Jayd, breathe. It's all over," Mama says, rescuing me from the water. My wet hair feels like snakes again, but this time it doesn't scare me. Instead, I am comforted by their return. The eldest ancestors are represented by the amphibians and therefore would never harm a hair on my head, let alone strangle me. The cold-blooded reptiles instantly cool my blood, and my vision is again my own. And what a powerful vision it is.

Epilogue

It's been two weeks since the debutante ball, and I haven't spoken to any of my friends for longer than the two minutes Mama allowed me to communicate that I'm all right and will see them soon. Today's the first day we've had to chill, and I admit I've missed my crew. Nellie's not here and neither is Rah, who's caught up in his hustle, but I'm glad to see Mickey, Nigel, and Nickey made it to the Westside Pavilion. There's nothing like shopping on a nice day to bring out the best in us all.

"Jayd, are you okay?" Nigel asks, hugging me tightly.

Mama gave me strict directions not to let anyone touch my skin directly, thus causing me to be fully covered when I'm outside of the house: no more arms and legs out until the restriction is lifted. My friends all look concerned at my altered appearance, but I feel better than I have all year long.

"Yes, I'm fine," I say, returning the love. "Please tell your mom I said sorry and thank you for everything."

"You can tell her yourself," Nigel says. "She wants to see you first thing on Monday. I know you didn't think this debutante shit was over, did you?"

"Yes, actually I did."

I greet Mickey and Nickey and follow them to a table in

the food court. We have only a few weeks left of summer, then it's on to our senior year at Drama High. I want to spend them doing everything I want to do. Mama called the school and told them to send my reading work home, which they did. Cheer practice is a whole other complication I'll have to work out when I return to camp in a couple of weeks.

"Jayd, it feels weird being in the mall with you looking like a goddamned nun," Mickey says, turning her nose up at my attire.

I feel strange, too, but it's all part of my transformation. At least it's happening now and not during the school year. Then I'd really feel out of place. I've already been down that road and don't want to begin my senior year like that.

"Do you have to wear that thing over your head? It might not be so bad if you had your hair out."

"Not until my five weeks are up," I say. I'm just glad to be out of the house. For the first seven days, Mama had me on lockdown in the spirit room. I couldn't do anything but study and sleep. I wonder if my diabolical twins had the same experience. I can't believe Misty and Emilio were initiated the same day I was. That's some irony for my ass.

"You and Nickey take a load off. We'll grab the pizza and drinks," Nigel says, holding Mickey's hand as they walk toward the long line of patrons waiting for the New York slices.

"Hey, baby," I say to my goddaughter, who smiles up at me. I know she understands my attire, unlike the gawking people around us. So much for people having an open mind about other cultures.

My phone rings with a general tone, and I check my cell: It's a picture message. I hardly ever receive picture texts or use the camera on my fancy phone. As the photo becomes clearer, my heart rate increases: It's a picture of Cameron kissing my man. As my vision predicted, they are outside showing their affection. I don't recognize the cell number on the sending end and I don't care. A picture's worth a thousand words—damn the confession. When Jeremy gets home tomorrow, I'm going to confront him once and for all. I know I'm not supposed to engage in heated discussions while healing from Esmeralda's attack, but I can't let this one slide. Whether it's the new Jayd or the old one, I'm too real to ignore my man's blatant disrespect of our relationship. I already got one broad off my back, and it looks like I've still got one more to handle before it's all said and done.

A Reading Group Guide

Drama High, Volume 13: Super Edition

THE MELTDOWN

L. Divine

ABOUT THIS GUIDE

The following questions are intended to enhance your group's reading of DRAMA HIGH: THE MELTDOWN by L. Divine.

DISCUSSION QUESTIONS

1. If you had Jayd's powers, how would you use them? Do you think Jayd uses her sight properly and to the best of her abilities?
2. What is your favorite personal attribute? If you could change something about yourself, what would it be, and why?
3. Out of all of the Williams women's powers, which do you identify with most? Do you think one is more useful than the other?
4. Sandy repeatedly crosses the line with Rah and Rahima, yet Rah has compassion for her because Sandy reminds him of his own mother. Is there hope for Sandy's recovery or should Rah do everything he can to keep his daughter away from her mother?
5. Mickey wants Nigel to be Nickey's father so bad that she doesn't care to nurture a relationship with Tre's sisters on the baby's behalf. If they were agreeable, do you think the aunts should have any rights to spend time with their niece even though the father's passed away?
6. Although Jayd's slightly younger than the other women in her lineage were when they fully came into their powers, she's ready and willing to wear her crown as the voodoo priestess she was born to be. How do you think this will affect her senior year of high school?

7. Jayd and Jeremy are exclusive, but they are young. Now that Jayd has developed a friendship with her new college friend Keenan, should she stay in a committed relationship or explore her options?
8. Have you ever traveled across the country or out of the country? If so, what types of things did you learn? If not, where would you like to visit and why?
9. Chance has been through a lot lately regarding his identity, and his girlfriend, Nellie, has been less than supportive. Do you think there's a time in a relationship when one of the partners can leave for selfish reasons, even if the other person really needs their help but doesn't know how to ask?
10. If Misty decides to become good one day, should Jayd befriend her again? Do you think she can be trusted?
11. Esmeralda has been beaten at her own game but not without the help of Emilio, Hector, Misty, and Misty's mom. Jayd has vowed to pay back her enemies, but do you think everyone but Esmeralda is an innocent bystander under her evil influence, or should they pay, too?
12. Jayd has a summer reading list and loves to read for pleasure throughout the school year as well. What are some of your favorite books (aside from the Drama High series, of course)? What do you like about them?
13. What is your worst nightmare/fear? Have you ever had to face it head-on? If so, how did you handle it? If not, how would you deal with it if you were forced to?

Jaydism #5

Rather than spend your money on expensive masks, try what's in your kitchen cabinet for a change. Take a teaspoon of raw honey and a teaspoon of molasses and blend them together. You can heat the mixture slightly to make it more pliable. Then, add a dash of ground cinnamon, a couple drops of fresh lemon juice, and a dash or two of sea salt. Mix well and spread it on a clean face. Leave on for at least fifteen minutes and rinse. Enjoy your glowing complexion. You can also use the mask all over your body for the smoothest skin ever.

Stay tuned for the next book in
the DRAMA HIGH series,
SO, SO HOOD

Until then, satisfy your DRAMA HIGH craving
with the following excerpt from the next
exciting installment.

ENJOY!

Jayd's Journal

The beautiful journal Mama and Netta presented me with to keep a record of my first year as a priestess is supposed to be filled with my spiritual transformation, not the same old shit regarding trifling dudes and the females they roll with. Instead of writing about my latest dream or other surreal experience while dressed in white from head to toe, I'm writing about my man's indiscretions. I wonder if all newlyweds worry about their cheating boyfriends during the honeymoon phase of their blossoming love.

As strange as it may sound, my initiation two weeks ago was my marriage to my spiritual mother, Oshune. Mama says there's nothing like being an iyawo—a wife to my head orisha. Mama explains it as the most important relationship I'll ever have. Now my head as well as my heart belongs to Oshune, and because her love and devotion knows no boundaries, she also belongs to me. According to Mama, my time as a newborn is short and sweet, not only because everyone dotes on me, but also because it's the most sensitive I'll ever be—spiritually, mentally, and physically. Maybe that's why my emotions are running wild over seeing a picture of Jeremy kissing Cameron. I can't think or dream about anything else since seeing the texted photo yesterday.

Jeremy's already left several messages to let me know he's on his way home and wants to visit as soon as possible, but I'm not sure if he wants to see me like this. So much has changed this summer, and it's more than my attire. I don't know if anything will ever go back to the way it was before, but what I do know is that the truth is coming out—the good, the bad, and the hood.

Prologue

After my shopping excursion with my crew abruptly ended yesterday afternoon with me plotting ways to kill Jeremy and Cameron once their plane lands on American soil, I went back to Mama's house and took a long, cool bath. It's more dangerous now than ever for my head to get too hot. If I have a dream about Queen Califia, Maman, or another one of my powerful ancestors breaking someone down with their sight, I'm liable to bring it back with me when I wake up. I might not be able to control myself when I look into Jeremy's eyes as he denies anything's going on with his side trick when I have the physical evidence to prove otherwise. And Jeremy's crippled mind is the last thing I need on my conscience right now.

My initiation has made my dreams more intense and my sight off the chain, but it's still in the beginning stages. But so far, seeing my dreams come to fruition is the most natural feeling ever—like breathing. I've decided to tell my ex, Rah, about my dream of his baby mama, Sandy's, insemination by another dude. She can try to tell Rah it's their second baby, but I know the real story, and she needs to come correct here and now. Rah couldn't join us yesterday, so we all decided to meet up at his place since crazy Sandy is MIA for the afternoon. Knowing Sandy, she won't be missing for long, so we'd better enjoy the peace while it lasts, because when she gets back, I'm going straight for the jugular.

"Your mama's a total bitch," Mickey says to Nigel, throwing the cloth diaper with remnants of baby formula all over it down on the table in front of the futon.

So much for a chill session vibing to Rah and Nigel's latest beats. I remember when the garage-turned-studio was the most serene place we could all hang together. Now it's yet another firing post for our collective drama.

"Mickey, the baby," Nigel says, caressing Nickey's soft hair.

She's the only one who can get any rest in here. That girl can fall asleep anywhere. Staying asleep seems to be her main problem.

"Nickey knows her mama's telling the truth about that evil woman," Mickey says, sitting in the chair next to the table.

She looks better and is back to her old self. As soon as I put some color on, I'm checking Misty's ass for giving Mickey unhealthy vitamins Esmeralda prescribed. For now, I'll have to settle for Dr. Whitmore expertly switching the tainted pills with his healing combination in time enough to save my vain friend.

"She's still my mom," Nigel says, reading the sports section of the newspaper at the work desk he and Rah share. Rah's busy counting his cash. He's been hustling harder than ever since his mom stopped chipping in for the rent and bills. But judging from the frustrated look on Rah's face, I'd say he's still coming up short.

"She ain't right, Nigel."

I wouldn't call Mrs. Esop a bitch, but she's not the nicest woman in the world. I've yet to face her after I bugged out at the debutante ball, and I know she's waiting patiently for an explanation. But what can I say? I never wanted to do it anyway. It's ironic how the universe has a way of working things out, no matter how much we try and plan otherwise.

"What happened now?" I ask, leaning across the futon and touching my goddaughter Nickey's toes. If she's dreaming, I want her to feel my presence and know that I've got her back consciously and subconsciously. Rah's daughter, Rahima, looks up at me from her spot on the carpet where she's surrounded by toys and smiles, knowing I've got her, too.

"Since I've been staying at Rah's house for the past couple of weeks, she's convinced my dad to cut off my allowance, saying I'm not earning it because I'm not home to do my chores," Nigel says.

"That's a cold move right there," I say, ever surprised at the depth of Mrs. Esop's swag. She knows she's a lot of woman to deal with and uses it to her advantage all day long.

"A bitch, Jayd. There's no other way around that shit." Mickey keeps it real all the time, damn the audience. "We're supposed to be saving up for our own place, but now we ain't got a damned thing to save."

Nigel and Mickey aren't even married yet, and Mickey's already claiming his money. We all know Mickey's not making any cheddar of her own.

"For real, Mickey—in front of my daughter, too?" Rah asks, looking up from his stacks of tens and twenties at Rahima stacking her blocks like they're money. He'd better be careful of the example he sets for baby girl, too. "Unlike your newborn, Rahima's talking and can repeat what she hears."

Like her mama's any better. If Rahima wanted to curse, she'd be a professional by now with the example she's got in Sandy. But I'm with Rah—not swearing around the little ones is best.

"I don't want to have to up my game, but our hustle's all I've got now." Nigel looks at his boy, and Rah recognizes the hunger in his eyes. They go way back to elementary school before Rah's dad went to prison. Nigel and his family were there for Rah when he had no parents at home and no food in the fridge, and now Rah's returning the loyalty.

"Y'all can move in with me," Rah says, throwing the last bill on the pile and leaning back in his seat. "Kamal's spending more time at my grandparents' house, and me and Rahima can chill in the den while you, Mickey, and the baby take my room."

"For real, Rah?" Mickey asks in disbelief.

It's not exactly what they had in mind, but it'll have to do. Living with Rah is much better than sharing a room with her little sister and sharing a bathroom with everyone else in her crowded household. There are two and a half bathrooms in this house—a good ratio for six people. That's the thing I miss most about being at my mom's apartment, but I can't go back until my time in whites is over. Luckily, it ends right before school starts, allowing me privacy to create my first-day-back outfit. I want to start my senior year off as fly as possible.

"Man, I don't know," Nigel says, shaking his head. "If Sandy's living here, it's going to be tough."

"That won't be a problem much longer, I'm sure," I say.

My friends look at me, wondering what I know, but I'm not giving up anything until Sandy gets here. I want to see Sandy's face when I confront her with the truth about her insane ways.

"Man, we'll work it out," Rah says. "Besides, I could use some help. My mom's been slipping on the rent lately. I should change the locks, but I can't since it's her house and all."

His mom is hardly ever here and only shows up to borrow money and weed from Rah. Sandy's just like her, which explains Rah's save-a-ho attitude, but some broads should be left out in the cold.

"All right, then, man," Nigel says, putting his hand out for his boy, who returns the gesture. "I'll get our stuff tomorrow. And here's something to make it official." Nigel pulls out five one-hundred-dollar bills from his pocket and hands them to Rah. Houses in this neighborhood cost way more than that, but I know Rah's grandparents actually own the house and only charge his mom about half of what it would normally cost to live here.

"Bet," Rah says, making Mickey's day. "Now, can we get this session officially started? We can leave the girls in here and move to the living room. I don't know about y'all, but I could go for a pizza or three."

Sounds like a plan. I'm glad our crew is somewhat back to normal, even if Nellie's presence is missed. She's too busy hanging with her new friend from church, who I'm convinced just wants to get in her panties, but I have to handle one broad at a time. Sandy's first on the list and then Cameron. The poor white girl won't know what hit her by the time I'm through. If she thinks I'm giving up my man without a fight, she's got another think coming. Unfortunately for Cameron, she picked the wrong boyfriend to jock. No matter where she and Jeremy are from, in my hood if you want a man who's already spoken for, you have to be willing to deal with the consequences. And I'm just the one to teach the trick how we do things in Compton.

~ 1 ~
Come Again?

I don't care if you don't want me /
'Cause I'm yours, yours, yours anyhow.

—Jay Hawkins

Not wasting any time, Mickey has taken all of Sandy's things out of the room formerly known as Rah's and put them in the hallway. Rah advised against it, but once Mickey gets started, there's no stopping her. I feel sorry for Rahima and Nickey. Both of their mothers are forces to be reckoned with, and with them living under the same roof, it's going to be a new storm every day. That's why as their godmother, I owe it to them to check the hussy once and for all. I just hope Rah sides with me instead of his sympathetic heart for Sandy's bull.

"What's up with y'all?" Sandy asks, stepping into the foyer and interrupting Mickey's moving session. She couldn't have timed her return any better: It's time to shut Sandy down, and Mickey's already started the process for me.

"Rah, what's this heffa doing with my shit?" she asks, stepping over her clothes strewn all over the floor and eyeing Mickey hard. After all the trouble I went through to get rid of the broad for Rah and his daughter's sake, I still can't believe he let Sandy stay here in the first place. I don't know what kind of spell she's got my boy under, but I'm just the sistah to break it.

"She and Nigel are living here now, Sandy. You have to take the couch until you can find somewhere else to stay," Rah says, almost sounding sad about his decision to put her ass in the living room.

What the hell? Mickey walks back into the bedroom to get more stuff, and Sandy looks on in amazement. I bet she never thought this day would come, but it's here and she'd better recognize there's a new queen of this castle.

"Rah, are you shitting me?" Sandy asks, collecting her lingerie, boots, and other work clothes from the floor. "I'm pregnant with your baby, fool, and this is how you treat me?"

Rah's silence speaks volumes, and I don't have time to let her manipulate the situation any further. Thank God I'm not Rah's girlfriend anymore, because I'd have to fight for him every day. Who, other than Sandy's Amazonian ass, has that kind of energy?

"Sandy, it's over," I say, moving from the couch to the foyer and letting it all hang out. I turn around to face an exhausted Rah standing by the front door. I don't need my mother's powers to cool his mind. What I'm about to reveal from one of my recent dreams is enough to freeze everyone in the room. "Sandy slept with Trish's brother, your supplier, Rah. And this is his baby, not yours." The truth settles in the still air like a quiet fart: No one saw it coming, but everyone's painfully aware of its presence.

"She's a lie," Sandy says, completely busted.

Nigel and Rah look at each other, knowing this shit ain't good. Trish's brother supplies them both, and they can't afford to have any beef with that dude, especially not over Sandy's trifling ass.

"Get to stepping, trick," Mickey says, throwing more of Sandy's things on the floor, which pisses Sandy off even more. Sandy charges for Mickey, who doesn't back down for a minute.

"Stop it, now!" Rah yells, holding Sandy back while Nigel gets his girl. What a mess, but as Mama says, real change rarely comes easy.

"Get your stuff and bounce, Sandy," I say, glad she has no more power over Rah, or so I think.

"Not so fast," Rah says, looking from me to Mickey to Nigel. "Like I said, Sandy, you can stay here until you work something else out, but don't get too comfortable. And I'll check with Trish to see if that nigga knows about you carrying his baby." Rah lets Sandy go, and she heads to the bedroom with some of her belongings in tow. Luckily, the babies are sleeping peacefully in the den, but not for long if they keep this up all night.

"Come again?" I ask as my neck snaps to the right of its own accord. Even my body can't believe what I just heard. "Why do you need to call your ex-girlfriend to verify the story when I just told you the truth, so help me Oshune?" I ask, fully offended. Rah and the rest of our crew should know that my confessions come from a much higher source.

I follow Rah into the kitchen as Nigel and Mickey continue to calm down in the foyer. This new living situation is too hood, even for me.

"Jayd, Sandy's got a problem. I can't just let her back out on the streets," Rah says, pounding his fist on the kitchen counter. "What am I supposed to tell Rahima when she grows up and finds out I let her mother get strung out?" Rah takes out a cup and fills it with bottled water before drinking it down in one gulp.

"You didn't let Sandy's grown ass do anything but take advantage of your kindness, Rah. Now it's time to let her deal with her own madness."

"I'm not a punk, Jayd. I'm just trying to do the right thing." I look at Rah, trying to navigate my way around his fragile ego, but there's no getting around it. He has a weak spot for Sandy, because he thinks he can save her, unlike his mother.

"The right thing for who? Because this is certainly the wrong thing for your daughter. Sandy's no longer your responsibility. You have to let her go, Rah." Seeing my vehemence for the situation, Rah finally comes to his senses and recognizes that I'm right. Even if his ego is suffering, he has to know Sandy took advantage of him in the worst possible way, and that shit can't be tolerated any longer.

When Sandy comes back into the foyer to collect more of her things, Rah heads her way and I'm right behind him.

"Sandy, on second thought, you have to get out. Tonight," Rah says, pointing to her stuff. "And Rahima's staying with me, so don't even think about trying to take her out of this house." Finally, Rah mans up.

"But, Rah, we haven't had a DNA test yet," Sandy says, defeated. "I know you're not kicking me out like this. Where are we supposed to go?" Sandy asks, rubbing on her stomach for dramatic effect.

"What you and your new baby daddy do with that baby is none of my business," Rah says.

I know he feels for her, but he feels for Rahima more now that he knows the new baby isn't his.

"But I told you, this is your baby no matter what that witch says," Sandy says, pointing to me.

"I told you about calling me that word, Sandy," I say, tightening the white wrap on my head, ready to defend my lineage as always. I'm forbidden from any type of altercation, but it's impossible to avoid in my life.

"Oh, my bad. I meant bitch."

Sandy's gone too far, but we all know it's her way of trying to hold on to what she's lost. But it's over for her.

"Get out, now," Rah says, opening the front door. She'd better hurry and collect her shit or it's going to be on the front porch from the way Mickey's eyeing the remaining piles.

"But, Rah," Sandy pleads.

I think she'd better call Trish's brother and see if she can stay with them, because this house is closed to her.

"Bitch, he said leave. That's our room now," Mickey says, pointing toward the bedrooms.

"This ain't got shit to do with you, so sit down and shut up before I shut you up," Sandy says. Little does she know Mickey's been holding herself back for almost a year while she was pregnant and is now ready to get live with the best of them.

"Look here," Mickey says, removing one oversized gold hoop from her earlobe and then another. "I don't know who the hell you think you're dealing with, but I don't give a damn about you—or your little baby, if you're really pregnant."

Sandy looks shocked as Mickey continues to remove her jewelry, obviously ready to throw the first blow if need be. If Nellie were here, she'd tell Sandy all about Mickey's love of fighting. That's how they became best friends in the first place. Nellie's too cute to get dirty, and Mickey loves a good brawl, making them the perfect cute crew of two before they met me.

"Nigel, check your trick before she gets her ass beat down, for real." Sandy looks on as neither of our boys move an inch. Mickey's got this and we all know it.

"There goes my baby," Usher sings from my cell on the living room table. I walk over and open the phone, answering Jeremy's call without thinking. I need to change his ringtone because that song's out of date for our relationship.

"Baby, I'm back," Jeremy says like he's all innocent and shit.

I have been waiting for this moment for weeks, and now

that it's here, I don't know which emotion to honor first, but it seems like my anger knows exactly what to do.

"I can't talk to you right now, Jeremy. I'm in the middle of something," I say without so much as a hello. I can hear Jeremy's shock through the phone, but I don't care how rude I'm being. If I had the time, I'd be much more offensive, so he should consider himself lucky.

"Jayd! Jayd!" Jeremy yells through the phone as I close the pink lid.

I erase Jeremy's name in my contact list and replace it with the words *Do not answer.* I've been too nice. If Jeremy thinks I'm going to be a fool for him, he'd better think again. I can't forgive and forget. Like Rah, the new and improved Jayd Jackson is no one's punk. Maybe my previous story line was different, but this is an entirely new book and a stronger me—damn the bull.

START YOUR OWN BOOK CLUB

Courtesy of the DRAMA HIGH series

ABOUT THIS GUIDE

The following is intended to help you get
the book club you've always wanted
up and running!
Enjoy!

Start Your Own Book Club

A Book Club is not only a great way to make friends, but it is also a fun and safe environment for you to express your views and opinions on everything from fashion to teen pregnancy. A Teen Book Club can also become a forum or venue to air grievances and plan remedies for problems.

The People

To start, all you need is yourself and at least one other person. There's no criteria for who this person or persons should be other than their having a desire to read and a commitment to discuss things during a certain time frame.

The Rules

Just as in Jayd's life, sometimes even Book Club discussions can be filled with much drama. People tend to disagree with each other, cut each other off when speaking, and take criticism personally. So, there should be some ground rules:

1. Do not attack people for their ideas or opinions.
2. When you disagree with a Book Club member on a point, disagree respectfully. This means that you do not denigrate other people or their ideas, i.e., no name-calling or saying, "That's stupid!" Instead, say, "I can respect your position; however, I feel differently."
3. Back up your opinions with concrete evidence, either from the book in question or life in general.
4. Allow everyone a turn to comment.
5. Do not cut a member off when the person is speaking. Respectfully wait your turn.
6. Critique only the idea. Do not criticize the person.

7. Every member must agree to and abide by the ground rules.

Feel free to add any other ground rules you think might be necessary.

The Meeting Place

Once you've decided on members, and agreed to the ground rules, you should decide on a place to meet. This could be the local library, the school library, your favorite restaurant, a bookstore, or a member's home. Remember, though, if you decide to hold your sessions at a member's home, the location should rotate to another member's home for the next session. It's also polite for guests to bring treats when attending a Book Club meeting at a member's home. If you choose to hold your meetings in a public place, always remember to ask the permission of the librarian or store manager. If you decide to hold your meetings in a local bookstore, ask the manager to post a flyer in the window announcing the Book Club to attract more members if you so desire.

Timing Is Everything

Teenagers of today are all much busier than teenagers of the past. You're probably thinking, "Between chorus rehearsals, the Drama Club, and oh yeah, my job, when will I ever have time to read another book that doesn't feature Romeo and Juliet!" Well, there's always time, if it's time well-planned and time planned ahead. You and your Book Club can decide to meet as often or as little as is appropriate for your bustling schedules. *Once a month* is a favorite option. *Sleepover Book Club* meetings—if you're open to excluding one gender—is also a favorite option. And in this day of high-tech, savvy teens, *Internet Discussion Groups* are also an appealing option. Just choose what's right for you!

Well, you've got the people, the ground rules, the place, and the time. All you need now is a book!

The Book

Choosing a book is the most fun. THE MELTDOWN is of course an excellent choice, and since it's part of a series, you won't soon run out of books to read and discuss. Your Book Club can also have comparative discussions as you compare the first book, THE FIGHT, to the second, SECOND CHANCE, and so on.

But depending upon your reading appetite, you may want to veer outside of the Drama High series. That's okay. There are plenty of options, many of which you will be able to find under the Dafina Books for Young Readers Program in the coming months.

But don't be afraid to mix it up. Nonfiction is just as good as fiction and a fun way to learn about from where we came without just using a history textbook. Science fiction and fantasy can be fun, too!

And always, always research the author. You might find that the author has a Web site where you can post your Book Club's questions or comments. The author may even have an e-mail address available so you can correspond directly. Authors might also sit in on your Book Club meetings, either in person, or on the phone, and this can be a fun way to discuss the book as well!

The Discussion

Every good Book Club discussion starts with questions. THE MELTDOWN, as does every book in the Drama High series, comes with a Reading Group Guide for your convenience, though of course, it's fine to make up your own. Here are some sample questions to get started:

1. What's this book all about anyway?
2. Who are the characters? Do we like them? Do they remind us of real people?
3. Was the story interesting? Were real issues that are of concern to you examined?
4. Were there details that didn't quite work for you or ring true?
5. Did the author create a believable environment—one that you could visualize?
6. Was the ending satisfying?
7. Would you read another book from this author?

Record Keeper

It's generally a good idea to have someone keep track of the books you read. Often libraries and schools will hold reading drives where you're rewarded for having read a certain number of books in a certain time period. Perhaps a pizza party awaits!

Get Your Teachers and Parents Involved

Teachers and parents love it when kids get together and read. So involve your teachers and parents. Your Book Club may read a particular book whereby it would help to have an adult's perspective as part of the discussion. Teachers may also be able to include what you're doing as a Book Club in the classroom curriculum. That way, books you love to read, such as the Drama High ones, can find a place in your classroom alongside the books you don't love to read so much.

Resources

To find some new favorite writers, check out the following resources. Happy reading!

Young Adult Library Services Association
http://www.ala.org/ala/yalsa/yalsa.htm

Carnegie Library of Pittsburgh
Hip-Hop!
Teen Rap Titles
http://www.carnegielibrary.org/teens/books

TeensPoint.org
What Teens Are Reading
http://teens.librarypoint.org/reading_matters

Teenreads.com
http://www.teenreads.com

Book Divas
http://www.bookdivas.com

Meg Cabot Book Club
http://www.megcabotbookclub.com

HAVEN'T HAD ENOUGH? CHECK OUT THESE GREAT SERIES FROM DAFINA BOOKS!

DRAMA HIGH

by L. Divine

Follow the adventures of a young sistah who's learning that life in the hood is nothing compared to life in high school.

THE FIGHT
ISBN: 0-7582-1633-5

SECOND CHANCE
ISBN: 0-7582-1635-1

JAYD'S LEGACY
ISBN: 0-7582-1637-8

FRENEMIES
ISBN: 0-7582-2532-6

LADY J
ISBN: 0-7582-2534-2

COURTIN' JAYD
ISBN: 0-7582-2536-9

HUSTLIN'
ISBN: 0-7582-3105-9

KEEP IT MOVIN'
ISBN: 0-7582-3107-5

HOLIDAZE
ISBN: 0-7582-3109-1

CULTURE CLASH
ISBN: 0-7582-3111-3

COLD AS ICE
ISBN: 0-7582-3113-X

PUSHIN'
ISBN: 0-7582-3115-6

BOY SHOPPING

by Nia Stephens

An exciting "you pick the ending" series that lets the reader pick Mr. Right.

BOY SHOPPING
ISBN: 0-7582-1929-6

LIKE THIS AND LIKE THAT
ISBN: 0-7582-1931-8

GET MORE
ISBN:0-7582-1933-4

DEL RIO BAY

by Paula Chase

A wickedly funny series that explores friendship, betrayal, and how far some people will go for popularity.

SO NOT THE DRAMA
ISBN: 0-7582-1859-1

DON'T GET IT TWISTED
ISBN: 0-7582-1861-3

THAT'S WHAT'S UP!
ISBN: 0-7582-2582-2

WHO YOU WIT?
ISBN: 0-7582-2584-9

FLIPPING THE SCRIPT
ISBN: 0-7582-2586-5

PERRY SKKY JR.

by Stephanie Perry Moore

An inspirational series that follows the adventures of a high school football star as he balances faith and the temptations of teen life.

PRIME CHOICE
ISBN: 0-7582-1863-X

PRESSING HARD
ISBN: 0-7582-1872-9

PROBLEM SOLVED
ISBN: 0-7582-1874-5

PRAYED UP
ISBN: 0-7582-2538-5

PROMISE KEPT
ISBN: 0-7582-2540-7